D1549858

BECAUSE

OF

YOU

I AM

SANDY HOGARTH

Matador
9 Priory Business Park,
Wistow Road, Kibworth Beauchamp,
Leicestershire. LE8 0RX
Tel: 0116 279 2299
Email: books@troubador.co.uk
Web: www.troubador.co.uk/matador
Twitter: @matadorbooks

ISBN 978 1838594 466

British Library Cataloguing in Publication Data.
A catalogue record for this book is available from the British Library.

Printed and bound by CPI Group (UK) Ltd, Croydon, CR0 4YY
Typeset in 11pt Adobe Garamond Pro by Troubador Publishing Ltd, Leicester, UK

Matador is an imprint of Troubador Publishing Ltd

For Janet, Michael and Stirling

Acknowledgements

An enormous thank you to everyone at Matador who have been so very efficient, friendly and helpful at every stage of the publishing process.

The novelists in the Leeds Writers Circle have been immensely helpful and supportive, in particular, Edward Easton, always answering my calls for help.

And the critique and support from Anna Glendenning.

Knowing little about the court system I contacted Leeds Crown Court and there found Yasmin Saldin and the answers to all my questions. My thanks, Yasmin

My thanks and love to Jane, Natalie and Siobhan, and Max, who has reminded me of the joy, curiosity and innocence of the toddler; to the friends who have never given up on me and most of all the love and belief of my partner, Katrina.

To my readers. I hope you enjoy this novel and I would love to hear from you via Twitter @sandyhogarth1, email: sandyhogarth1@btinternet.com

Who in the world am I? Ah, that's the great puzzle.

Lewis Carroll, *Alice in Wonderland*

1

September 1991

What had I done? Stitch by stitch, I had unpicked myself.

Pee in my pants: wet, warm.

A forty-six-year-old woman. Afraid. Locked in a small box in a moving vehicle.

I opened my eyes, raised a finger to each teared cheek.

I was someone else, an observer. Then the observer vanished too, took my life with them.

No matter.

A road unknown: London to somewhere.

Gates clanged, the sweatbox shuddered, stopped.

Voices, laughter, cigarette smoke.

Hot, too hot. I slammed the toe of my shoe against the door. Pain. Slumped back into the unforgiving seat. Shut my eyes.

Cuffed and led to the steps and down. Gates opened and locked and pushed into a large room.

Uniforms, searches, orders.

An automaton.

Escorted down the long corridors, keys on the officer's belt locking and unlocking; banging. Eyes examining me as if a piece of dog shit. The whispers had started.

'Yours, Oldfield, your new home.' The screw placed her hand on the small of my back and pushed. She was young, a mother perhaps.

I clutched the regulation plastic bowl, cutlery and mug, roll of toilet paper, sickly-smelling soap, blankets, sheets and one towel, to my breast. Arms too short.

A plastic sack sprawled on the floor, spewing out my few belongings.

Behind me, the door banged shut. I jumped, shouted out.

The lock turned. Laughter.

Soon the corridor echoed with emptiness.

Same routine, different prison. Months at the other place had almost taught me subservience, to keep my head down, choose my friends carefully, be someone else. I knew the rules, had been a fighter. Once.

That is what got me here.

My cell: small, fetid, stinking of bleach, body odour and worse. An iron bed with skinny mattress and pillow, both stained; a small table and chair and, at the far end, a stainless steel sink with toilet attached.

I stood, minutes. Maybe hours, unmoving.

Four years, the man in the wig had gifted me, for a premeditated act of revenge.

2

The other sentence was forever.

I emptied my arms onto the table, onto the floor, and climbed, fully clothed, onto the bed, dragging one of the blankets over me.

Sometime later – minutes, hours – I opened my eyes, threw off the blanket, swung my legs over the side of the bed and slumped over my knees. The sun slipped in through the high cell window, timid, finding its way onto the opposite wall, oddly split by parallel black lines.

I scrabbled through the plastic sacks on the floor and found the photograph and the drawing.

A door slammed. Footsteps; the flap in my door flung open.

Eyes.

Meds four times a day. The pills made me slow, stupid. I echoed inside, so I hid the small ones in my mouth and later flushed them down the toilet. There was a trade in pills, in almost anything. In fantasies. I might accumulate my own stash of white dreams and watch it grow, until I had enough. What was it like to die? Was it dreaming, letting go? I wanted to believe in God, in heaven. Could not.

Could I will my heart to stop?

Banged up: nights, days. No matter.

Everything by the rulebook. Home: a word I had forgot. Inside.

I dragged my nails up my arms, tearing at the cross-stitch of scars, longing for the pain to take away the other, the boy whose name I could not say; small legs pedalling on that too-big bike, head turned back to me, mouth opening, closing. His words.

My words.

He came to me in the noisy dark, with its shouting, banging.

Nights. I stared up through the blur of the window searching for one star. My boy loved the stars, wanted to take Rabby, his brown furry rabbit, and fly into the night sky. He flew, but that was different.

It was Jake, his father, my husband, who was good with stars. Star-man.

I howled loudly enough to send myself mad, except I was already there, took up my own chorus, thrust out my chest, filled my lungs.

I pounded on the door. Laughter pounded back.

A scream. Mine, the same as on that day.

I begged some Sellotape from a screw and stuck his drawing on the wall above the meagre table, where I could see it from my bed. Stars and one word: "MumMum". His tongue would have been running across his lips, the pencil scrunched in his exquisite small hand.

Oh, for his touch. His photograph was in my pocket; he went everywhere with me. And so did his words; not those a mother wanted to remember.

I wrapped my arms around myself, let my head fall.

I dreamt of him most nights. Last night we were at the seaside. His sturdy short legs waded into the shallows, Rabby hanging from his left hand, disappearing beneath the waves.

'Teach Rabby swim,' he'd said, his eyes solemn.

A wave, a dark giant, crushed the horizon. I screamed, 'Come back. Stop. Come back.' I couldn't move, had fallen to the sand.

4

He waved without turning around. I heard his thin, small voice: 'Bye, MumMum.'

In the mornings I said, 'Hello, sun,' even if it was behind a cloud, and wished it good night. My boy taught me that.

I was because of Jake and my child and their love. The still points of my life.

Time. 'Once upon a time.' That was how my father began his stories. Except his last one when he had a secret so big it carried him away. I was fourteen when he abandoned me. I had loved him utterly. Was that when the unravelling began, or was it because I ignored the one who might have prevented it, my mother?

In my head a cacophony of cymbals, of singing: *"Run rabbit, run rabbit, run, run, run"*.

What was the past? Daily rewritten, reimagined.

The cell walls crept ever inwards.

Alice Oldfield. Prisoner No. A45306. Category B prison, somewhere in the Midlands. September 1991.

2

24th June 1983

A man held out a book, his fingers long, milky white.

What was I thinking at that exact moment? The direction of my life? Unlikely. Or the lack of it? Also unlikely. Friday, 24th June, 1983: a date to be etched into my life calendar.

A blue-sky day. I smiled, at strangers, at myself, whoever that was. Alice Reynolds, thirty-seven; hated the Tories and the failed left, consistent in her inconsistencies.

The Iron Lady had recently won a landslide victory on the back of the Falklands War, and Sally Ride, the first American female astronaut, had just returned from space. How I envied Sally. It should have been me. A dreamer always.

I had remade myself after my mother's funeral nine years ago: night school for those long abandoned A-levels, a BA from the Open University, and had distinguished myself in the Library Association exams. I was in a hurry, had always been that, yet without much purpose.

I passed my early days in the library in the basement of the large red brick building on the main street, with its fully stocked shelves and loyal readers, tearing up discards and sorting. And upstairs, filling shelves.

My promotion changed all that.

I liked to think I was imaginative, open-hearted in the books I chose. My life outside the library slipped away as I walked through the door – perhaps because it was such a slim, insubstantial thing – past the books, lightly touching my favourites, pausing to pull odd ones from the shelves and read a few pages, then, my feet tapping over the carpet, to my office where I settled myself behind my desk, handbag in bottom left-hand drawer. Yet I often took my work to a desk in the children's section, playing at work there, listening to their conversations, their quick-fire frustration when the book they wanted was not there, or the cries/screams of joy at treasures discovered. I understood their short fuses. I was a little like that, impatient with life.

And I watched them sit on the floor, book in hand, instant absorption. Their world secret, uncluttered by our baggage.

Ten or fifteen minutes first thing each morning in the library stacks grounded my day; my special time, for me alone. I wandered, starting at A and pausing invariably in front of the letter W. Virginia Woolf, VW. Early death in her family life: mother, brother, father. Loss. Is that what drew me to her? And her writing, which I loved.

I stretched out my hand to touch the spine of *Orlando*, Virginia's love letter to Vita.

VW had struggled with mental illness all her life, her "madness", her family called it. My Open University supervisor, an old man, said he'd met VW once, called her special, a groundbreaker, a feminist and a great writer. She had Leonard, the man to whom she wrote, *I owe all the happiness in my life to you.* I envied her that.

The library was my domain. I was thirty-seven, still struggling to be the best (my father's command), and a little lonely.

That was where he found me, the man with the book. I had noticed him over the last weeks, seated at the same desk tucked away at the back, had branded him "not my type", not that I was looking, had almost lost the habit.

He was tall, stood pole-straight as if wanting everyone to notice his superior inches.

I pulled back my shoulders. I was 5 feet 3 inches tall, two inches less than the average height for a woman in this country. I noted people's height, was a collector of odd facts, a one-time collector of odd words, but that is another story.

His navy suit was bespoke, I was sure, a thought accompanied by the slightest curl of my lip. Expensive, yet he wore his clothes almost carelessly. And there was something gangly, awkward about him. His face was long, thin and pale like his hands, his hair black and thick, brushed back from a high forehead.

Half a dozen years older than me, I judged.

I had two smiles: the real and the pretend, but smiles can mean anything. I gave him the pretend; the bare parting of the lips, the eyes a little curtained, and glanced up into his wide-set eyes, monk-grey, gentle, and something else.

'John Clare,' I said, running my fingers over the book's cover. '*I Am*, my favourite Clare poem.' Then I offered him the real smile, my small heart-shaped face, pixie it had often been called, dividing into two small hillocks, without the dimples I had once craved, and my green eyes tendering the same delight as my fully parted lips with the small gap between my front teeth.

His laugh, almost a shout, bounced off the books, hovered as if choosing the one on which to settle. The old men reading the newspapers looked up, wondered.

I had known only one other man who laughed like that and he too had a hint of shadow that sometimes flickered, oh, so briefly, in his eyes, eyes that I had once trusted. My father.

'Is that you too?' the man in the suit said, in a low, soft voice at odds with the laugh. When I knew him better, I sometimes ignored the words, simply bathed in the music of his voice.

'Perhaps.' Although I hadn't really thought that until now. 'The peasant poet,' I said, and might have added, and the deranged.

He shifted from foot to foot. 'An advertising man,' he said, with a hint of apology in his voice. 'John Clare is an indulgence.' He flushed.

'A necessary one.'

I liked him for John Clare and for the flush.

'Jake, Jake Oldfield.' He put out a hand that was soft, womanly almost. His grip was firm, holding my hand overlong as he ran the other hand through his wavy black hair and his lips stretched over a wide mouth. It might have been a strong face except for the softness of the eyes. His eyebrows were perfection, and his slightly overlarge nose reminded me of VW.

'Coffee?' He waved his pale, slender hands round the library. 'You must get out sometime.'

I swallowed a laugh and looked at my watch. Midday.

'Give me five minutes,' I said, surprising myself. 'Alice Reynolds.'

'I know,' he said.

In my office I checked my lipstick and touched, for luck, the orange flower that I always wore in my dark brown hair just above my right ear. My hair sat bushy (striking, I considered) on my shoulders. My mother had made the flower and I had stolen it. I patted my green seersucker blouse and looked down at my mid-length cream skirt.

'You'll do.' I smirked at myself as I carefully followed the line of my lips. Good mouth, full lips and, just as I turned away, I glimpsed the sort of excitement in my eyes that I perhaps hadn't seen since I was a kid.

There was nothing in my diary for the weekend. Indeed, there was no diary. It had depressed me to see it so naked, so I had binned it.

I had grown too accustomed to myself, not overly fond, rather a habit. Those early years in London, I had been young, careless, brave, reckless. Then dullness crept in. I had become dull decades too soon but disguised it well. My colleagues and my few friends saw me as fun, successful.

Only love really surprises. And dreams. I had neither right then. I existed.

I pulled out my handbag from the desk drawer.

'I'll be back after lunch,' I said.

Anne looked up from her desk and a list of books she was annotating and over at the large clock on the wall.

'Bit early. Hungry?' She gave her soft chuckle.

Nearby, the bevy of oldies, mostly men, regulars who came in to get out of the cold or read the newspapers; to borrow a book from time to time or more often, to pluck one from the shelf, sit, read briefly and replace it, carefully.

Mr Williams was my favourite: tall, slim, upright of stature despite his age, at least eighty, always standing in front of the thrillers, leaning forward, peering. He made a pretence of searching but it was only Le Carré he read, in date of publication rotation, then starting back at the beginning. I envied him his clarity of purpose. We called him Le Carré.

And Rosemary, bent almost double and with two sticks. She must have read every romance we stocked.

Jake Oldfield was standing just inside the library entrance with its imposing red brick portico. We left together, through the glass double doors and down the four steps to the pavement, watched by Anne, the old men and Rosemary.

We stepped out into the warmth and sun.

He pointed across the road to a cafe, the only one nearby and as modern as the library was old, with glass tables, hard plastic chairs and decent coffee served in different-sized cafetières. Suddenly self-conscious, I moved a little away from him and we walked, not quite side by side, the ten or fifteen yards along the pavement before crossing the road to the glass-fronted building. There we cluttered the doorway, awkward.

You've lived too long on your own, I remonstrated with myself.

We stepped inside and I headed straight for my usual table in the corner.

The boy behind the counter smiled and waved.

Jake followed, then stood, looking around. 'So this is where you hide away.'

'Not hide. Well, sometimes.'

He placed his briefcase and brolly on a spare chair and stood. I pulled out a chair, sat and wondered, not for long, what I was doing. I had forgotten the way of this.

'Coffee, thanks, black.' I twinned his earlier flush.

He took his wallet from his jacket pocket, straightened and walked to the counter, returning some minutes later with a tray and a large cafetiere of coffee, two cups and saucers and one plate. 'Thought you might like this.' He pointed to a slice of carrot cake. My favourite. Clever man.

I didn't hesitate, picked it up and took a large bite. I wiped my mouth with the back of my hand, forgetting the paper serviette, and sat back. I was not especially fussy about food.

'Thanks. You not indulging?' I added, pushing my plate an inch or two towards him. 'Help me out,' not meaning a word.

He shook his head. 'All yours,' and leant across to the empty table next to us and picked up a blue election leaflet.

'You didn't vote for her?' My voice was redolent with disapproval. *Not a good start,* my inner self remonstrated. I could tell from the expression on his face that he had.

'A landslide, Callaghan's fault, and I couldn't stand Michael Foot.' He interlocked his elegant fingers, released them and started again.

I wanted to place my hands over his, to still them. 'The Falklands saved her. She's after our souls,' I said.

'That's okay, I don't have one.'

'She's St Francis running amok, bringing disharmony.' I recalled the St Francis bit from her 1979 speech. I'd ignored Maggie and politics until the sinking of the *Belgrano,* steaming out of the exclusion zone, for God's sake. The *Sun's* headlines, *GOTCHA,* had got me going, not in the manner it intended. I joined a demonstration then forgot all about it. I was like that; a bit of a chameleon, changing my mind daily on the serious things like government, the end of society, nuclear war, IRA bombs and the rubbish piling up in London's streets. It was simpler to live in books.

I fiddled with my right earring, my favourites: three small stars, graduated in size, pink and silver.

'I didn't vote for her. I didn't vote for anyone,' he got out, muddied by that loud, outrageous laugh.

I grinned at him, wiped my mouth with my serviette this time, and picked up my coffee cup. Wrong again.

'Civic duty,' I murmured.

'I know.'

Cups rather than mugs were the cafe's one nod towards classiness.

He leant back and looked across the road. 'You're surrounded by books,' he said. 'I envy you that.'

A bit obvious. 'I'm a librarian.' That smirk again that I kept trying to lose. 'Late starter.'

He waved a hand towards the library. 'Makes a break from the day job.'

I raised my eyebrows. 'So what's that? The day job?' I

filled my mouth with cake, mostly the thick slab of icing that smothered it.

'Advertising.' His fingers, locking and unlocking.

'Aha,' I got out, through partially chewed cake. No wiser.

He released his hands and tugged the cuffs of his shirt down.

'Explain. TV ads or what?'

He was silent a moment, then said, in a measured tone. 'I have a carefully selected group, ten or twelve. I ask them what they think about something, about brands of cars, for example, or which brand of frozen peas they prefer; ask them to dream aloud, tell me their prejudices, their hates and loves. It's fun,' he said, his arms on the table, his hands still at last.

'I bet it is.' I meant it, although didn't really understand. I believed he would persuade them, with his gentle eyes, his elegant hands and his sonorous voice, to reveal their innermost secrets.

'And then?'

'Our minds are crowded and it's crowded out there.' He waved at nowhere in particular. 'We have to take people by surprise to get their attention, so we tell them stories. It's my job to find the words for those stories.'

'A writer,' I interrupted, feeling a little envious.

'Not what you mean. My stories get translated, by someone else, into adverts, campaigns, the things you see on TV.'

His teeth were so perfect I wanted to run my finger along them.

He took a silver cigarette case from his pocket, clicked it open and held it out.

'No, thanks.' I'd given up years back. Another life.

He lit his cigarette and blew a perfect smoke ring.

A laugh, no, a silly girly giggle escaped me, the sort I despised. 'The cigarette lighter was invented before matches.'

He looked surprised.

'That's me. A show-off.' That sounded worse than I'd intended so I added, 'I like to collect odd facts.' I couldn't stop myself. 'Leonardo invented scissors.'

'Ah, Leonardo,' he said. 'I thought I knew everything about him.'

We sipped our coffees and the cafe filled with the lunchtime crowd, including Anne, who hurried through the door, saw us, hesitated then walked to a table some distance away. She kept her hair very short, almost an Audrey Hepburn look of decades back. 'No time for hairdressers,' she'd said. 'Kids.' She had four, so her life was pretty full on. She and I lunched here often.

I had the reputation of a workaholic, not a skiver with gorgeous men.

'I'd like to work surrounded by paintings,' he said. 'Like you with your books.'

They were *my* books. That was how I saw them.

'Then work in an art gallery.' I wondered how his blue suit would go down there.

'It's just one painter, Mark Rothko.'

'What about him? Never heard of him.' I knew little about art, wasn't much interested. I shifted in my seat, checking on Anne, wishing she would leave.

'Most people haven't.'

'VW,' I offered.

15

He turned his head to look out of the cafe and at the cars parked on the kerb.

'I don't drive.' That awful giggle again. 'Virginia Woolf.' I leant back in my chair, hands on the table.

The corners of his eyes wrinkled and he ran the fingers of his right hand through his black hair. 'Ah, *Who's Afraid of Virginia Woolf?'*

'Not really. VW thought the birds sang in Greek, and Adrian, her brother, called her The Goat.' I didn't say that I'd fallen in love with a photograph of her years ago, when she was twenty, a side head shot, her dark hair in some sort of bun, her eyes and face, dreamy, wistful. Fell in love with her and with her books.

He shook his head.

We leant towards each other, our hands wrapped around our coffee cups. '*Mrs Dalloway.* Clarissa, she married Richard instead of Peter, took the safe option, not the passionate. And there was the question of the Sally Seton kiss, no restraint.' Was it Vita Sackville-West VW was thinking of when she wrote about the kiss? I might have turned this into a VW lecture.

He looked puzzled.

'The best moment of her life. She should have gone for the passion.'

'Would you have gone for the passion?'

'Of course,' I said, and wondered.

'The best moment?' he asked, looking thoughtful.

'Yet to come.' What a flirt.

'There's hope then,' he murmured, a smile in his eyes.

'Perhaps.'

'He paints huge.' Jake's eyes shone.

16

He made it sound as if this Mark was his best friend. I'd never heard of him. Not surprising. I wandered into the National Gallery occasionally, if near there and had time to waste. That was about it with me and paintings.

'Mark Rothko. He seems to be talking to me, only me.'

I understood that.

'He is clever and difficult, he can be allowed that; self-taught, a genius,' Jake almost whispered; words too important, too personal to be spoken full voiced. 'It's his colours: pinks, blacks, oranges, purples, reds; ordinary colours made special. He puts them together in ways others haven't, can't. They take your breath away.'

Many words, I suspected, for a quiet man.

'Great blobs of colour that grab you by the balls.' That flush again.

'Yours, not mine.' My laughter came quickly, surprising me, a silvery, tinkling thing. It stopped abruptly, leaving a look of slight surprise on my face.

'Your metaphorical ones then,' he said, showing his perfect teeth and lightly touching my hand.

'You want to crawl into the colour and the blur.' He ceased speaking for what seemed a long time, but can only have been a minute or two. 'Suicide, cut his wrists, found in a pool of blood.' He paused a moment and then, 'A Jewish mystic, into Nietzsche, Greek mythology.'

'VW too, the suicide bit. A large stone in her pocket, walked into a river, was afraid of her depressions, voices. *Dearest, I feel certain I am going mad again.* Her last letter to Leonard.'

'Tough,' he said. 'Perhaps I'll read her.'

We two, speaking to ourselves, to our memories, our dreams. What were my dreams? Had they vanished with

17

my father? I had come from my small northern hamlet to London, twenty-one years ago. A silly sixteen-year-old, dreaming of London and the Beatles and finding my father. Once there, I had not chosen wisely.

Jake broke into my reverie.

'I have some reproductions of Mark's paintings in my flat. I got them in New York, not as good as the originals but it would help you understand him.' He added, 'And there's the heath.'

I stared at him. His eyes told me he was serious. I almost laughed out loud at the cliché. Madness.

I stood up and walked, rather too quickly, over to Anne, who was busy with her usual large slice of carrot cake.

'I'll be back by four,' I said.

'Gorgeous. I've seen him around. So it was you he wanted, not the books.'

3

We left the cafe and, with quick steps, walked to the station and the Northern Line.

We sat side by side, in an almost empty carriage. Silent.

Was he regretting this adventure? I hoped not.

Out at Hampstead, the deepest platform of the underground system, into the bright sunshine.

He took my hand.

I smiled up at him.

We passed pubs and cafes and people sitting in the sun; noisy, content. Part of me wanted to stop, join them. Already I was becoming someone else.

'The Village. Marx lived in Hampstead,' he said.

I squeezed his hand. 'Is that a recommendation?'

'Guessed you'd like that. We could walk on the heath later, see the City of London in the distance.'

I was almost totally ignorant of this part of the city. Some of the streets were cobbled, just like The Street back home. But that was where the similarity ended. Hampstead was stuffed with the rich.

A slight awkwardness fell between us, and Jake filled it with details of the places we passed, naming the pubs and restaurants, naming exotic dishes I had never heard of, pausing slightly outside the ones he judged good. I didn't really listen.

I lived alone now, considered myself happy in a cerebral sort of way, had a few friends, a job I loved. My wild London years were now a scant memory and I had made good on my promises to my dead mother. I wasn't overly reflective about my life's direction.

I glanced up at Jake, saw his lips moving. He was someone I might trust. I moved a little closer.

'The pools, fed by the River Fleet. We could swim.'

I shook my head. 'Not me. I'd drown.'

He squeezed my hand. 'I'd save you.'

I believed him.

We turned left into a street, away from the shops, and then through a small gate and down a bricked path to the solid oak door of a three-storey building.

'It's small, the flat, suits me. I'm away a lot,' Jake said, over his shoulder, as I followed him up a narrow, curving staircase to the top floor. He unlocked the door and stood back for me to go inside.

I took a few steps and stopped, took a deep breath. The entire front wall was glass and through it tumbled swathes of green. In the distance, London, sprawled like a kid's messy toys, punctuated by skyscrapers. I hitched my handbag further up my arm.

'Four miles to Trafalgar Square.' Jake pointed.

What was I doing here? Casual sex didn't frighten me, yet there was nothing casual about this man, his hands on my shoulders, tugging me over to face a cream wall. And a painting.

A blast of colour, no, darkness, enfolded me.

'He wanted it to hit the beholder.' The corners of his mouth stretched.

'It's done that.'

'*Red on Maroon.*'

'I can see,' I said, almost before he had finished speaking. The base colour was maroon and in it floated, hazily, a large red rectangle, itself containing a narrower maroon rectangle, a sort of window.

'There's another.'

He turned me to face the other wall.

Too soon. I was still drowning in the first, wanted to cry out 'wait a little.' Or 'save me.' I didn't understand what he was showing me yet my heart did, somehow.

'*Four Darks in Red,*' he said with love in his voice.

This one was dark reds, brown and black, as the title promised. I stared at it, trying to see what he wanted me to, could feel nothing, only blurry blocks of colour that a child could slap on.

'Critics hammered him, said his work was dead. They didn't understand. You have to just let it take you over.' He spoke the last in the manner of an instruction.

I tried. Failed.

'He called his colours performers, wanted his paintings to be miraculous.' Jake was stumbling over his words, yet did not seem a stumbler. 'A lustful relationship between the paintings and viewers. It was a wet New York day. I wandered into a gallery and through the rooms. Nothing much interested me until I saw that one.' Jake pointed to *Four Darks in Red*. 'I stayed in there, with the Rothkos, until they closed. And since then I've read everything there is about him, seen as many of his paintings as I can.' He spoke softly, not looking at me.

Could I compete? I wanted to.

He took his hands from my shoulders and led me the few steps to the glass wall. I was glad to escape the paintings, was beginning to wonder if this was a mistake.

I looked up at him, at his soft, generous, mouth, girlish in a way, yet only at certain angles. His eyes were like my father's, but unlike his that were often half empty, Jake's eyes were for diving into. His clothes were too posh for me but I forgave him that.

'I dream about his paintings sometimes. Wish I could paint like that.'

'Have you tried?'

'I will one day.'

I moved a little away from him and dumped my handbag on a small table.

'They don't do much for me, sorry.'

'You're not trying,' he chided, placing his arm around my shoulders, then letting it drop. 'Never mind,' he said. 'Tea, coffee?'

'Coffee, please.' I plopped onto a leather sofa, tucking my legs beneath me, and ran my hand through my hair. The room had a deep cream carpet, warm, and two leather armchairs and a sofa. Beside each chair was an oak coffee table, and in one corner a standard lamp, and on the wall beside it, a low bookshelf.

I stood and walked over to the books. Large art books including half a dozen on Rothko, a mix of biography and his paintings and a dozen or so other biographies: Churchill, Roald Dahl, Peter Sellers, John Lennon and Mick Jagger among them. At one end of the bookshelf was a full rack of records and a gramophone. A quick flip through the titles revealed mostly jazz, except for a stack of Elvis. On the mantelpiece was a photograph in a large leather frame: a woman, standing a little stiffly, and two small boys, one either side, both in school uniform. The woman had a kind face and anxious eyes. She was tall and slim, wore a long-sleeved dress and an expensive-looking necklace. I recognised Jake with his thick black hair standing to one side of her. The other boy, a little older and taller, was fair-haired and smiling. Jake was solemn. There was something strained, even unhappy about the photograph.

'My mother, James and me.' Jake came in carrying a tray with two mugs, milk and sugar and two glasses of white wine. He placed it on a table. His voice was quiet, flat. '1947. I was eight.'

I did the sums. He must be forty-four, seven years older than me.

He'd taken off his jacket. His waistcoat was patterned with large blobs of colour, not unlike the Rothkos, and bound with orange trim.

'The colour of your flower.' He pointed to his waistcoat. 'It's a full moon tonight,' he said. 'Twice as many dog bites as at other times.'

'Mad, like us.'

'Ah, Cheshire Cat, don't disappear.' Jake's face was soft, mischievous.

For a moment, I heard my father, reading *The Adventures of Alice in Wonderland*, doing all the voices. A white rabbit with a pocket watch, a dormouse, the Duchess and the Mad Hatter. And the Cheshire Cat: *It doesn't matter which way you go... so long as I get SOMEWHERE.*

Daddy (I despised that word now), the man I had loved, then hated and tried to forget. I had skipped down a rabbit hole of his making. Or was it my own?

'We'll have to stay in,' I said, as I stretched out my hand for the coffee and milk, feeling giddy, un-Alice like.

I poured milk into my coffee but didn't pick up the mug. Instead, I stood and walked again to the glass wall. People were running, walking, on the large swathes of grass below: groups, couples, loners. And dogs, and kids playing some sort of ball game. Excited voices, shouts, laughter.

'Boudicca is buried somewhere there, although others say she's beneath Platform 10 in King's Cross Station.' He held out a glass of white wine.

I lifted it to my mouth: chill, exquisite. I abandoned the coffee, drank large gulps of wine.

Jake sniffed, sipped.

'I imagined you standing here with me one day.' He shifted from foot to foot. 'I watched you pull a book off the shelf and read a little, then you left it, jutting out slightly from the others. I found it, John Clare's poetry. I fell in love with him too.'

The "too" rang in my head, bells pealing.

He took a mouthful of wine. 'I kept coming back, hoping to find you, the woman with the pert breasts, small feet, green eyes and a perfect nose.'

'Nasophilia,' I whispered, and stood on tiptoe to kiss him, feeling the fullness of his lips, and my own longing. 'Obsession with noses.'

'Just as well you told me.'

He took my wine, held both glasses by the stems in one hand and with the other led me from the room.

A wardrobe lined the right-hand wall, on the opposite side a dressing table, both pure white, and a brown leather-covered stool. In the middle of the room, a large bed with a grey damask bedcover and two small white bedside tables.

Two more Rothkos on the walls. I turned away from them to the glass wall looking onto the heath. Heavy curtains pulled back either side.

It was perfection.

Later, I found the bathroom, also pure white, tiled from floor to ceiling. No messy toothbrushes, pots of make-up, overflowing bins. Everything tucked away behind shining cupboard doors.

Jake placed the wine on a table and stood in front of me, his eyes locked on mine. He gently took the index and middle fingers of my right hand, separated them from the others then held them for a minute or two, his long, slender fingers round my two small ones. Then he pulled the few pins from my hair, ran his fingers through it, came to the tangles, stopped, picked them apart.

My skirt dropped round my feet, blouse following.

I found his trouser belt, unbuckled it, ran my hands down his slim hips.

He took my face between his hands and put his lips on mine. A little later I ran my tongue over his exquisite teeth. We fell, together, onto the bed.

My hands over his chest, following the river of hair down; his mouth on my breasts so my nipples tingled, begged, my head empty of words at last. No hurry: tongues, hands, fingers, penis, clitoris, wetness. My cry so deep, so elemental. Tears slipped from the corners of my closed eyes and from his. A musky smell swaddled us both.

Afterwards, I ran my hands through his hair. He lay perfectly still, surprise and joy in his face. Something in me paused, fell away.

My clothes lay strewn across the floor; his were neatly folded on the stool.

The disbelief in Anne's voice tumbled down the phone in the late afternoon. 'Good for you,' she said when my excuses had meandered and finally ceased.

Sometime during the evening Jake left me and returned with more wine and crackers and cheese.

'We could go to the Village to eat.'

I shook my head and patted the bed.

*

Saturday morning, very early, still dark, that exquisite moment of not quite sleep and not quite awake, a gentle simmer.

Jake had thrown off the covers in the night. I gazed at his body, longing to touch him. Instead, I slipped out of bed into a the room lit by slivers of moonlight, walked to the glass wall and stood, naked, gazing out over the lights of London. I'd never been to a circus as a kid, but right then London looked like a lit-up big tent: sparkling, magical, dreamlike. Behind me, the resonance of Jake's gentle snoring.

I wrapped my arms round my breasts and smiled at the heath: soft, silver, safe.

4

Jake's long limbs, at angles that should have been uncomfortable, sprawled on the bed, covers thrown back. He stirred, offered up odd snuffling sounds.

I trailed my fingers over his belly and down, watched his body reassemble, eyes slowly open, saw the love flicker and swell.

'I'm hungry,' I teased.

'Breakfast in ten minutes, ma'am,' he said, and pulled me down.

Later, we sat on the carpet in front of the large window, our knees and hips touching. On a tray beside me, a perfectly cooked soft boiled egg with two slim slices of toast and butter. I cut the toast into thin sticks and dipped them in my egg. Soldiers.

Jake knocked the top of his egg with his spoon, removed the shell with finger and thumb and dipped his teaspoon in.

It was some time after noon.

We didn't go outside. The heath was too crowded.

Saturday evening, although day and night had blurred, we lay, side by side.

Jake rolled over to face me. 'I had a brother once.'

I waited.

'James died, when I was still a kid, thirteen, a yachting accident. He didn't get out of the way of the boom. That's what they told me. Pa was at the helm.'

I held him close, willing him to go on.

'That day, he knew I was scared, knew I hated it, told me to play sick. He went instead of me.' His voice trembled round the edges. 'He didn't want to go, only went so I didn't have to. He shouldn't have died.' Jake's voice broke. His eyes were shut, his lips tight. Pain enfolded him.

'It was not your fault, Jake, believe me, please.' I tried to wrap myself around him. He was stiff, unresponsive. 'You were just a kid.' I knew my words wouldn't count.

Nothing could.

'That's not what I believed.' After a moment, he added, 'He never spoke to me much, my father, and after that, even less.'

I sat up. 'You weren't there. Your father. What a bastard.' My voice smacked back at me from the glass wall.

He pulled me down to his chest.

'I should have been. The wrong one died.'

I almost told him then, that my father had left me, had run.

Jake lay still.

'For Pa, shaking hands was the most loving thing he could manage, when I left for boarding school. "Get you out from under our feet," he said to me, not to James. A bit of a joke that, as we hardly saw anything of him and Ma, just brought out for a few minutes at their dinner parties, us dressed up like idiots. We were performers. When he wasn't working it was golf or the Masons.'

'Your mother?'

'At his beck and call, I suppose. And she was into the church. And then he bought this yacht, to impress his mates. He told me I had to learn to sail. "Will make a man of you," he said. I could hear the contempt in his voice.'

His long white fingers locked and unlocked. 'James was three years older, looked out for me, especially at school. I was safe there until he left.' He stared at the ceiling. 'I was skinny, shy, no good at what mattered: rugby, cricket, debating clubs…' He laughed, not the loud outrageous version but a sad, smothered thing. 'I wanted to collect butterflies, beautiful, delicate creatures.'

I held him tight. I knew a little about butterflies, about one in particular. And this man was like no other I had known.

'There was a small wood in the school grounds and a pond,' he said. 'I spent hours there with a net, exploring. It was my secret place, just me. James was a rugger star, good at everything. He loved boarding school, was House Captain. I hated it but it was better than being at home.'

I ached for the sadness, the self-deprecation in his voice.

'The photograph,' I said, waving in the direction of the other room.

'Taken just before I left for boarding school. I was eight. Ma, she was a real lady.' The love in his voice was clear, insistent. 'She loved her gardening.' I felt his face move, briefly, into a smile. 'But he bullied her too. She tried to tone Pa down a bit but it was my brother they both wanted, not me.'

I lay still, numbed. I had never given much thought to being an only one. I had the kids in The Street, my gang.

'I missed James, still do. I don't know. Life would have been different had he been around.'

'I bet you were the clever one,' I said.

'I suppose so but somehow that didn't count.'

He sat up. I heard the click of his cigarette case, the lighter, followed by a deep inhalation. 'They wished it had been me.'

'You can't know that.'

'I might as well have not existed after…'

He lay back down and placed the cigarette between my lips.

'I wasn't worth staying around for. My mother first, died. Then he did, just after I graduated.'

I took him in my arms and we lay like that for a long time. Still.

I sat. 'Let's go out,' I said, pulling him up. 'A walk on the heath.'

We hadn't closed the curtains, and a full moon enticed.

'You're mad, Cheshire Cat,' he said as he leapt out of bed.

I wriggled into one of his sweaters that came halfway down my thighs and into my skirt and shoes.

Outside, he led me through a couple of streets and onto the open ground.

'Come on,' he said, setting off too fast. 'Kite Hill.' He carried a small rug over his arm.

A gentle breeze coaxed us up the slope and a tough half-hour later we stopped.

Breathing heavily, I made a resolution to get fit. I was good at that sort of resolution: the unlikely ones.

He turned me round the way we had come, pointed. 'St Paul's Cathedral.'

The distant city was ochre in the moonlight.

'The tall building next to it, Guy's Hospital.' He turned half right. 'And over there, one of the ponds.'

He sounded bright, manic.

He spread the rug on the grass. We lay down, curled into each other. The moon teased, hiding itself from time to time, then surprising with its bright orange glow.

'Your father,' he said. 'What was he like?'

It seemed silly to speak of my father's tales of rabbit holes, deep in the earth where everyone would bow and curtsey to me and I could have chocolate for breakfast, for every meal if I wanted.

'He brought chocolate home every week, Terry's Neapolitans. None of the other kids had any.' Our mothers were careful with food and with most things. It was a habit they would never break; the war had taught them that. My father was different. I suppose he didn't really belong in The Street.

'Rationing,' Jake said. 'It went on forever. Bet you were popular.'

'And at Christmas, we had the largest tree in The Street. It was huge, with all the lights and stuff.'

A small cloud dimmed the moon for a minute or two. I waited.

'He called me "Princess", I said, in its dreamy light. 'Princess, and promised to take me in a small plane, round the world and to the desert.'

'Daddy's girl,' Jake said.

'He wasn't like the other men in The Street. Different cars, most weeks,' I said. 'Just trying them out, he'd say. That's what he did, sold cars.' I was murmuring to the stars.

'The street?' he asked.

'You mean my accent? The Street, up north.'

A couple of dozen houses, stuck out in the countryside, squashed together, two-storied with chimneystack and two pots atop steeply pitched roofs and four lace-curtained windows facing onto the cobbles. Tall, skinny buildings running back to small yards. Tin baths hung on the sides of sheds and garden gates set in the high glass-encrusted back walls that led into dank back lanes.

I took a deep breath. I didn't want to go there. My shame surprised me. 'He came home on Tuesdays, left us Saturdays, 5pm sharp, the same every week,' I told Jake.

Sometimes, he didn't make it home until later in the week, or not at all.

I heard Jake's intake of breath, then his voice, replete with love and tinged with sadness, 'Ah.'

*

A Friday at dusk. I was sitting on the stoop, utter silence all around. Eleven years old and soon to start at the Grammar in the nearby town. It was September 1957. He was late, three days late.

The stoop, the cleanest in The Street. My mother saw to that as if it was some stupid competition. On hot summer days, the women sat on the stoops in clusters, smoking, pots of tea in their hands, rollers in their hair if it was a Friday, dressed in apron or housecoat.

I wriggled, to let the blood flow back.

My bike with its blocks on the pedals leant against the wall of the house behind me. Lights shone from ground floor windows of the houses onto the cobbles. The Street didn't bother much with curtains. Cabbage smells from Jenny's house drifted over and I covered my nose with my hand. I hated cabbage, got the starving children of Africa lecture if I refused to eat it. The African kids could have it.

I had been daydreaming about rabbits, although not the White Rabbit of my namesake.

I waited there for him every Tuesday evening, in my best dress if it wasn't raining, the dress with its blue daisies smocked across my small, flat chest, my Daddy dress. I wore ribbons in my hair, one above each ear, and on my feet, white socks and black patent leather shoes.

I looked down at my scabbed knees, put the finger of my right hand under the edge of the biggest scab and picked round its edges until it lifted off, bit into its saltiness and spat onto the cobbles.

Through the open door behind me I heard the bang of pans.

'You get yourself in here, Miss,' my mother shouted.

Miss was another word for trouble. She usually called me Pet. She was always like this when he wasn't home on Tuesdays. I hated him too, those times.

I laughed out loud and didn't move. He would be home soon.

I shivered and wrapped my arms round myself then touched, in my pocket, the marbles I'd won from Billy that afternoon. In the other pocket, the penny. It was flat and thin, no longer round, the Queen's head crushed. The railway line was not far away.

'Three days late,' I chanted to myself, getting crosser with every word. I would run away, that would show him. 'Three days late, three…' It was a Friday.

I had a promise from my father for tomorrow. My heart beat a little faster.

'What's the time, Mum?' I shouted.

She banged down another saucepan.

A car door slammed.

'Hello, Princess.'

'I'm not your princess.' His hand was on my head, his fingers deep in my hair. I looked down at his shoes, could almost see myself in them.

'Not talking, ah well.' He took his hand away, dropped his cigarette, grinding it out with his shoe, dragged a box from his pocket and dropped it in my open, ready hands.

I tore it open and prised out as many chocolates as I could cram into my fist.

'Better tuck it away, save it for later. Our secret.' His voice caressed.

'Jenny said you weren't coming back.'

'Well, she was wrong, wasn't she? I'm here. Business, you know.'

I didn't know but was certain he would never abandon me.

I gave in, reached for his hand. 'You promised you'd take me hunting tomorrow.'

'So I did, Princess, so that's what we will do. Now let's see your mother.'

'She's cross,' I whispered and might have told him that she sometimes cried when he left us every Saturday.

He picked me up, slung me over one shoulder, his bag in the other hand, and walked into the house. Hanging upside down. I pummelled his chest with my best shoes. With love.

'You haven't asked,' I mumbled, mouth crammed with chocolate, my head banging against his back in time to his steps.

'What haven't I asked?' he said, although the smile in his voice told me he knew.

'The word.'

'So what is it?'

'Funambulist,' I shouted.

'You tell me.'

'Rope walker,' I crowed.

'That's a good one.'

I slipped off his shoulder, stood close. Mum walked towards us, her apron covering her full liberty skirt and white long-sleeved blouse, her wet hair tied loosely back (it was hair wash day), no lipstick. Her feet struck the hall floor hard. A plump woman with features that had once been soft. 'Tom,' she said. 'You're home,' and thumped back down the hall.

*

I took a hold of myself, dragged myself back to Jake. 'Playing bombers,' I said. 'That was what I loved best.' Flying down the street with arms outstretched, ducking and weaving, and killing.

Jake looked puzzled.

I scrambled to my feet and swooped and whooped in grassy circles around him. The moon sailed out from behind the clouds and applauded with its bright glow.

'That's what my father did in the war,' I said, out of breath, looking down at him. 'I bet you've never been up there, the North. It can be a bit bleak and wild but,' I drew breath, 'it was home. I loved it once.'

I flung myself down and wriggled so I was almost in his lap. 'Outside toilets. Not us, though.'

'Ah, posh.'

I ignored the teasing in his voice.

'Most of the men worked at the factory, and the women stayed at home.'

He lifted my hair and kissed the nape of my neck.

The Street. He wouldn't understand it. Life had been easy then. Or is that the lies of memory?

'A dark, cobbled street,' I said, 'two rows of terraced houses in the middle of fields.' Surrounded by fields and sheep and stone walls; an etiolated black stain on the northern countryside.

'Our house was on the sunny side.'

He heard it, the pride, and dug me in the ribs.

'The sun didn't often make it to the cobbles,' I said. 'We loved the dark corners, the old air-raid shelter at the end, full of rubbish. And my best friend, Jenny, lived next door.'

'Ah,' he said, 'best friends,' in a tone that made it sound as if they were an odd species or something on the telly.

'And two doors down, Billy.' Billy died not long after I left. TB. Tall, skinny Billy with a mop of curly ginger hair. We had played doctors and nurses in the air-raid shelter. He was always the doctor with his pretend stethoscope. No touching.

'And Mrs Jackson.' Her red and sweaty face, her eyebrows and forehead always smeared with flour from wiping them with her green pinafore. 'She gave us cakes, lived next door to Deaf Old Smelly, was too fat to fit on the pavement so had to walk on the cobbles and never stopped telling us they hurt her feet. She was always baking.'

Cats found their favourite ledges on the sunny side, and the dogs waited for the children to come home from school.

I had to spill it all out, my Street life.

'Our school was just a big house, twenty-five kids. The headmistress called us one big family. We ran along the country lane behind the houses, across the stile and through the field to it.' The girls hand in hand, our own small herd. The cows looked up from tearing at the grass to watch us and the boys whacking at the hedges with sticks.

'Lucky you.'

Around four in the afternoon, The Street was alive with shouts and screams, with hula hoops, hopscotch, skipping ropes, yo-yos and footballs. Handmade carts raced down the rough cobbles, and bikes. We used bad words for the fun of it, but whispered for the threat of having our mouths washed out with soapy water. And we pulled faces, watching the wind to see if it would change and we would have that face forever. Disappointment always.

'There were woods nearby. With hobgoblins, stoats, Moley and a white rabbit,' I said.

'Of course.'

'We kept ourselves to ourselves.' We were a tribe. There was a small town to the west, with a brown river running through it.

I murmured to Jake, 'The red admiral.'

Jake smirked. 'The butterfly. Red bands, brown/black wings, white spots near tips of its forewings.'

'That's it, the entrance exam for the Grammar. I gave them an adventure story of a pirate with a patch over one eye. All the other kids wrote about the butterfly.'

Jake kissed me. 'Good for you, something different. Bet they loved it.'

'The Grammar,' I said, 'I hated it, didn't fit in, the only one from The Street.' My school uniform wasn't quite the same as the others. My mother made it. The stares, the derision. Perhaps not, perhaps all in my head.

'My only friend at the Grammar was Hannah. She was French.' I hesitated. 'I fell in love with my French teacher, Miss Simonsen. She told us to question everything.' I had been sure she was speaking only to me. She'd asked me what I wanted to be. 'A poet,' I'd said.

I had lost that hope over the years.

I sat up, pulling the blanket with me, holding it tight around my shoulders. London in the distance was dreamlike. The Street was real just then.

'My Alice,' Jake said softly, although there was no one to hear. 'Full of surprises.'

Was I his Alice? I didn't yet know but there was a perhaps.

I rolled off him and sat up. I was getting cold. The new words were just one of the many things I stopped bothering about when my father left.

'Your father sounds great. What happened to him?' Jake's voice was wistful.

'He left us when I was fourteen.' How easily those words slipped out. The night of the school play. I couldn't bear right now to go there.

'That was tough,' Jake said.

'I gave up,' I said, meaning my father, and held Jake's hand tight. 'Fell in love with the Beatles instead.'

I refused to let my mother cut my hair. It grew until it was on my shoulders, curly and bushy. I didn't bother tying it back. Yet all these years later, I still brushed it every morning and night, fifty strokes each. She taught me that.

'A couple of years after he ran, I left for London, to find him.'

'And you never saw him again?'

I was silent a time. Jake was a patient listener, indeed, a patient man I had quickly learned. 'Once, at my mother's funeral,' I said, finally. 'She was fifty-one and he was living in the States by then.'

'Tell me,' he said.

'An old man,' I said, 'He'd got fat.' I heard the contempt in my voice and was a little ashamed.

Jake leant forward and kissed me. 'Princess,' he said.

I stopped his lips with my forefinger.

We were silent a minute or two, until I turned back to him and said, 'He loved me.' I let my words reverberate in my head, confusing. 'He wasn't around much, but I'd got used to that.' A lie.

'And your mother?'

'She blamed the war, said my father was different when he came back to her, changed. I blamed her for my father's absence.'

'Not good.'

'Yes, I was wrong, a kid.' I paused then said, 'She loved him, even after he abandoned us.' I added, 'And she loved me but I never noticed until too late.'

'I'd like to go there,' Jake said. 'To The Street, wherever it is.'

'You can't, it's pulled down. Rose Avenue,' I murmured. 'A brand-new housing estate. Mum was the last to leave The Street.' She'd never thought of Rose Avenue as home.

Tower blocks littered the fields between The Street and the town, concrete boxes streaming upwards: tall, ugly, punctuated by rows of windows and accommodating thousands. "Streets in the sky", the newspapers called them. And a little further out, a large estate of hundreds of expensive houses. Tarmac streets ran like sores along the valley. Shops changed and multiplied, and big sums were offered to The Street, a lifetime's dream of cash. Glossy brochures of bright new houses with gardens front and back, ensuite bathrooms, bright kitchens with fridges, freezers, the latest in cookers. Housewives' dreams slammed through letterboxes and pored over and discussed by the women. Hope and change thrummed up and down the cobbles. Most took the cash and moved to the tower blocks. The Street was kicked aside like a child's plaything, to be reduced to rubble.

I stood in front of the Rothkos many times that first weekend, breathed in the deep, strong colours: floating, lustful. It was the red that pulled me in, away from the blacks. I sometimes imagined I was Mrs Dalloway. She thought that even living one day was dangerous. Perhaps it was.

I returned to Wimbledon on the Sunday afternoon. I needed clean clothes, I needed space. Jake was leaving for New York early the next day.

I wondered, for a brief second, if I had made a mistake. Another man who was always elsewhere.

'I know where to find you,' he said, when we hugged at the station.

5

After Jake's house, mine looked a mess. It was a mess.

I took down the Van Gogh *Sunflowers* poster and the menu from the early days of the Hard Rock Cafe. The corkboard went, with its randomly cluttered postcards: the Eiffel Tower, the Mona Lisa, St Mark's Square, the Spanish Steps, beaches on the Greek islands and many others.

The 1960s and 70s went into the bin.

I tore up a photo of myself wearing hot pants and with permed hair and kept the Provencal pottery I'd bought when bumming through France. It had taken too much effort to get it back to trash it. The fridge magnets with the silly sayings went. I hadn't noticed most of that stuff for years. Lost years. I'd run from place to place, made friends, lost them. Without the evidence I might have believed I'd imagined those years. Were they good? I didn't know. I'd believed they were.

Two photographs on the mantelpiece survived the clear-out. One, a grainy black and white of my mother and father on their wedding day. The other, not much less grainy, of ten-year-old me, standing in my Sunday best dress, my hair with a ribbon either side and wearing a cheeky grin. I smiled at my ten-year-old self, put them both away in a drawer and swept back the years, waves of memories.

*

My exam results were out. Passes in English and French were not enough. It was the summer of 1962, the year when Kennedy and Khrushchev drove the world to the brink of nuclear war, although that was to pass me by. 'Marilyn Monroe is dead,' I'd told my mother across the kitchen table, my voice wet. 'I'm going to London to live.' I was going to dye my hair blonde, beg or steal white fur coats and long white gloves and wear bright red lipsticks.

'You're just like him,' she said, turning to look at me, misery and anger in her eyes, her bottom lip trembling.

She put down her knife and fork and pushed her plate of sausages and mashed potatoes away. 'Well, I mightn't notice you've gone. You've barely spoken to me since he left.' A small brittle laugh. 'Not that you spoke all that much before. Just like your father. The Street not good enough for you.' She slumped in her chair. 'Why London? What do you know about London?'

For a wild moment I wanted to say, 'The Beatles are there.'

It was 832 days since my father had left. My notebook proved it, each day crossed off, neat columns of figures in totals of twenty.

'A runner,' she said. 'You'll be back before the year end. London's full of girls like you.'

How would she know? She'd never been there.

I swung my hair around over my face. She hated my long hair. It was my greatest joy then, my pathetic rebellion.

She turned away from me, picked up her pack of Players, shook one out, lit it and put it to her lips. She pulled hard, then breathed out, smoke slipping from between her lips. 'You secretive little thing. Don't think you'll find your father in London. You always were headstrong.'

It was her eyes, replicas of my own, that troubled me most: wet, miserable and loving.

'You still love him,' I said, my face screwed up, my eyes almost closed. 'How can you?'

'You haven't been in love, Pet, really in love,' my mother said. 'It can hide for a while but it's still there. He loved you. You can't ever have doubted that.'

She stopped and smiled, was somewhere else. 'The dance. He was beautiful, Tom was, standing by himself smoking. All the girls were after him. He was in his Air Force blue-grey jacket and trousers, pale blue shirt and dark tie, leaning against the wall of the hall, a little apart from the other men. Us girls, dressed in our best, in a huddle, waiting to be asked to dance. He chose me. We danced to Bing Crosby. I knew that night he was the one.'

I looked away.

Twelve years later, she was dead.

Those early days, when I first arrived in London, living in a bedsit in Earls Court, my accent had marked me out as from somewhere else. I had a powder compact in my new handbag and a transistor radio that I carried everywhere,

45

plastered to my ear. I knew little to fit me for my new life; thought I knew everything.

My body then was still a child's with small, firm breasts, no Marilyn Monroe.

Before leaving The Street, I had tamed my hair into braids that hung on either side of my head, nestling in front of my shoulders. I was proud of them.

Within a month they were gone. A hairdresser, held a braid in her hand, scissors in the other.

'Are you sure?' she asked.

'Audrey Hepburn,' I murmured. A little shyly, humming *Moon River*.

The girl laughed. 'You saw it too. *Breakfast at Tiffany's.*'

The cinema compensated a little for my loneliness.

I couldn't copy Hepburn's clothes, a stretch too far from my mother's homemade skirts and dresses, but I had my ears pierced and bought earrings to compensate for my shorn head. I chose a pair of dangly stars.

I was cutting away, throwing away my mother and The Street.

Part of me believed I was special, that London would falter and bow down before me, a sixteen-year-old who had failed at school and left the Grammar early. I had lived through the lives of the heroines of books, had been warned by Miss Simonsen about my over-vivid imagination. I'd wanted Paris, the city of Simone de Beauvoir, but the closest I could get was to buy a pack of Gauloise cigarettes at the newsagent's at King's Cross station.

My first London meal: a tin of tomato soup, 1s 3p, and most of a loaf of sliced bread, 1s 8p. If I lived on that sort of food, I had about enough money to last me three months.

I was a little afraid.

People, strange people. I smiled at everyone. Few smiled back. I said 'Hello' and they looked puzzled, or away. Perhaps they heard the fear in my voice.

So many houses, cars, people and noise. I missed the moon and the stars, hated the black sky populated by harsh streetlights. I wanted to go up in a plane, or some sort of spaceship, just to see how far you'd have to go to get away from the lights of London.

For ever, probably.

I bought a rubber plant, just like the one I had at home.

The big freeze, the coldest winter on record for 200 years. I bought a duffle coat and desert boots.

I knew little of tourist London: the galleries, Buckingham Palace, Westminster Abbey, the churches. It was the parks I loved, the open spaces, especially Kensington Gardens with Peter Pan, the statue, a bronze boy playing the flute, standing on a tree stump, surrounded by animals and fairies, playing a violin.

I learned to stop saying hello to strangers; I learned to not look them in the eye. No one cared what I did. Both lonely and liberating. No rules, nothing predictable, no love.

*

Che Guevara and Simone de Beauvoir posters covered the walls of my bedsit. I read *Private Eye* each fortnight to be in the know, but missed most of the innuendo. I danced in dark basement clubs to Beatles' music: *Love, love me do*.

I bought fashion magazines and a bright red plastic mac and several mini skirts, and trousers so wide at the bottom that I couldn't see my shoes. I threw out the skirt and dress my mother had stitched on her Singer sewing machine and the jumper she had knitted. I threw out the shame.

I was everything at once: a communist, a feminist, a bohemian; was really just copying everyone around me. Always searching for my father, peering at unusual cars, flash cars, looking for a driver in a check jacket and a bright red tie.

I started a letter to my mother but couldn't find the words so sent a postcard of Buckingham Palace. Went home, for brief visits when she threatened to come to London.

I learned to type, got a job in an office where the bosses, all men, seemed old, and how they lorded it over us secretaries. We stuck up for each other, went to the pub and were shrill about abortion and a woman's right to choose. What did I know about it all? Nothing; it didn't matter. I professed free love although still a virgin, and it began to look as if love was free because no one wanted me. My pay was eight pounds a week.

I drank indiscriminately, excessively. Blank nights fuelled by Benzedrine and whatever pills were offered.

The years passed. I was one of London's lonely people. I listened to the Beatles, daydreaming of bumping into Paul McCartney, or into my father.

My mother died and left me Rose Cottage and more. I had money, lots. That was nine years ago.

On one of my random bus trips round London I discovered Wimbledon Common, glimpsed water and large swathes of green backed by woods. I rushed off the bus, almost tumbling down the steps. Inner London wiped out the countryside and the birdsong.

The young estate agent described the house as a fantastic opportunity for a family: three well-appointed bedrooms, welcoming entrance hall, paved driveway for off-street parking, private back garden and close to the common with its grassland, birch wood and history; desirable neighbourhood, excellent schools... Estate agent speak.

Far too big. He didn't ask about my family. I had no children, didn't want any, just wanted out of my dark flat and the crush of Paddington.

My house was tall, thin, and made of brick; pushing purposely upward for three floors with its two bathrooms, one more than I needed, and two more bedrooms than I had a use for. I had no car to park at the front.

I moved in and two of the walls of the sitting room were soon lined with books. I refused to give any away, except to friends who might treasure them. Few books left the house.

I made the top room into my study. From there I could look down into the nearby back gardens: the neighbours, acquaintances or strangers. I bought a functional, plain teak desk from Habitat and a chair to match. Teak bookshelves lined the wall. I planned to spend long days and nights up there writing.

I passed my days working in a library and my nights in my bedroom in the house I'd bought and lived in lightly. The study was rarely visited.

One summer evening, shortly after I moved in, I wandered up to the open green of the common and the woods, past several ponds, until I found another smaller one, surrounded by birch trees. On its edge stood a solitary grey heron with long neck and dagger-like beak.

Herons, roasted at medieval banquets, a wingspan of six feet or more, and the fat of a heron killed at full moon was once believed to be a cure for rheumatism.

The heron and I would be friends, even though he was far more beautiful and elegant than I.

Loners both.

I had friends but they lessened in number when I failed to return the calls, forgot birthdays and Christmas cards.

I couldn't say exactly when I slipped into this almost solitary existence. I believed I was content.

I worked, I went home, and seldom climbed the stairs to my study.

6

I lay curled on the sofa, my head in Jake's lap. He sprawled, in tracksuit bottoms and a tee-shirt, his legs stuck far into the room.

'Coffee?' Jake offered.

'Tea, please.' I snuggled back down into the warm space he had vacated and waited.

Four Darks in Red on the opposite wall embraced me, enfolded me in a fierce love.

It was a couple of weeks after that first weekend.

I had never put my past deeds under too close scrutiny, hadn't been in love all these years, not like this. To be in the same room with Jake, to touch in passing, to share a glance, to know what he was thinking, to know that no one else, nothing else, mattered.

'A small perfect flower,' Jake called me.

If he moved away, left the room, no matter for how brief a moment, I touched him lightly on return, to claim him.

I was safe.

Jake placed two mugs on the small table.

I dragged myself upright, picked up my tea. It was a bright, sunny day, the sort that suited the chasing away of shadows. I stared into the sun until my eyes blurred.

'There was someone that mattered to me,' I said. 'Years ago, before Neil Armstrong said those words about mankind. I was young, silly.'

Rob. For some time I had wanted to tell Jake. None of the others had mattered.

'Tell me,' he said, tenderness in his voice. Jake was a little like Rob, in body and perhaps background, although Rob did his best to hide his family.

I met Rob in one of the clubs somewhere on the King's Road and fell in love with his shoulder-length hair. He came over and kissed me on the mouth, put one hand on my breast and with his other gave me a joint. He wore an earring, something I also marvelled at back then. And a long Afghan coat. I fell in love with that too. He was the most beautiful man I had ever seen.

'Rob, he was a poet. That's what he claimed, but when I asked to see the poems he said they weren't ready and I wouldn't understand them.'

'Oh, yes,' Jake murmured. 'I've met men like him. All bullshit.'

'I didn't know much about sex. Just as I was leaving for London, my mother said, "Don't let any man touch you down there," and pointed to just below her tummy, although it sort of turned into a wave.'

He bent forward and lightly touched his lips on my forehead. 'I didn't get that. It was as if sex didn't exist. We all arrived, flown in by a stork.'

Back at his squat, Rob and I had made love in a very large bed. He called me "bitch".

Exciting.

What else could I now remember? The beating of my heart. And, I had to admit, the disappointment. The sex wasn't a beautiful thing, not what the books had hinted at.

A girl walked into the bedroom as Rob and I fucked. I turned my head to look at her. She was beautiful, tall like Rob. She sat on the edge of the bed and watched.

When he rolled away, the girl lay down beside me, putting out her hand to feel the pink-tinged wet between my thighs.

'Look after her,' Rob said to the girl as he strode out of the room.

She did.

I never saw him fuck Ellie so I don't know if he called her "bitch". Later, I noticed that Ellie had fat ankles.

We became friends.

Rob said make-up was demeaning, wasn't feminist, so I stopped wearing it. I threw away my paltry store of cheap cosmetics. He gave me cigarettes that smelled different and made me feel good. We moved on to acid, always seeking the ultimate.

Anything was possible. Neil Alden Armstrong had stepped on the moon. One small step and all that.

'Rob said he was a terrorist,' I said to Jake.

'Against what?'

'Too many children in the world.' Rob's ideals were like his poems: fluid creatures of the moment. 'We lived off food from the bins or shop-bought food Rob brought home, mostly soya beans, brown rice and heavy bread. We joined the CND, Greenpeace and the Labour Party, a good triumvirate; went to the meetings, met the same people and discussed the same things: war, peace, the pound in your pocket and Barbara Castle, the first woman appointed Secretary of State.'

'Yes, I remember her.'

'How could you not?' I chided.

I found yoga. Rob refused to go, said it was a girl's thing. Ellie and I went twice a week, practised daily. Ellie lent me a copy of *The Female Eunuch*. We had much to say about the subservience of women. We were, oh, so serious.

'Germaine Greer,' I said to Jake.

'Ah, the mad woman.'

'Not really. "Do what you want and want what you do",' I quoted from *The Female Eunuch*. Why had it taken so long for me to find that out? 'Women, handmaids in the more important work of men,' I added.

'Can I be your handmaid?'

'Always.' I held out my hand and he kissed it.

Rob threw the book in the fire. Germaine would have laughed at that, would have said it made her point. I thought about standing for parliament, to change things, although I wasn't clear exactly what things. Rob had sniggered when I told him.

'He went back to Oxford,' I said, leaving Ellie out of the story. 'To posh parents like yours.' He cut his hair, took out his earring and left, wearing a mid-blue three-piece suit, shirt and tie. Ellie went with him. She was pregnant, said his parents had bribed him.

'Poor Rob,' Jake chuckled.

It had taken me months to see that his eyes were empty. He had been a delusion, part of the London glamour, and I had been a fool.

'He was different to anyone I'd known. That was what I fell for.'

Jake leant down and kissed me.

'And you?' I touched Jake's face. 'What about you?'

'That boy at school,' he said. 'I was scared of girls, of anyone. A boy seemed safer.' He looked away.

'Girls, women?'

'One or two, nothing serious. One that Papa would have approved of. We bored each other. I was waiting for you. No, I wasn't. I'd given up.'

'So now it's you and me,' I said.

'Always.'

'Cross your heart and hope to die.' That silly giggle again.

We showered together or climbed into his long bath. My fingers travelled his white body, through the hairs on his chest, over his belly, and teased his flaccid, floating cock.

He washed my hair; I washed his. He bathed and dried me the way I supposed a mother did a baby.

I held him close. 'I love you,' I said. The words surprised me.

My love for Jake was locked away in a box of wonder. Just we two.

He leant over to the table and passed me the box of After Eight mints. I took three, and the papers fluttered to the carpet. Jake picked them up, murmuring, 'Your handmaiden.'

7

I had grown to think of love as an ad hoc thing, a parcel, delivered, opened, discarded. I knew already that Jake had all of me. There was nothing more. I wanted to burrow into him, know him like I knew myself. Did I know myself? Perhaps not.

I had been a little spiky, hard-edged. No longer. To be loved by Jake was all I needed for the rest of time.

I returned from the library each night, longing for him, a little fearful that he might have vanished.

I had been a moderately careless dresser. Now, each morning, I laid out my clothes on the bed, found the right accessories, preened, stretched my neck, imagining it to be unusually long, like those of famous actresses. A little common sense trickled through as I spat "peacock" at the image.

We ate out a lot. He ordered raw steak, and if he wanted to torment me, he had a raw egg on top. He ate tomatoes whole, bit through their tight protective skin into the pulpy seeds and flesh inside. No salt.

When he didn't feel like cooking, we had pizza from the new place that had just opened. Or a takeaway curry. The pubs didn't appeal to either of us.

Our weekends were gentle, leisurely. We shared our dreams, spending long hours over dinner with good wine, often with talk of our dreams.

'A bookshop,' I said. 'I'd like to have a bookshop. I'd stock it with all the books I love.'

'Full of VW,' Jake laughed.

'Of course. But a few others.'

'A painter,' Jake said, oh so softly.

'Indubitably.' I stood, pulled his face to me and kissed him.

We discussed, in a roundabout way, moving into one place, acknowledging that it was ridiculous living on opposite sides of London. Neither of us wanted to live in its heart. Jake's work took him away too often, mostly to New York. He loved it there. Odd that, as he was so quintessentially English. At those times, I returned to Wimbledon.

'Can't someone else go?' I grumbled.

'I love what I do. I do it better than anyone else.'

He didn't often boast.

'I'm a witch.' I added, 'I miss you.'

Every time he left I felt abandoned. Knew myself to be pathetic.

We roamed London together, becoming cinema buffs, mostly to the Hampstead Everyman. We weren't very subtle in our choices. I took him to see Meryl Streep in *Silkwood*. We argued about the ending. I was the activist

Karen, the conspiracy theorist, so of course the car crash was no accident. I couldn't persuade Jake. He was too soft, looked for the good in things, yet James Bond films were his favourites. Almost all our videos were James Bond films.

'You, James Bond,' I said, 'me, Meryl Streep.'

Our lives fluctuated around two very large patches of green and ponds. Reluctantly, I admitted to the heath's superiority with its thirty ponds.

On the day Neil Kinnock became leader of the Labour Party, 2nd October 1983, and saved the party, so some papers claimed, although it proved later to be a rather different story, Jake rented out his apartment and moved to Wimbledon.

He placed his arms around me, leant down and put his head onto my shoulder. 'I love you, Mrs Jake,' he whispered.

'I love you, Mr Alice.'

My street was quiet. Few cars passed down it or parked on the kerbs. Our neighbours were elderly strangers.

Except for a couple of dull landscapes, bought on impulse somewhere, probably a street market, the walls of the rooms were largely bare. I took down the paintings and we spent a week deciding where his Rothkos would go. Three ended up in the sitting room, one in our bedroom.

I ran my hands over my books. I could have borrowed most of them from the library, but that was not the same as having them line my walls. I took down enough to make room for Jake's, carted them off to the charity shop and showered him with VW's novels. He read *Mrs Dalloway*, pronounced himself in love with Clarissa.

He brought his jazz records and player to Wimbledon. I had to admire the mellifluous tones of their playing, often near weeping with the beauty of it. I'd heard of Duke Ellington but not the others. I loved them, even considered taking up the sax, then remembered. As a kid, I'd persuaded my father to buy me an expensive violin and took music lessons. I was hopeless. One day, on the way home from school, I carefully placed the violin under the seat of the bus and got off.

The first meal I cooked for us was boeuf bourguignon followed by cheat's crème caramel, both from Delia's *How to Cheat*. I followed those with a rather boring lamb stew that would last three nights.

All were passable, nothing more. Jake said all the right things about my food then, standing behind me one evening in the kitchen, put his arms round me and murmured, 'Let me cook, I love it.'

I gave in immediately. He came home the next Saturday with a slab of beef, placed it on the kitchen worktop with olive oil, a bottle of brandy, two glasses of red wine (one for the dish, one for him), thyme, parsley, a small strip of orange peel and a cup of black olives. All neatly laid out. He leant over the recipe, carefully checked the ingredients, read out loud, 'Three and a half hours to cook.'

I stood on tiptoe and kissed the back of his neck. He barely noticed.

He brought much of the flat's kitchen with him: his knives in their block, "the magnificent seven", as he called them, his pans that made mine look as if I'd found them in a rubbish dump, and other pieces of cooking apparatus that I'd never seen.

He brought home exotic fruits: mango, passion fruit, papaya.

And figs. He squeezed them daily for ripeness, then, starting at their pointy tops, peeled the skin downwards, strip by strip, finally placing the whole thing in his mouth.

He did something similar with avocados, the peeling part, then nibbled them, like an oversized mouse, round and round until he was left with the stone.

I watched, not tempted. His voice was a smile, a song that I wrapped myself in.

Jake changed everything. I had been a pretence before. In shop windows I saw someone else reflected. Happy eyes stared back, a hint of surprise in them.

I could tell him anything, wanted to tell him everything. Our world was high-walled, protected, mysterious. Perhaps another planet. Just the two of us.

We watched TV, curled together on the sofa. *Yes Minister* was his favourite programme.

'That's because you're like him,' I said.

'Who?' His smile told me he knew.

'Jim Hacker.'

We both loved *Cagney and Lacey*, Jake because it was set in Manhattan. For a time, I wore cowl necks. We both hated *Dallas*.

He employed two young men to decorate the rooms, except my book-lined neglected study at the top of the house. My dreams of escaping (from what?) to the top of the house had quickly died.

The house echoed with him, whether or not he was here, its air soft, caressing.

I started talking to my neighbours and the people in the street, smiled unknowingly, and most surprising of all, I became reasonably tidy around the house.

I waited each evening for the sound of his footsteps, the scent of his aftershave and his arms around me.

He left the hand basin covered with fine bristles after shaving, and on the weekends, he got out the ironing board.

The first time I laughed. I'd never seen a man iron.

'School,' he said, 'then university.' He hung an exquisitely ironed shirt on a coat hanger and pulled another from the basket, mostly full of my yet-to-be-ironed clothes. 'Don't do women's clothes,' he said.

My clothes tended to pile up until I had no choice.

He believed in homeopathy and herbal stuff. I went to a straight-up doctor. He went to a chiropodist. I told him that was for old men who could no longer reach their feet. He cut my toenails. What greater love could a man have?

Jake read the newspaper from cover to cover, *The Times*. I glanced at the headlines. And he read biographies, usually of great men.

On politics we agreed to disagree.

He loved sleep. I didn't, so read far into the night, pausing at the dull parts to gaze at him, wonder at the love that had tripped me up.

Spitting Image took over from *Yes Minister* as our favourite TV viewing. Bland, boring Geoffrey Howe talking to sheep; Norman Tebbit as a leather-clad skinhead; Edwina Currie as a vampire, and best of all of them, Cecil Parkinson, fucking every woman in sight, unimaginable as that was. We made love afterwards on the settee, still laughing.

He painted my toenails deep red, carefully unscrewing the top of the bottle and scraping the brush on its side. He then applied the polish in wide, bright strokes, big toe first, total concentration on his face.

'It's as close as I'll get to being a painter.' He cocked his head. 'He'd like the colour.'

'Have you done this before?' I had good feet, neat, despite the winklepickers and high heels I invariably wore.

'Never.'

In someone less honest, the vehemence of his tone might have covered a lie.

He wanted to come with me to shop for clothes. I refused. 'Do you want me to come with you to your tailor?'

'Of course,' he said.

He made me laugh.

I kept his feet on the ground.

8

A cold March day, 1984

Jake perched on the arm of my chair, smelling of Old Spice, dressed in his favourite weekend wear: cream turtleneck sweater and khaki slacks. A delicate sun lit his face and his love. Nine months since we met. Joy was when we were together. The rest was waiting.

On the nearby seat, *The Times* shouted the end of British coal. We were not to know then how prescient this was, or how many of the communities would never recover from the closures, 187,000 miners on strike.

'A rabble-rouser,' Jake had declared of Arthur Scargill.

'No one should work in those conditions. Southerner.' I demurred but without my usual vehemence. My fight seemed to have vanished. Perhaps that was what love did.

The sitting room was large, well proportioned, a couple of Jake's Rothkos on the walls, another lined with books. Sofa and two armchairs and a cluster of small tables. A plain rug in front of a gas fire. The dining room table was at the far end with a door opening to the kitchen, offering glimpses of the back garden.

Jake was smoking, the ashtray on his lap, the cigarette between first finger and thumb, the back of his hands facing towards his lips.

My dream had flickered and grown. If you'd asked me about babies even a year ago, I would have laughed. Work was good. I was calmer in everyday life than I had believed possible. Still over-hasty, still a little angry.

I tried to sound composed. 'I have a favour to ask, a big one.' I looked up at him.

'Granted.'

That was always his answer to my requests, a bit of a joke between us.

I took a deep breath and leant into his side. 'A baby.'

He opened his eyes wide, threw himself against the back of my chair and let rip that outrageous laugh of his. 'A baby. I thought we'd said...' He laughed again, but this time there was a hint of nervousness. 'No kid wants me for a father.'

'Why not? You'd be a wonderful father.' I had turned thirty-eight a few months back and time was running out. Jake never asked me about the pill once we agreed I'd take care of it. 'I'd take a couple of years off work. We can afford it.' I almost laughed. I'd always despised women who thought of babies in terms of cash.

'I don't know. I just can't see it. And my job, I'm away a lot. How will you manage?'

Well, it was out. Nothing was going to change. His absences, I hated them. Perhaps I was wanting to patch them over and, in truth, I saw this as yet non-existent baby as my affair.

'You really want that? It would be tough.' A little of the fear receded from his eyes.

The battle was won.

'No girls,' he said, slipping off the arm of the sofa, pulling me to my feet and then onto his knee. I nestled there, a baby bird. 'A boy would be good.'

'Do you mean that?' I asked, so quietly, I almost missed my own words.

He took my face between both hands. 'Marry me,' he said.

'Of course.'

That night we made love, gently, nervously, as if for the first time.

I woke late the next morning. Jake had left already for an early flight. There was an envelope on the bedside table, *Alice* written on the outside.

I leant against a pillow and somewhat nervously opened the envelope. Inside was a sheet of paper covered in Jake's elegant green scrawl.

My love (Mrs Jake),

Soon it will be our special day. The two of us side by side, holding hands. We will say the words, the legal ones. A formality.

I haven't known love like this before. You make me real.

Oh, my love.
Your Jake (Mr Alice)

He had stolen my words. It was me that was real, at last.

We had met late, we compromised, loved; would never part, of that I was sure.

No mention of the other. It would happen.

Eleven months and a few days after meeting in the library, we married in a registry office: Tuesday, 8th May, 1984.

I wore a new cream linen dress with a Venetian necklace Jake had given me. And bright green high heels, the orange flower in my hair. Hats weren't me. Jake had a new suit made, navy as always. A tie of reds and purple blobs of colour. And a new waistcoat, trimmed with our orange.

Anne was a witness, and David, Jake's boss and a drinker of many malts.

We agreed to love each other forever. And all the other words. They were not real, only my Jake was that. We exchanged rings: plain gold bands.

We ran down the steps, holding hands, skipping like kids. A small crowd outside, waiting, with the next couple.

An expensive lunch for the four of us.

David and Jake spent what seemed like hours discussing which bottles of wine to order, then sniffing and swirling while Anne and I got on with what mattered: talking.

She wouldn't give up. 'Babies,' she insisted. 'Or you'll regret it.'

I smiled.

The taxi pulled up outside the house.

We stepped out, still holding hands.

'This way. I've something to show you.' I pulled on my jacket and started up the hill, running awkwardly in my heels.

The sky was blue, pretending, the spring warmth meagre.

Jake caught me up. 'Where are we going?'

'You'll see.'

We hurried up the hill, past the pond spotted with gulls. An early butterfly flurried past. 'A monarch,' I said.

Jake stared around.

'Not the king, husband. A butterfly.' It had orange and black wings.

'Ah.'

'They taste with their feet, can see some colours. Their skeleton is on the outside, water inside.'

'So I've married an encyclopaedia.'

'Of course,' I said.

We ran on, hand in hand.

'I think I'd like the caterpillar stage. All they do is eat. It first eats the leaf it was born on,' I said.

Deep in the wood, I found him, the heron, beside the pond.

'There,' I said, 'my wedding gift.'

The heron put its head up, stared, preened, stood tall.

Jake took off his jacket and laid it on a thick bracken bed.

We'd said the words earlier. There was no more to say right then. I wanted to invade his life, live his secrets, uncover him.

I held him tight and watched my tears drop on his smart new suit.

Mr and Mrs Oldfield.

9

Jake obsessed with my belly, splaying his fingers over it, spreading them wide, fussing.

'I'm pregnant, not dying,' I protested but didn't really have a clue about this pregnancy business.

He persisted, leant down to place his ear on it. Did he expect a song?

I surprised myself by trying to do the ordained things. I ate the right foods, except for the Cadbury Creme Eggs and the Black Forest gateau that Jake brought home too often. Oh, and the Arctic Roll. Now was the time to eat for two.

I gave up on the antenatal classes. Everyone wanted to tell me what to do and I didn't take easily to that. The other women were too young, made me feel old. I bought all the books on pregnancy that I could find and soon threw them away.

Every morning, I examined my belly, willing it to swell.

Soon enough I hated the huge knickers, blossoming breasts and my small waist lost in this balloon, my skirts and trousers too tight.

The sonographer put some cold gel on my belly, ran a probe over my skin. Jake and I watched the black and white screen. She seemed to make sense of it, I couldn't.

'All looks good, Normal. Come back between eighteen and twenty-one weeks. We can check any anomalies then.'

Anomalies, the risk of Down's. An older mother like me. I refused the test. My baby girl, Rebecca, would be perfect.

Names. I considered Miranda, meaning wonderful, Prospero's daughter, but opted for Daphne du Maurier's Rebecca. I was done with *The Tempest*. I didn't discuss them with Jake.

I bought baby clothes, exquisite little dresses and shoes and much else.

Mostly, I was insanely joyful, except that I spent too much of my days and nights peeing. No one warned me about that.

The kicks were slow in coming, were rather a flutter or a dance.

Daughter. How I loved that word. I wanted the whole world for her.

My mother. She must have felt the same when she was carrying me. 'I've always loved you more than my own life,' she'd said, putting a cigarette to her lips, on the day of my last visit to Rose Cottage. 'You'll understand one day.'

As I began to show people started treating me differently, strangers and friends both. London softened.

I was losing my identity, or was I finding it?

'It will be wonderful. Children,' Anne said, a messianic look in her eyes. She often regretted out loud how quickly her own four were growing up, feared their leaving home to take up their own lives and empty hers.

'Just one,' I offered.

'Perhaps,' she said.

Work segued into maternity leave. Part of me hated leaving the library and my friends there. Anne demanded to be godmother.

'I don't believe in God.'

'That doesn't matter.' She hugged me.

I wasn't overly clever about this pregnancy business. My brain had gone into stasis.

10

I had to get out of the house.

A Sunday, very early in the new year. Time had slowed to a still point.

Jake was away. I minded but there was little I could do about it. Each evening I waited by the phone. When it rang, I alternated between happiness and anger, asking myself if he really loved me. If he did, he wouldn't leave me.

I had become a bit of a nag.

I picked my way up the hill towards the common, holding my belly with both hands. I was never fast but hated being so slow. I could no longer fit into any of my trousers so had to wear loose-fitting skirts with an elastic waist, and generous sweaters to accommodate my breasts, which seemed in competition with my belly.

At the first pond, I carried on across the green to the woods and through them to another pond where I knew I would find some large rocks. I'd watch the water and the birds, although it was early in the year. It was dry but very cold. I was well wrapped in a thick coat and wore fur-lined boots. Being pregnant kept me warm but not my feet.

A man walking towards me smiled. At my belly.

At the edge of the next pond I walked round its end towards the rocks and stopped.

A woman sat on my rocks with her legs crossed, showing off plump knees and thighs encased in stockings. Her jacket could not disguise the generous curves of her body. Her blonde hairdo was enormous, towering Madonna-style, and her wrists and neck were adorned with large, glittery gems.

She waved, then stood. 'Sit here, you look tired, not surprising.' She pointed to my belly. 'Take the weight off your feet.'

Her eyes were deep blue and the flesh of her neck took a shortcut to her chin. When she was old her chin would disappear into it. I frequently imagined what I and others would look like when transmogrified into old age.

She held up a book and raised one eyebrow. 'I get away for peace and quiet and to read. The boys.'

I'd always wanted to do that eyebrow thing, but mine insisted on unison.

'*Mrs. Dalloway.*' I said, unable to keep the surprise out of my voice. 'When I was a kid, at school, I called myself Clarissa for a time.'

'Good, we'll be friends.' She stopped. 'Sorry, I can be a bit of a bully sometimes. Sorry. Beth, Beth Cuthbert.' She put a plump ring-encrusted hand to her mouth. Stood, quickly, lightly, her flesh falling downwards, stretching her dress.

Her knees were dirty and her stockings torn.

'I know,' she said, following my eyes. 'I hunt,' she said. 'Not the right clothes. Couldn't help myself when I spotted this beauty.' She held out a green-grey clump.

Perhaps she was mad. I shook my head. 'Wouldn't have a clue. Alice Oldfield.' I sat, easing myself, and my belly which had its own separate existence, down onto the rock. 'Hunt?'

'Mosses, my work, an old habit. I can't come here without the gear.' She pointed to a small backpack. 'If you'd come half an hour ago, you might have found me on my knees in the woods over there. Not a lovely sight.' Her breasts shook with her laughter. A crimson wool skirt covered broad hips.

'Look.' She took my arm and pointed to mallards swimming on the pond. Flashes of bright orange legs, contrasting with glossy green heads.

She settled herself beside me. 'It's not fair.'

'What's not?'

'The males have the colour. The females are so dull. Thank God we're not birds.' Her laugh was a "I don't care what you think" semi shout.

I turned to her with a smile. The North was in her voice. 'My part of the world.'

'My mum still lives there. What about yours, your mum? Her first grandchild?'

I shook my head, answered slowly. 'She died, years back.'

'Sorry,' Beth murmured.

We both sat and watched the birds.

'How long?' She pointed to my belly.

'Four weeks.' I was beginning to wonder if this was real. 'I live down the hill, love coming up here. There's usually no one about.'

'Ah, so I've spoilt it for you.'

I shook my head.

'Boy or girl?'

'Girl.' I had told them at the hospital that I didn't want to know the sex.

'Lucky you. I've got two boys, holy terrors. Mind you, I adore them.' A soft breeze carried her love and her words, dancing, into the sheltering trees.

She dug into her pack for her wallet and pulled out two photographs: two smiley blond kids.

'Ben is three, wants to be loved by everyone. Matthew five, at school. He's a serious kid, like his dad. Amazing how quickly they become their own little creatures.'

'Lovely.' I meant it, although Anne was always showing me photographs of her kids and I'd never paid much attention.

'I can't be too long. Pete will be driven crazy by now.' A giggle. 'That's how he found me, on my knees in a wood. I'm lucky, he works from home a lot.' She looked at her watch. 'I said I'd be home an hour ago.'

'Jake's in the US right now.'

'That's tough. When's he back?'

'In time, I hope. He doesn't like being away right now. Work.' Jake fretted, about me being on my own, about the birth, about everything to do with pregnancy. Underneath it all, I suspected it was the threat of impending fatherhood.

I wondered sometimes, what we had done.

I stood. 'I've strayed too far. I'll have to go back. Pregnancy and bladders.' I was like an incontinent old woman.

Beth stood, unexpectedly quickly, shoving her wallet into her bag and slinging it over one shoulder, the book in her other hand. 'I'll walk some of the way with you,' she said.

Her heels were higher than mine and her tight skirt restricted her walk, so she took short steps, chubby knees flashing as we passed through the wood and across the green to the pond on the road and the top of Montgomery Hill.

Beth didn't stop talking, about her boys: mad for sport, football especially; good at schoolwork… until, 'Sorry. I'm going on about them. I do that.'

I loved the pride in her voice. My little girl would be a world-beater.

'That's okay,' I said. We had reached the pond near the road.

'I go this way.' Beth pointed towards the High Street.

'Do you always kidnap strangers?' I asked.

'Only interesting ones.'

'How do you choose?'

'Oh, I'm good at judging people.' The skin on the corners of her blue eyes crinkled. 'Here, you have this. It will give us an excuse to meet again.' She held out *Mrs Dalloway*.

I had no idea where my copy was. That and much else.

'Give me your phone number,' she said. 'I'd like to see her when she comes, and you could bring her to meet my boys. They should have had a little sister. It didn't happen.'

She wrote my telephone number on the back of her hand with a biro.

Back home I sprawled on the sofa, feet up, hands on my belly, an immense globe on which Jake might have drawn a map of most of the world.

Dusk had fallen, the cowardly fleeing of the light too soon.

I smiled to think of Beth, hoped she would telephone. We could be friends, although I knew nothing about mosses.

I would have a little girl, would take her to ballet lessons, would read her fairy stories, watch her smile. I would tell her I loved her, bask in her love. Strangers would marvel at how alike we were. I would give her everything, my life if I had to. I had it all planned.

She would be tall like her father, or perhaps not quite so tall, would love Mark Rothko and VW and be brave, adventurous. Never afraid.

I used the remote to turn on the TV, not caring what was on. 'Not long now,' I whispered to her, and felt a small kick.

11

17th February 1985

Two trees clad in bridal gowns, side by side; no grooms. Shrubs, shrouded lumps of white.

Heavy snow. Stillness, muffled sound. Soft swishing of the ambulance through slush.

Snowflakes fluttered down, past the hospital window.

Pain unending, transformative, its chalkiness. I put out my hand for Jake. Empty.

'Push,' urged the midwife. 'Push.'

Someone screaming. Me.

Much, much later, a smile unfurled across her round, tired face, 'You have a son, Alice, a lovely boy.'

I turned away, hid my tears.

A boy. That was why he had torn his way out, fighting.

What an imagination deficit. I had bought all the girly stuff for my daughter, a replica of me, a little one that I would love forever. A bit like a kid dressing a doll, a thirty-nine-year-old kid.

The midwife held out her arms. I hesitated, then took him, held him tight against my swollen breasts, held him clumsily.

He opened his eyes and stopped crying.

'Snow,' I pointed a half-free hand to the window. My first word to him. Each flake unique, hexagons on their wayward descent.

As always, I had slipped into a new life too carelessly.

I would teach him love, teach him not to fear, teach him to take the world in his tiny hands and triumph. I would keep him safe. That was my promise to him.

I touched his hand and he wound it around my index finger. The exquisite perfection of his feet and hands, the unblinking gaze of his eyes. His tiny nostrils, so small, so tentative; his full lips.

A boy. I laughed out loud. The midwife smiled and sat heavily on the chair beside the bed.

His face, as yet unwritten upon, with eyes of wonder and perplexity, offering a doubtful stare. He took my nipple in his mouth, his small hands pressing on my breast.

A mother. I buried my wet face in his belly, his hands on my head, his legs flailing. I listened to his odd noises, trying to work out what they meant. He was telling me something.

'Adam,' I whispered, holding him tight to my breast, our hearts beating in tandem.

I was in love. Again.

Adam Oldfield, born on 17th February 1985, at 8.12am.

12

Jake's key in the front door.

I ran my hand over my hair, wishing I'd made more effort. It was tied back in a ponytail and I was wearing old tracksuit bottoms and a milk-stained sweater. I had been home from hospital a day. We were both exhausted, my boy and me. I woke to feed and change him, ineptly, and fell back asleep beside him.

Yet I didn't want to sleep, I wanted to gaze at him, hold him to me, feel myself melting with joy and astonishment.

Jake's aftershave scented the hall as I reached up and sated my lips with his, felt the roughness of his cheek.

'Oh, my Alice, I should have been with you. I didn't get the message until too late. Fools.'

I heard the anger, knew my own.

'How could they? Idiots. I caught the first flight. I wanted to be with you. Oh, my lovely girl.'

I put a forefinger to his lips. 'He was in too much of a hurry to meet us. You're home.'

'Was it bad?'

I nodded, didn't want to go there. And I didn't speak of my early efforts at nappy changing, of poo up the back of Adam's vest. Jake placed his arms round me and nibbled one of my ears.

'A boy.'

I held Jake, feeling the skin of his face stretch as his smile widened, then I ran back to the sitting room and plucked Adam from his carrycot.

'Your son.' I held him out.

The long, slim fingers of one of his hands curled around Adam's nappy-fat bottom, the other under his head, and the white shawl hung down the front of Jake's trousers. His grey eyes flickered from the baby's face to mine, beads of perspiration on his forehead catching the light.

'He won't break,' I laughed. 'He likes you, I can tell.'

I could still feel Jake's arms wrapped round me, his lips on mine.

'Adam Oldfield,' Jake said. 'Adam,' he repeated. 'That's good,' his voice trembling and joyous. 'My son. Look, he's smiling.'

Adam's head had turned towards Jake's voice.

I shook my head, with that superior mother-knows-best look. 'It's wind, just wind.'

'Does it hurt him?'

As if in answer, Adam began to cry. I held out my arms. Jake kissed him gently on his forehead and surrendered him, smelling of my milk and something else, something rich, fresh, himself.

'I'm so sorry,' he said, 'so sorry.'

I leant over Adam to kiss Jake again. He was home. Part of me had expected him not to make it back, the untrusting part. Yet now he was here we were a family.

'I should have been here. I promised.' He stood, looking down on us.

'I missed you,' I said, although I hadn't. The birth had taken all of me. 'I love you, my Jakey.'

He took my hand and kissed my fingers. 'He's beautiful.'

'A boy,' I said, as if I'd known all along, despite the drawers upstairs replete with girls' clothes.

In the sitting room Jake dragged his armchair over the carpet and sat so our knees almost touched. He eased a silver cigarette case from his inside jacket pocket then stood to extract a lighter from his trouser pocket.

I unbuttoned my blouse and moved Adam's small mouth to my optimistic nipple. A quiet, trouble-free baby, the midwife had said.

'Wish I could do that.' Jake's voice was a little tremulous.

My head shot up, saw the wonder in his eyes.

'You'd be good at it.'

'I shall buy him a bike.' His eyes shone.

'Whoa,' I said. 'He's three days old. You'd best wait a bit.'

Jake took off his jacket, leant over and laid it on the back of the sofa.

I gazed at our son's small concentrated face then at his lightly curled fingers on my breast. For a moment I was back in that schoolroom, at the Grammar, Miss Simonsen writing on the blackboard: "*One is not born, one becomes a woman.* Simone de Beauvoir".

I had become. It had taken a very long time.

'His hands are so small,' Jake whispered.

He went back to the hall and returned with an expensive-looking camera.

'All that hanging around at the airport. I saw this.' He fiddled for a moment then took a photograph of Adam and me.

It wasn't particularly good but Jake had it framed and placed it on the mantelpiece.

A magnificent cot with soft satin padding round the bottom half of the wooden sides, bedding to match and brightly coloured plastic balls hanging above it, dominated Adam's room, next door to our bedroom. Jake had bought it from Harrods, weeks earlier. A brown rabbit, not white like the one I had carried around until so tattered it got thrown out, sat on the pillow in the cot. A courtesan in waiting, his brown legs dangling. I had spotted it in one of the many shops I wandered in and out of.

There was nothing girly about the rabbit. The shop had been full of pretty dolls with long blonde hair and sparkly dresses, and teddies with bows at their necks. The rabbit wasn't particularly beautiful but somehow right.

I told myself Adam was too young for his own room yet, would be lonely. He could sleep in his carrycot beside our bed. When he was a man and I was growing old, he would leave me, but not until then. I had that feeling, the sort of feeling that is never wrong.

We sprawled on the sofa, Jake, freshly showered and shaved. He'd demolished much of a bottle of wine and we'd shared a pizza from the place on the High Street. Adam was asleep upstairs, the baby alarm set. It was strange not to be with him, made me anxious.

'Our son,' Jake said, as he raised his glass.

'So tell me about San Francisco.' It was Jake's first time there, a change from New York.

'Wonderful. The bridge, stretching forever over the water. Well, two miles but that's a pretty big bridge, and boats, fishermen's boats, dozens, and cars. Cable cars, and hills.' He added, a little sadly, 'I miss the Rothkos. They seemed the point of all that travel.'

I didn't care about the Rothkos. I had Jake back.

He left the room and returned with a small red bottle in his hand.

My toenails were a mess.

'Put them here,' he said, as he laid a small towel over his knees.

The next day Jake brought home a teddy almost as big as Adam, a blue bow at its neck, large black eyes. Adam stared at it and turned away.

'It's big,' I said to Jake. 'Give him time.'

Adam never did like that teddy.

The snow had gone when I lifted Adam, dressed in a cream romper suit, cardigan, bonnet and mittens, into his Silver Cross pram with its large wheels and hood, his rabbit beside him. I tucked in the blankets around him and he lay there quietly, watching, waiting, his eyes flickering. It was a cold March day, the pavement slippery. We strolled, or Jake strolled with long confident strides, pushing the pram straight up the hill while I half ran, sort of skipped, my legs about a foot shorter than his, my hand tucked into the back of his tracksuit bottoms. I wore warm trousers, a sweater and thermal jacket, plus boots, gloves and hat. The hat seemed to puzzle Adam, or perhaps it was something else.

My breasts were milk-heavy, too big for my small frame.

It was a weekday, so the common was almost deserted. Hundreds of seagulls stood on the iced-over pond. I looked at Adam and whispered, he seemed to like whispers, 'I'll take you skating in a few years.' I would hold his small hand and we would glide over the ice. Always a dreamer. A skater I was not nor ever would be.

We strolled round the other side of the water, turning away from the wind, following the path to the woods, to be surrounded by oaks, beeches, silver birches and others I couldn't name. I shuffled my feet through the dead leaves.

'He's ours,' I murmured.

The grey heron would be waiting for our son, standing on the edge of our pond. I would take him another day.

Later in the year, house martins and swifts would be soaring over Rushmere Pond, and deep in the woods there would be mallards, coots, moorhens, greater spotted woodpeckers. And nuthatches running, head first, down the tree trunks. I would show him everything, empty my head into his.

On the way home, Jake ran ahead, pushing. Snatches of a song I didn't know drifted back up the hill. Joy and recalcitrant stomach muscles were slowing me down.

13

Those first days after Jake came home, we played at perfect families. Adam woke once or twice in the night and I would pluck him from the carrycot and place him on my breast or between us in the bed. He would still be there until he needed another feed.

Jake never managed the nappies but walked or nursed Adam for endless hours. I expressed milk into bottles so Jake could feed him in the early mornings if I was asleep. I claimed the night feeds, claimed the magic of just Adam and me in the half dark, our very own world, unassailable. Then, in the mornings, half asleep, I listened to my two men. Jake would be kissing Adam on the forehead, murmuring 'keep safe,' and 'I love you,' or, sometimes, if I'd had a hard night, 'be good for Mummy.'

Later, Adam would lie in my arms, sucking on my breast, great gulps of bluish milk, while I sat, propped up on pillows, gazing at the top of his head, at his chubby legs and arms, wondering how they could possibly extend, be those of a boy then a man. Part of me wanted him to stay just as he was, perfect. I was in love with his miniature fingers and toes with their tiny nails, with his neat bum hidden under the bulky nappy, but most of all with his rosebud lips.

He slept and drank and woke at 5am every morning. What sort of genius of a son did we have who could tell the time, be so consistent? His twisted, red, wet face mostly turned to joy when he saw me, or was it triumph? I changed endless nappies and Adam wee-ed in my face. A little girl would not have done that.

'My Adam,' I whispered.

I'd stopped thinking about the library shortly after Adam was born. Anne had laughed at my conviction that I was carrying a girl. 'You might be in for a surprise,' she'd said.

She arrived at the house a day after Jake got back, bringing flowers and toys and excitement.

'What did I tell you?' She bent to kiss Adam on the forehead. 'He's wonderful, a boy.' She couldn't resist a small note of "I told you", in her voice. 'You're tired. I know what it's like. I won't stay. Bring him to see us. The oldies are asking after him.' Her eyes smiled. 'I think they wanted a girl.'

Jake took photographs, dozens. They lay in a box, unsorted. Sometimes I flicked through them. Too late for my mother, but my father, he would love his grandson. I could hear him telling stories of brave little boys. I had no idea where he was.

The time came, too soon, when Jake put on his navy three-piece suit, a white shirt and tie. He loved his ties, first laying out on the bed, a half dozen. Yet more often than not, he selected his favourite: navy with small orange dots.

In the evenings, he opened the front door calling out, 'Where's my boy?'

Adam's eyes shone as he offered his no-teeth smile.

Once the boy was in bed we switched on the TV. It didn't much matter what was on. I was soon asleep in Jake's arms, Darby and Joan.

I wheeled him down the hill to the library.

Hands reached out for him.

'He's beautiful,' Anne cried. 'Give him here.'

Mr Williams and the oldies gathered round, said the right things. I basked in the praise. Adam looked perplexed but content.

Later, I carried him in my arms around the stacks. We started in fiction, an enormous room with the shelves laid out in slightly odd patterns, in the middle and then around the walls. I started at A, pulling out books at random, whispering that he would love this place as I did. We ambled through the alphabet until we reached W. I told him he would read Virginia Woolf one day. 'You will read all her books, you'll love VW.' It was something of a command.

In the children's section, I found Beatrix Potter and put *The Tale of Peter Rabbit* to one side. And *Alice in Wonderland*.

Daily he changed. Everything in his eyes became a question followed by joy, smiles or a growl of distaste.

14

Adam was almost four weeks old when the doorbell rang, a long, determined peal. I had been considering, somewhat desultorily, tidying the house. Reluctantly, I opened the door to a bright early spring day that I had barely noticed, and to Beth in a yellow sleeveless dress, her blonde hair loose on her shoulders.

I checked her knees. They were clean.

We two, a goddess and a frump. She had telephoned to say she was coming and, of course, I had forgotten.

It was almost lunchtime and I was in my dressing gown, splattered with vomit, dribble and more. Slippers on my feet, scantly washed hair pulled roughly back in a rubber band. I was fat and couldn't be bothered dieting. I stepped back and tried to rub off some of the most obvious splatters.

'Ah motherhood.' She leant forward, over an armful of flowers, a small cardboard box and handbag, to offer her cheek. 'Been there.'

There was something indefinably graceful and charming about her. Her lipstick was bright red, her eyebrows drawn on and three pink bracelets jangled on her right wrist.

'Offerings,' she said with that laugh, which lit her blue eyes. 'Motherhood, nothing prepares you for it.'

'Down the hall, the kitchen,' I pointed. It was marginally tidier than the sitting room, although I couldn't remember if I'd washed the breakfast dishes. Adam was bawling.

She placed the box on the kitchen table and looked round the room. 'A vase?'

I waved at a cupboard. The sun shone through the dirty back window, dishes were heaped in the sink and the floor was scattered with a spill from my breakfast cereal, replicating my dressing gown.

'He'll be footy-mad, I expect. Mine are.'

I didn't have a clue about football and I suspected Jake didn't, either.

'Those are for you,' she said, pointing to the box. 'Don't share them. Sorry it's taken me so long to get here. You know, families.' She hurried towards Adam. 'What do I see?' she stage whispered. 'Is it a mouse, a lion?'

He stopped crying and stared.

I opened the box: four croissants: big, beautiful. I wanted to stuff them, one after the other, in my greedy gob.

'They're good for you,' Beth said over her shoulder as she picked Adam up. 'Anything French.' I was to learn that food and Beth were synonymous, carefully selected items of joy, mostly cream or butter or both.

Give me five minutes,' I said, a smile in my voice.

'Don't bother for me,' she said. 'I've seen worse. I was a total slut when mine were babies.'

This woman, this almost stranger, I half loved already. I opened a cupboard. 'Mugs.' I pulled open another. 'And coffee here.'

She laughed, 'What happened to the little girl?'

Adam looked up in surprise. Well, that's how I read it, not what the books say, but of course he is smarter than any other baby in the world.

Ten minutes later I was back, skimpily washed, dressed, brushed hair and a smattering of make-up. Beth was sitting on a chair, her skirt rucked halfway up her thighs, Adam in her arms, snuggled into her large breasts, gazing up at her.

'I love little boys. You'd think I'd know better, with my two holy terrors at home, well, at nursery and school right now, probably getting into trouble.'

There was coffee in a mug beside her and evidence of a missing croissant.

'All talk, that's me, I couldn't resist,' she said, brushing the crumbs from her skirt with her one free hand. 'He's exquisite, clever you. I expect you're exhausted. The first one is tough.'

'No more kids for me,' I said, pouring some milk into my coffee and stuffing an oversized piece of croissant into my mouth.

'Oh, you'll change your mind.'

I didn't tell her that I had been lucky with Adam, that there could be no more.

'You learn to duck, with the second one, the vomit.' Beth giggled. 'I went a bit mad when I had Matthew, my first. Thought I was losing it, didn't have a clue. All the other mums loved telling me what to do, where I was going wrong. I wanted to kill them, silly bitches.' She added, 'You must be doing something right. Look how contented he is.'

Adam had been an entirely different boy two minutes before she rang the doorbell. And Jake and me: I could barely remember those first halcyon days of tenderness, of exploration of each other, of joy. Adam took everything we had to give.

'Stick him in front of the television. Plenty of programmes for little ones. Not such a big sin,' she said. 'I promise you, it will work.'

I despised people who watched TV during the day.

Beth and I talked the remainder of the morning away, about her boys and her job as a botanist. She had given it up when she got pregnant with Ben.

'Too many field trips,' she said. 'Still obsessed with mosses. You saw the evidence.' She looked down at her knees. 'But I couldn't bear to miss out on a second of my boys' lives. Well, some of them were pretty vile, I could have done without those.'

All the time with Adam on her knee. Perfection, barely a whimper from him.

'I'll get back to work soon. Pete's a good dad but spoils them.' Her smile erased the criticism. 'Another botanist but plants and medicine. Mosses are my thing, bryology.'

I was impressed. Science does that to me.

We finished the croissants. 'I'll bring my boys when he's a bit bigger,' she said, and kissed Adam on the forehead, then hugged me tight.

15

My nipples cracked, became angry, sore, and I had black circles under my eyes. I sometimes tried to cover them with make-up, mostly didn't bother. I'd even given up on the ritual hair brushing, made do with tying it back, not too clean, in an elastic band.

Jake came home to a dirty house, his clothes in a pile, still unwashed. He bathed us both, wife and son, his eyes full of love, and I regaled him with every small detail of my day, or on the phone if he was away. It was sharing, and punishing for his absence. Adam took all of me.

'Wrap him well,' the midwife had instructed. 'He needs to get out every day.'

So I took Adam for daily walks in the grand pram.

Women, young and old, stopped me in the street, admiration followed by advice.

Did I have something written across my forehead that said "novice mother", or was it in the way I pushed the pram? I waved or nodded to other women out with their babies. They were everywhere. Most wanted to boast of their own baby's achievements, were lying, should be put in the stocks and smeared with baby poo.

I sometimes found myself, erratically and rapidly, crossing the road, a half wave over my shoulder. I was too brave, not brave enough; despaired over the smallest thing and the next day triumphed. Often I smiled, more often I wept. I was exhausted. The midwife had warned me. And everyone else. The real know-alls were those who had never been anywhere near kids. When Adam slept, I did, always fearful when I woke that he might have disappeared. Sometimes hopeful, shamed.

I pushed him up the street to the first pond on the common, claiming my favourite seat, always vexed if someone got there first. Adam sat on my knee, the empty pram beside us.

'Marbles, you'll love marbles.' It came out as something of an instruction. 'And hide-and-seek. Coming, ready or not,' I shouted. Adam opened his eyes wide. Passers-by, startled, turned to us then smiled. 'We hid in the coal shed,' I whispered, 'or if it had just been dustbin day and the bins were empty, I got in one of those, a bit smelly. Or down the railway embankment. We weren't supposed to go out of the back lane. Those were the rules.'

What an inane creature I had become.

I talked to him all the time, mostly gibberish. About The Street, that the road was made of cobbles, small paving stones, all different, stuck together, cobbled; that they came from stream beds, although there were no streams nearby and they made hopscotch difficult. 'Hopscotch, you won't know what that is. When you're a bit bigger I'll teach you.'

So much I wanted to share with him. Everything.

'Your grandfather was a war hero.'

He listened with solemn eyes.

I didn't speak of my father's promises, although I still dreamt of America sometimes.

'Perhaps,' I whispered to Adam, 'you will fly to the moon, one day, to the stars, where the gods live. Zeus, the god of the sky. Orion, the lonely wanderer searching for love.' Too sombre for one so small and innocent. So I offered, 'Or walk on the moon.'

I buried my face in Adam's stomach, kissed his round lips, nibbled his toes to make him laugh. I read to him from the pile of picture books Anne brought almost weekly: *The Magic School Bus, We're Going on a Bear Hunt,* and best of all, *Guess How Much I Love You.* And many, many more.

Those were the good times. Then there were the others: his eyes screwed shut, his face red, the room filled with his screams. Oh, how they perplexed and terrified me. Sometimes angered. Were they wails of hunger, fear, wet nappy, too hot or too cold or even boredom? Slowly I learned to interpret them. Somewhat.

Lunchtime would find me still in pyjamas, endlessly loading the washing machine and trying to work out what I was doing wrong. Daily I chastised myself for being a bad mother. I held him on my lap, against my breast, cried with him. I was fat, ugly; my skin broken out in rebellion.

Time passed and his stares took on meaning. He smiled at Jake when he came in, puckered his perfect lips. Each day

I was full of wonder and each night I fell into bed, exhausted, knowing my sleep would be short.

I discovered the baby sling and carried him, his face on my breast, his head below my chin, our hearts twinned. I loved the feel of him, his hands just above my armpits, his knees spread wide. 'Adam,' I whispered. He stirred then settled.

Beth was right about the television. I propped him in front of it for an hour or two each day with the sound off, crawled onto the sofa behind him and slept.

When the fridge needed replenishing we staggered 400 yards up the hill, to Dick's, the small grocer's. I was his best customer, easy to please.

Adam's knees and one hand on the floor, then the other, his head up. He was crawling. Too soon he would become his own person, standing straight, steady on his feet, concentration on his face. Laughter. Would keep his secrets. I would die for him, a million times over.

16

Rain splattered the window, tapped, demanded in. Jake paced. He had a neat bum, I had to give him that, had admired it the first time I saw him.

'You don't have to go, you're running. I bet you've always run from the difficult stuff.' This was my bitch voice, bitch words. 'I need you here, at home like any other father. He's yours too.' I looked up at him. 'It's for too long.' I was managing life a minute at a time.

It was late, too late. I needed to be in bed. Instead, I was on the sofa, knees scrunched up to my chest, my arms tight around them, revisiting the same argument.

'I have to go,' Jake said. He was sitting beside me. 'I will miss him, you must know that.' The pain in his voice told of truth. And some anger.

'Then don't go, get another job.' Distance made being a good father easy.

Unreasonable, I knew it.

'I've looked,' he said. 'There's nothing. My clients ask for me.'

'Lucky you,' I snarled. 'Mr Indispensable. Where this time?' I loaded the words with scepticism.

'San Francisco again. We are opening an office there.'

My head slumped onto my knees, again. What was he trying to tell me?

'It's major, a US office will make all the difference, and almost half our clients are there. There's a promotion in it for me if I don't make a mess of it.'

'A month, and after that?' I said.

'I don't know. We need the money.'

I snorted. That was rich, coming from him, yet true. I'd been spending big, credit cards bills falling like leaves from my hands. Anything for Adam.

I turned away. How could he leave us? A treacherous voice in my head whispered: *Perhaps he wants to.* 'I don't do babies,' he'd said, in another life.

'It isn't easy for me, either,' he said, his voice rough, hard.

He was good with Adam, more than good, wonderful, more patient than I was but he flew in and out. The day-in-day-out stuff he didn't know.

I looked into his face. 'Is there someone else over there? Another woman. Perhaps you're like my father.' My voice was becoming more shrill by the minute. 'Can't you see? I can't do this on my own. He needs both of us.' Then the tears rolled. 'I'm a rotten mother.'

He leant over and pulled me to him. I resisted then gave in.

'Of course there's not. There will always be only you. I don't want to go, but it's what I do. I'll miss you and the boy.

Terribly.' There was a tremble in his voice, tears in his eyes. 'My life began when I met you. If you really don't want me to go, I won't, but I will lose my job.'

There was silence between us.

'Go, Jake, I'm sorry. I'm so tired, so useless.'

He turned to me. 'You're not useless. You're a wonderful mother. I know I get all the good bits. I can see how exhausted you are. I'll be back soon. I promise.'

He kissed me, gently, tenderly, almost like our first kiss. 'I love you, Alice. You must know that. There will never be anyone else. I will miss you both.' His voice broke.

*

Life calmed, or I did, or perhaps I became more expert. And Jake came back from the US sooner than I'd expected.

I didn't have to hurry back to work but I would go back. Soon.

On a sombre day, a sky with barely enough blue in it to make a sailor boy's suit, my mother's expression, Adam took his first step. It was a couple of months after his first birthday.

She would have loved to see that, see everything about Adam. I longed, often, for her advice.

He walked – a small exaggeration, but mothers are permitted that – towards the grey heron which stretched, flapped one wing in applause. I knelt beside Adam. 'Another,' I urged, 'another,' and he did, his tongue sliding across his lips. Five more uncertain steps, then to sit with a bump on a small hillock.

I took him in my arms and let my tears fall on his perfect head.

His first word, or the first I could understand, was Rabby, as he held the brown furry thing in his small arms. He was more easily parted from me than that creature.

MumMum came some time later.

He was his own person.

I read *Peter Rabbit* to him, over and over. 'Peter,' he would say, pointing to himself and putting a small fist over each ear if I tried to read anything else. He wore the blue jacket, his "Peter jacket", and crawled or tottered to the bushy corner of the garden, chuckling, ''scape, MumMum.'

At the bottom of the back garden there was a hedge and a minute shed with a seat in front of it. If the weather was good, we sat there to read.

I cleared out a small little-used room just off the kitchen and turned it into Adam's playroom. Within a day or two, his small low table was covered in drawing paper and pencils lying around on the floor. He sat on his heels at the table and drew for hours, strange, coloured scribbles.

Lego was strewn over the floor. 'No, MumMum,' he shouted when I tried to tidy it up.

The click of Lego being put together and dragged apart told of pieces carried in his pocket.

He loved hiding: the kitchen cupboard behind the waste bin, dark and smelly (smells never bothered him), and the bushes at the very bottom of the garden. He had a large cardboard box in one corner of his playroom, his official hiding place. When he was curled up tight, he only just fitted in. It was hide, no seek.

I poured into his ears (sometimes his eyes wandered, signifying enough) everything I had learned in life.

Inconsequential rubbish or stories of the Greek gods. Stories and more stories.

And when Jake came home and picked him up, I might as well have not existed.

Jake bought a chair from an antique shop and we put it in one corner of the playroom: his wishing chair. We read there at night before he went to bed. Or he sat on his own, turning the pages of his favourite book. The wishing chair took over and he was off to the Land of Goodness-Knows-Where, or the Land of Slipperies. Or to the moon, the stars. Flying.

'Daddy, stars. Go, Daddy,' he shouted to Jake.

That was the beginning of his obsession with the stars.

I bought him spaceman pyjamas and had to return to the shop to buy another pair.

17

Jake came and went and adored us both.

I sometimes imagined him bumping into my father in America. Ridiculous, yet I could hear my father saying, 'I have a daughter in England. I called her Princess.'

Joy was in Adam running to hug my legs, or running away giggling, looking over his shoulder, mischief in his eyes. And in the way his tongue moved across his lips as he concentrated on his train set, a present for his third birthday.

I temporised about sending him to nursery.

'He needs to go,' Jake insisted. 'Get to know other children.'

Jake didn't often insist so I listened. I wasn't sure, wanted my freedom and wanted to be with Adam. Having your cake and eating it, my mother would have said. I could go back to work. I was missing the library, the books and the company.

The room at the nursery was large with small tables around its perimeter, a big one in the middle and mats scattered on the floor.

She looked young, Nicola, the woman in charge. 'Young, good with the kids,' I told Jake that evening. 'Adam made straight for a table with sheets of paper and coloured pencils. He was still on his own, drawing, when I left, and he didn't cry like some of the other kids.'

'He told me he went to school,' Jake said. 'I asked him what he liked about it and he said, 'Drawing, Daddy. And Lego. I was a bit like him.'

A week or so later, Nicola said Adam was not a joiner but she thought he was happy.

I returned to the library to job share with Anne. The mechanics of it worked well between us yet I worried.

'He'll be fine,' Anne said without my saying anything. 'I know what it's like. They live in your head all the time. He's a good lad.'

Beth had also gone back to work so I saw less of her, but she still came to take Adam on moss hunts.

Adam ran to the open door shouting 'BethBeth,' and his chubby legs didn't stop until he banged into hers and he'd flung his arms round them.

A moss hunt.

Beth had given him a small backpack which held a packet of envelopes and pencil and a small bottle of water with a spray nozzle to wet the mosses if too dry. Round his neck on his lanyard hung a small lens.

'A bright kid,' she said. 'Wish my two were as interested.'

They would return a couple of hours later both with grubby knees and half a dozen envelopes filled with samples.

Then the serious work would begin on the kitchen table and there would be much laughter as Adam's small fingers plucked the moss from the envelopes and I heard serious talk of mosses.

'Brown sedge,' Beth said, pulling out a dry lump from an envelope. Adam nodded, repeated, 'brown sedge.'

I picked up one envelope after their first exploration and recoiled at Adam's shriek. 'BethBeth and Adam.' He had us all compartmentalised.

She never did bring her boys to play.

Then school. He called it his "big school" and stood on tiptoe raising one thin arm high in the air. 'Big, big,' he said, wriggling his fingers. 'Adam be tall like Daddy. Daddy taller than anyone in the world.'

After a week he demanded a pair of sunglasses, although the summer was long gone. 'So they don't see me, Adam see them.'

I bought him a pair but the teacher made him take them off in class.

'Am I a weirdo?' he asked a few days later.

'A bit different, good different,' I said.

'I like weirdo,' he said, and wafted around the room making whoo-whoo noises.

'Smile,' Jake told him. 'A good smile can get you out of trouble.'

'Teacher shout stop smiling.'

18

'A surprise for you, little man,' Jake said, placing the parcel on the kitchen table.

'What it, big man? What it?' Adam tore at the parcel. His small fingers weren't strong enough for the box so Jake helped. I was sitting in my usual eavesdropping seat at the table.

'You'll see,' Jake said.

Jake pulled off the tissue paper.

'What is it, Daddy?' he shouted. 'What it?'

Jake extended the telescope's three short legs, pushed the eyepiece up and down a few times and set it up on the bench at the window.

Adam's eyes were shining. 'Stars, Daddy, for the stars. Thank you, Daddy.'

That evening was cold, bright, a cloudless sky replete with stars.

'Where's the rabbit star, Daddy? Adam want rabbit star.'

'I don't know, son.'

'Where?' Adam shouted, his hands moving.

'Maybe there is one, son, and we haven't found him yet. We'll keep looking.'

'You Star-man, Adam Star-boy.'

'That's right, Star-boy.'

I heard the fatigue in Jake's voice. Jet lag.

'School tomorrow,' Jake said, 'just a bit longer.'

Adam started to spin, shouting, 'A bit longer, Daddy, a bit longer. Star-man, Star-boy.'

They found the Great Bear, although Jake later told me he wasn't sure.

'A good god,' he told Adam, 'threw the big bear and the little bear far up into the sky to keep them safe. Mother and son.'

'Daddy and son, Daddy,' Adam said, dismay on his small face.

Jake and Adam perched on their seats under the window overlooking the back garden, but mostly they were outside, wearing coats and woolly hats and gloves. They could be there for hours until I called them in, usually way past Adam's bedtime. The telescope became their nightly obsession.

I found a book on the stars in the library and Adam sat cross-legged, the book on his lap, his finger pointing at the stars on the page or waving his hands. Rabby sat cross-legged beside him.

'Bed,' I called to Adam.

'No. Adam stay here with Daddy.'

'When you are a big boy, you can stay up later.'

'All night?' he asked, not one for compromise.

'I suppose so.'

'Promise, promise, MumMum,' he persisted. He slipped off the bench and ran over to hold my legs.

'Promise.'

'Will Adam be really old, MumMum, like you and Daddy? Really old?'

'I guess so,' I smiled.

Adam shook his head. 'Adam never get old,' he said, and giggled. 'Live in a palace in the sky.' He giggled. 'Mercury, Venus, Earth, Mars, Jupiter, Saturn, Uranus, Neptune, Pluto.'

'Good boy,' I heard Jake murmur. 'The right order.'

The stars were Jake's territory. I knew almost nothing about them.

When they were star watching, Adam whispered to Jake if I went near them, looking at me over his shoulder, mischief in his eyes. They sat in a row, the three, in descending size: Jake, Adam, Rabby.

I bought Adam a new bedspread, covered with stars, and watched his face when he saw it laid out on his bed. 'Stars, MumMum, stars.'

A month or two before his sixth birthday, we built a snowman together, the three of us. Adam stood with his hands outstretched waiting for the flakes to fall on them. Or he put out his tongue.

I found a carrot for a mouth, cut it to look a bit real, a plum for a nose and a couple of pieces of coal for the eyes.

Adam stared at the snowman then ran inside. A few minutes later he was back, looking flushed, in his hand an old pair of his sunglasses.

'Adam and snowman,' he said.

Jake took a photograph of him standing next to his snowman, both in dark glasses in the white land.

Jake still worked in the US but the trips were usually no more than a week or two.

'Are you flying to the stars, Daddy?' Adam asked him when he saw Jake's case beside the front door. 'Daddy promise to take Adam in an aeroplane, flying, flying. Mercury, Venus, Earth, Mars, Jupiter, Saturn, Uranus, Neptune, Pluto.' He kicked the case. 'I hate you, Daddy.'

Jake picked him up and held him above his head. 'No, you don't.'

Adam kicked and screamed. 'Daddy has long legs. Adam has little Daddy-long legs.'

Jake missed him, held him tight on his return.

'I'll take him to see the Rothkos and we'll walk the mountains, perhaps the Alps,' Jake said, with a look in his eyes not unlike Adam's. 'And camp, high up.' He waved, also a little like Adam.

I would be running up the mountain after them, alone, far behind.

19

16th February 1991

'Your birthday tomorrow, Adam. Cake after school.'
I was washing up while he finished his tea at the kitchen
table and Adam, still in his school uniform was pushing his
macaroni cheese around his plate. It was always a battle, no,
a war, to get him out of his uniform before bedtime.

'Will Adam live with you forever?' he asked, through a
mouth so full I wasn't sure that I had heard properly.

'You shall, my pet, until you are grown-up anyway.'

'Grown-up,' he said, and pushed his chair back. He
smiled and picked up his glass of orange juice. Some spilt
on the table.

'Watch your clothes.'

He kept on chewing, holding his glass of juice. He was
wearing his sunglasses, wore them everywhere: dull days,
bright days.

'Six tomorrow,' I said. 'Big boy.'

He stood on tiptoe and raised one hand.

Adam was steadily becoming his father, slender and with strong, black hair. He seemed content, although a little friendless at school.

He was still always last to the school gate in the afternoon and still ran to hug my legs.

Mr Donovan said he was the best boy he'd ever taught.

'He say I'm a genius,' Adam said. 'Genius. Sums. The best. Adam will be a space walker, an astronaut. Go with Rabby.'

Earlier that day, I'd come across an old television clip of the moon landing from twenty-two years ago.

When Jake got home and we both had glasses of wine in our hands, the three of us sat down to watch it, Jake and me on the settee, his arm around me, and Adam a couple of feet from the TV.

Adam didn't move until the end, then turned and looked at us, trembling with excitement.

'Adam going to the moon? Adam go there with Rabby.'

'When you are a bit older,' Jake said. 'How will you get there?'

'Wings or build rocket. Can you throw me to the stars, Daddy?'

'Too far.'

Adam looked disappointed.

We watched the moon landing again.

'What will Adam eat? Can Rabby come too?'

'Stardust, you'll eat stardust,' Jake said, while I was still thinking about it.

'Rabby?'

'Stardust too.'

'Take telescope?' Adam asked.

109

'Why would you want that?'

'See you and MumMum.'

'Ah. Then you can take the telescope,' Jake said.

20

17th February 1991

The next day I woke, smiling. Put out my hand for Jake. Empty space. I shut my eyes, listened. There were quiet movements coming from the kitchen downstairs. I yawned and snuggled into the pillow then remembered. It was Adam's birthday. I sat up. He was born six years ago on 17th February 1985.

I hadn't understood what life could offer before Jake, before that first day when I'd stood in front of *Four Darks in Red* and hated it. I had found myself in Jake. Well, perhaps I still had some way to go on that road but don't we all? And then our boy. I wondered how I could have thought my life something worth living before Adam. That sounded dramatic, even in my over-active imagination, but I would die for him, anytime.

A glorious almost two years, just Jake and me, then Adam. Nothing prepared me for motherhood. That was the way I went about everything, leaving all to chance.

In bed I stretched, looked at my watch.

A curious half-light filtered through the curtain. Silence then the muted slushing sound of car tyres. Snow.

Jake's feet outside, stamping. The smile in my life, one of my two smiles.

Running small feet, the door slammed open.

'Snow, MumMum, snow.' Adam put out his arms and flew around the room to the window, pushing aside one curtain. 'Snowman, MumMum.' His feet were bare and he was standing in his underpants, his mouth wide, showing the gaps at the front where his second teeth had not yet come. 'Happy Birthday, Adam, my lovely boy.'

He didn't move, his nose pressed against the glass.

A snowflake smacked itself on the window, spread, slid down. Others followed, dawdling, half suspended.

'Tiny ice crystals,' I said, 'sticking together.'

He ran over. I opened my arms.

He jumped on the bed and bounced.

'Ice crystals, ice crystals,' he shouted, his strong, small legs working, hands waving. 'Snowman, MumMum, snowman.' Rabby swung from his left hand.

Just as suddenly as he'd got onto the bed, he jumped off and ran to the window, his nose again on the glass. His lips and his fingers moved. He was counting the falling flakes.

I swung my legs over the edge – sturdy legs, not bad for a forty-five year old – walked across the carpet and knelt beside him, leaning my head on his shoulder. A thin covering of snow lay on the garden, individual flakes meandering down.

On Adam's face, a mixture of dreaminess and concentration.

'Happy birthday Adam. Get dressed then Daddy has a big surprise for you.'

He dragged himself away from the window. The bedroom door slammed behind him, his thin voice receding. 'Surprise, Daddy. Surprise.'

I waited, seated on the bottom stair, while Adam dressed.

'Almost ready, Adam?' I shouted up the stairs. 'Hurry up.' We were going to be late for school.

'Birthday, birthday,' he sang.

'Birthday or not, we are late. Get a move on.'

He stood at the top of the stairs, hopping on one foot, a sock in his hand, shoes beside him.

'Be careful, you'll fall.' I put out my hands.

He grinned and sat with a bump on the carpet. 'Birthday.'

Moments later, his feet thundered down.

'Birthday, MumMum, birthday. Where Daddy?'

'Outside, waiting for you.'

I pointed to the front door. 'Put on your coat and your hat. Gloves.' He hated gloves, lost them constantly.

He stood on tiptoe and dragged his coat off its special peg, put it on and his hat, shoved the gloves in his pocket.

'Gloves on.'

He giggled.

I took them from his pocket, handed them to him, one at a time, then hauled open the front door.

Arctic air coursed in. It was times like this I wished I could drive, although his school was only a few streets away. I wasn't much interested in cars. Jake's expensive model sat on the paved area outside the house, used only on weekends and often not then. Adam loved it, and occasionally, when he nagged hard enough, I took the keys and let him sit in the driving seat, to reach up and hold the steering wheel, making his vroom vroom sounds.

Adam stopped after a few steps outside and stared into the sky, cupping his bare hands in front of him. Snowflakes settled in them and on his long, dark eyelashes.

'Snow, snow, birthday.'

It had snowed six years ago today.

Jake rounded the corner of the house, pushing a bike, stopping on our small patch of grass.

'Adam,' he called, in a voice as gentle as the falling flakes.

Adam looked around and began to spin, his eyes singing.

I shoved a pair of shoes on my feet, my thickest coat, a scarf and a hat that Jake said made me look like a garden gnome. He couldn't imagine what it was like to be short. I'd dressed in a hurry, no make-up, felt naked.

I ran outside and gasped. The beauty and size of the thing. The bicycle was sleek and fast-looking. And big. Adam had a history of falling, although seemed to do himself little harm. On the swings and climbing frames in the park he was fearless.

'Mine, Daddy, mine,' Adam shouted, wonder and joy in his voice. And he ran his hands over the wheels, the handlebars and the saddle of the green bike. 'Mine, Daddy.' He found the bell on the handlebars: shining, tempting. It rang and rang. 'Ding-a-ling,' Adam shouted.

'Yours, son, all yours. Do you think you can ride it?'

I placed my hands on Adam's shoulders. He shook them off.

'Want to try it out?' Jake said, and held the bike while Adam clambered on.

I clenched my hands. He looked so small and fragile. Jake held the saddle while they did a few small circles on the grass.

'Let's go, birthday boy,' Jake said, his head close to Adam's as he pushed the bike through the garden gate and up the street a short way, Adam's knuckles on the handlebars standing out white while he pedalled.

Jake's hand gripped the saddle. 'Clever boy. That's it, you're riding your bike.'

'Faster, Daddy, faster.'

Soon they were back.

Jake lifted a protesting Adam off and leant the bike against the wall. Adam clung to his legs.

'Happy Birthday, big boy. You can ride it to school through the park.' He bent to put his hand on Adam's head.

I stared at Jake. 'Is that a good idea? The weather…'

'Oh, he's tough. He can handle it.' Jake pulled his hat down over his ears, wrapped his scarf tight, buttoned his overcoat and picked up his briefcase. 'Fish and chips, your day, you choose. And be careful with that.' He pointed to the bike, then smiled at me and held me tight. He was bulky in that overcoat, yet I clung to him as if we were both naked.

'Perhaps we should wait until you're home so he can get the hang of it.'

'Don't fuss.' There was an edge to his voice. We were all late. 'Hold the saddle, don't let go and he'll be fine.'

'Come with us, just today…' I said, waving vaguely at the bike.

'Sorry, Aly, I can't. I'm late already. He's fine on it.' He took my face in his gloved hands and kissed me hard.

Adam looked up at us both and grinned.

21

The breakfast table was laid: a bowl of Coco Pops for Adam, a treat; and muesli for me. I'd stayed up late the night before, making his birthday cake, a spaceship. He'd love it. I reminded myself to buy the candles on the way home.

I held out the milk but Adam hopped down off his chair.

'Bike,' he called over his shoulder and ran out the back door, wiping his mouth with the back of his hand.

I glanced at the kitchen clock.

A few minutes later he was back, standing at the table, his face flushed, waving his hands.

'Bird,' he said, 'bird,' and held out his hand. There were two small feathers on his palm. He raced back into the garden, coatless, snow still gently floating down.

I ran after him.

Just beside the back wheel of the bike stood a bird, its wings dulled, its head drooping, unsteady eye glazed as it stared up at us.

'Pick it up?' Adam asked.

I shook my head. 'It's sick.' I shivered and held Adam's bare hand.

The bird, diminutive, dying.

'Greenfinch.' He knew all the different birds that came to our garden, and their calls.

The greenfinch hopped, less than half a dozen steps, and stood in the shelter of my foot, leaning gently against it. A snowflake landed on its head. I put my hand to my mouth to stop myself crying out, spoke to him, told him I was sorry he was ill, that he was a beautiful creature. I almost let the God word slip in. Adam gazed up at me and back down at the bird, his eyes full.

The snow now deadly.

It seemed a lifetime but must have been less than a minute when the bird fell sideways, onto a bed of snow, its upward-facing eye empty.

'Your little spade, Adam, in the shed.'

The earth would be too hard. The tiny body lay at my feet. I reached into my pocket.

Adam ran back with the spade. I pointed to a spot under a bush where the snow had piled a little deeper. It would do for now.

'There, Adam, he's only small.'

I wrapped the greenfinch in my handkerchief, content that it was one of my best and pristine. A miniature shroud.

'Will God look after him?' Adam said, his voice shaking. 'Will he give him birdseed like I do?'

The school must tell him about God. We didn't. 'Yes,' I murmured. 'He will be happy. There will be other birds with him.' I neither knew nor cared what I was blathering on about.

Neither of us felt like finishing breakfast. I put the milk in the fridge and left everything else as it was – an unfinished birthday breakfast. I rebuttoned Adam's coat, picked up his schoolbag and my handbag and slammed and locked the door behind us.

'Mine,' he protested, reaching out for his bag.

'I'll carry it today. Hurry, Adam, we're late.'

'Bike, MumMum.' He ran towards it, clambered on, using the wall as a prop.

I grabbed the saddle. It felt heavy, unruly.

'Don't, MumMum. Don't.'

'Just until you get the hang of it. Don't go too fast. The paths will be slippery.'

'My bike, birthday,' he screamed at me, his face flushed and screwed tight.

We set off down the street, his thumb moving back and forwards, the bell's cacophony ratcheting apart the soft, damp air, the still falling snow. The ginnel was only a few yards down the hill, narrow, high-walled on both sides and unlit. We turned left through it.

Already out of breath, I tried to tighten my grip on the bike's saddle.

'Slow down, Adam, not so fast,' I shouted.

His legs slowed, not for long. I pulled back hard.

'Big bike, big bike, birthday boy.' He was singing.

At the ginnel's end we stopped. I caught my breath. Adam stood up on the pedals.

We crossed a quiet suburban street, up a small hill and into the park and the trees.

Adam whooped.

Shoes, heels too high, little purchase on the slippery path.

Snow fluttered through the trees, blurring the light, and car headlights shone on the tarmac in the distance as his small legs turned through a lacy white curtain. The park had an ethereal feel, a mixture of white magic and dark trees. The snow beginning to clump on the edges of the path. No one else on the path ahead.

I had a busy day at work, was running a "to do" list through my head.

Adam was getting the hang of the thing. I glanced at my watch: ten minutes to the school bell.

I tightened my grip. My hands; pathetic, weak things. I cursed, cursed Jake for his grand gestures, his foolishness. Okay for him, he had sauntered off to work.

Adam's bum, when not standing on the pedals, was on my thumb, and my fingers under the back edge of the saddle were beginning to numb.

'Slow down, Adam, slow down.'

'Let go, MumMum, let go,' Adam shouted, looking back over his shoulder, the large front wheel wobbling.

The school bell rang. We were close enough to hear excited shouts, car engines. Glimpses off to the left, of the crowns of stately buildings behind the high brick wall.

Cars would be parked all down both sides of the main road, dropping off.

I concentrated on keeping my grip on the saddle.

His small legs were turning fast. I wanted to kiss them. His tongue would be moving over his bottom lip, his eyes shining.

'The road,' I shouted.

'Let go, MumMum, let go.'

Jake should be here. He'd bought the damn thing. I was out of breath, my hand was cold, the fingers and thumb loosening, beginning to slip. I tightened my mouth as if that might help: strong lips, strong fingers.

A heavy truck rocketed down the road.

'Slow down, Adam, slow down.'

I pulled hard on the seat. Nothing slowed.

Faster, faster.

'Let go. Flying, flying.' He turned and shouted at me. His eyes spilling fury, hate.

Words. More words.

I shouted back.

Hand suddenly empty.

The bike slewed away, towards the trees, low branches smacked him.

Me: screaming, falling; bags flying, gravel mincing the flesh on my knees. Onto the heels of my hands. I jerked up my head. Couldn't move.

'Ding-a-ling. Ding-a-ling.' Boy and bicycle hurtled along the dappled path, round a bend, and disappeared. Small legs turning, turning, the world turning.

His face, his eyes. His words.

'Adam. Wait,' I screamed. He'd wait at the road. I'd taught him never to cross without me.

I opened my mouth wider. No sound left it. On my feet at last. Running. Into the open.

The squeal of braking tyres.

A bike and boy flying, flying.

Time, slow time, no time.

The road. Nothing moving except a bicycle wheel, spinning, spinning.

Metal on metal, metal on flesh.

In the middle of the road, a car, slewed across the road; a small white face at a window, open mouth.

A mangled green bike lay on top of a pile of clothes; a dark, expanding pool flowed from under. Not my boy. He was hiding somewhere. He would run out from the trees shouting, 'Hiding, MumMum, hiding.'

I looked again. Couldn't breathe, swallow. Ran, hauled at the bike.

A car door slammed. Crying from somewhere.

Strangers knelt beside me, touched me. I shook them off.

The front wheel of the bicycle, still spinning, spinning. Unknowing.

Noise, screaming, mine, others.

Then silence. Adamantine.

My heart, too big, drowning me; a woman knelt beside a pile of clothes.

A woman stood behind me, weeping.

My boy. His uniform torn, he would hate that. His body splayed, shapeless. Had lost his bones. Snow had been pushed into a small heap next to his feet. His sunglasses lay beside his head. Broken. He would want them at school.

Under everything, the flood, the blood.

I sat on the tarmac. I had to hold him, gather him in my arms, tell him everything would be all right. That I would mend his torn jacket.

Pulled to my feet, gently, caressingly held. Voices.

Mothers shut their eyes and some prayed, opened them to gather in their own children. Held them tight in their arms, shielded their young eyes.

Flashing blue lights. Sirens.

22

Someone took me by the arm, bundled me into an ambulance. My boy was already there, deadly white. He had left his life blood behind, on the tarmac.

The men had their backs to me.

'Take care,' I cried out as the ambulance swung round a corner, yet wanted to shout faster, faster. He was strapped down, strangely still. A monitor bleeped and the mask over his face hissed in its own language.

I wanted to hold him. He was mine. I leant forward and someone pulled me back, spoke words I didn't understand.

I pulled against my straps. Be careful, he's small. The man in the seat next to me touched my arm, pain in his eyes and resignation. I cursed every time we stopped, could not see out.

Doors opened. He was wheeled out of the ambulance. I followed. Swing doors, a maze of corridors.

Groups of people sitting. Department names: Cardiology, Neurology, Orthopaedics, ENT and more. Where was the doctor?

Two nurses appeared. One took my arm. I tried to shake her off, stay with my boy. She nudged me gently through a door. I resisted. She half pushed, half led me to a chair.

I refused to sit. 'Where is he? I have to be with him.'

'A cup of tea, Mrs Oldfield.'

I wanted to slap her.

Moments later, she was back, holding out a cup and saucer. 'Drink this, it will help.'

I ignored it. 'My husband.'

'I understand that the school has contacted him.'

I didn't believe her.

'I'll check. Please drink the tea, Mrs Oldfield. Please sit.' She pulled a chair close to me, and a small table, placing the cup and saucer on it.

Her breathing was too loud.

I sat, leant forward, the tea untouched. I sat. Five minutes passed. More minutes. Too many.

I got up. Jake, Jake, where are you? I stood, took the few steps to the window, pressed my forehead against the glass. It had stopped snowing.

He had flown through the air but he was tough, always falling and scrambling to his feet.

I paced.

I sat.

The door opened. Jake.

I lifted my head to stare at him.

'They said…' His words were strangled, his hands clenched and unclenched, his eyes wild.

His long, loose limbs carried him fast across the room. He knelt on the floor and wrapped his arms around me as I sat, ramrod stiff, hands still, lips tightly closed. Through the mist I saw his shaking shoulders. He lifted his head. What is it, I asked myself, that makes the sight of a man weeping so cataclysmic? I had never seen him weep; he had me.

There was something wrong in my head, I was someone else.

He squatted back on his heels. 'Tell me it's not true. Our Adam. An accident, they said. What happened?'

'A car, the bike.'

He dropped his head into his hands. Sobbed.

The door swung open. A man entered. He wasn't wearing a white coat, but a smart suit.

Jake got up, dragged a chair next to mine, pulled out a handkerchief. He took my hand.

The man pulled up the other chair.

'I'm sorry,' he said, voice sonorous, soft. 'Adam suffered an epidural haemorrhage. There was no pain.'

What did he mean? I had seen him breathing.

'There was nothing more we could do. I am so sorry.'

I screamed, stood, ran at him. He was ready, put out his hands, spoke words I didn't hear. I beat his chest. He permitted it.

The unmoving pile of clothes on the road. Adam had never been so still. I wanted to laugh, bend double with laughter. It was impossible to resist.

I bent over my knees.

'I want to see him,' I almost shouted as I raised my head, ignoring the wetness of my face.

'Of course. We will have to wait a few minutes,' the man said. He looked up at the nurse standing just inside the closed door.

Jake sat utterly still.

We followed the doctor down a corridor, and another and another. His head turned back to us, his lips moved.

Through a door into a small bare room. A bed in the middle, a nurse standing near the window.

Adam, a sheet pulled up to his chin, his arms lying at his sides on top of the sheet. He always slept on his side; he wouldn't be comfortable on his back. His face was clean. He had never been so neat. He looked young, younger than his six years, beautiful. His hair, the hair he refused so often to have cut, was wild, poking out in curled strands from a white bandage encasing the top of his head. It would be all right, I had a comb.

He often copied Jake, brushing his hand through his hair.

His watch was gone. It was big, with a second hand. He knew the time to the second. He would miss it. I'd buy him another. A couple of hours ago, I had spat on my handkerchief and wiped the remnants of his breakfast from the corners of his mouth.

'I'll leave you,' said the doctor, 'with your son.' He quietly opened the door and left.

The nurse didn't move.

I pulled a chair to the bedside and took Adam's hand, pressed it to my lips, then to my eyes to close off the flood. His perfect little hand. I didn't let go. Not then.

I gazed at him, almost like the first time I'd held him in my arms. His body, except for his arms and face, was shrouded. His small lips were full, relaxed, his chubby cheeks had fallen back a little, away from his perfect nose. He was the best thing I had done with my life and now…

Jake. I had seen wet eyes, a hand hastily rubbed across his face, but not this: loud, gasping sobs, full rivulets of tears running down his cheeks. I wanted to tell him to be quiet.

I leant over my boy, breathed in deeply, and again. Foreign smells. I kissed his lips, stood, straightened. Let go of his hand, placing the arm back beside his body, turned to Jake.

'She killed him.'

'She?'

'The woman in the car. She killed him.'

Jake's voice notched the air, rushed in shockwaves at me. 'That fucking bike, I'm an idiot.'

His pain seared me, doubled my own. He stood beside me. We held hands and stared down at our dead son. Small drops splattered the sheet. Jake bent and placed a kiss on Adam's forehead.

I looked down at my knee and murmured, 'I let go.' My boy, my boy, what had I done?

23

The peal of the front door bell split the air.

I was in the sitting room, the place I passed hours; dissolving into a small ball.

Jake was in the kitchen. I willed him to stay there.

His footsteps in the hall, the lock turning and the soft swish of the door swinging across the mat.

'May we come in?'

I didn't hear Jake's reply; perhaps he didn't speak.

A few moments later, two police officers blocked the sitting room doorway. The man walked towards me holding out a plastic ID card. I'd never seen a real one. I just nodded, looked away.

'Detective Sergeant Collins,' he said. He was short, stocky, or maybe it was in contrast to Jake.

The woman behind him held out her card.

'Detective Constable Wilkes.' She looked decent and anxious. I wanted to ask her if she had a son.

'How can we help you, Sergeant?' Jake asked. I loved him dearly at that moment for his firmness.

'I'm sorry,' the DS said, 'it's about your boy, Adam.'

I didn't speak, saw Jake move his head, indicating two

chairs, heard him offer coffee. He always offered coffee, never tea. They both accepted, the DS saying, 'milk and two sugars. please.' The woman asked for black, no sugar.

Jake left the room and I listened to the kettle being filled then boiled, the clatter of crockery.

And our breathing.

'Your son was six, I believe,' DS Collins said.

Footsteps from the kitchen.

'It was his birthday,' I said.

The DC looked away.

Jake walked towards us, carrying a tray with two mugs on it, a milk jug, sugar bowl and a couple of teaspoons. His mouth was tight. The tray shook a little.

The woman spoke for the first time. 'I bet he was excited.' She looked at me.

I didn't answer.

'Tell me about the bicycle. Had one before?' the DS asked.

I didn't know how to answer that. He'd had a baby bike, years back. All kids could ride. Couldn't they? I looked at Jake.

'Of course,' I said.

Jake set the tray down on a small table. No one hurried. The DS – already I hated him – poured his milk and took two teaspoons of sugar, dribbling it into his coffee.

Was he counting the grains? How lovely, an afternoon tea party. I had to pull myself together.

Rain started to beat on the windows. Jake sat beside me, took my hand.

Adam's exquisite small legs pumping.

I was on the ground, then running.

128

The inspector stirred his coffee. 'Your route was through the park, I believe.'

I said nothing. Jake squeezed my hand. We had lost our special handhold.

There was silence. Jake shifted in his seat, cleared his throat. I pulled my hand from his.

'I understand this must be very painful for you, but we need to go through everything on that day,' the DS said. 'We have a number of witnesses who say your son came out of the park very fast, on his own. The driver,' he looked at his notebook then continued. 'The driver of the car says the same.'

My head shot up. I stared at him.

'Were you with him, Mrs Oldfield?'

I paused a moment before saying, 'I was with him until I fell.'

'You fell? On the path through the park?'

'Yes.'

'Is there anything else you can tell me?'

I shook my head.

Jake looked at me.

The DS turned to Jake. 'I don't believe you were there, sir.'

Jake nodded, flushed.

The DS made a note, turned back to me, shifted in his seat. 'The weather conditions were bad, the snow. We are still carrying out our investigations, Mrs Oldfield. If you remember anything, please get in touch.' He held out his card.

I ignored it so Jake took it.

'She killed him,' I said.

DS Collins stood, his coffee barely touched. 'There will be a post-mortem and the body should be released within a few days.'

The DC hadn't touched her coffee. She walked across the room, put her hand on my arm. 'Please get in touch if there is anything.'

Hang her, I wanted to shout.

Jake showed them out.

A woman knocked on the door. Jake was out on one of his endless runs, anything to get away from me. The letter box clicked then her voice, 'Mrs Oldfield, could I speak to you, please? I'm from the *Wimbledon Observer*. I'm so sorry about your son.' There was a pause, then her weapon. 'I'm a mother too. I know how you must feel.'

I wanted to run to the door, place my hands around her throat and strangle her, watch her face turn red, then purple, stop her breath.

Nobody knew, nobody.

I didn't move.

The story was front page in the newspaper.

LOCAL BARRISTER KILLS BOY IN ACCIDENT OUTSIDE SCHOOL

Local boy, Adam Oldfield, was knocked down and killed on his sixth birthday while riding his bicycle outside the Primary School. He died not long after arriving at the District Hospital.

Witnesses saw Adam cycle at speed from the park opposite the school, riding out from between parked cars onto the road. His mother ran out a short time later.

The driver of the Range Rover, Mrs Rosamund Beresford, a barrister at Lincoln's Inn Court, does not appear to have been speeding. It is believed that the car skidded on the icy road. It was snowing heavily at the time.

There have been accidents outside this school before and this newspaper has previously raised the issue of cars parked on both sides of the road, at school drop-off and pick-up times.

There was a photograph of a woman, her hair in a bun; clear-eyed, a strong face. She wore a silk blouse and a long string of pearls. Success and confidence sang, even from the grainy black and white newsprint.

24

'I lost my grip.' The fingers of my right hand picked away at my left thumb. 'I don't know what happened. It was snowing but that wasn't it.'

I didn't mention the other.

Jake put my hands in his, gentle with the thumb.

'I'm the fool, always have been. The bike... And the snow,' he said. 'I have been away...' His voice begged. 'I missed so much of him. I always believed...' Despair darkened his eyes, etched new lines on his face.

I turned away.

We slept with our backs to one another.

We ran out of clean mugs. I studied the soapsuds, slowly moved the brush around: a picture. Cut the suds in two, a machete sweep. Lifted hands from the sink, stared at them, wrinkled, glistening with round white balls that slithered and fell. Whose hands were they?

Falling.

A loud crack. A glass falling apart.

Casseroles turned up on the doorstep; and fruitcake, apple pie and much more. Some with notes from strangers. I threw the food in the bin, didn't read the notes. Jake washed the dishes and put them back on the doorstep.

People I didn't know filled the house. Jake offered drinks, the strain on his face for all to see.

My words didn't come.

I was rage.

Jake put out his arms to me. I turned away.

I passed days in the wishing chair, felt the boy leaning back against my legs. Yet, he was not there, must be hiding in the shrubs at the bottom of the garden, under his bed in the darkest corner. He could no longer fit in his special box.

I crawled into his bed, made a shroud of his sheet.

MumMum, a planet-sized word.

I slept in his bed nights, and often through the day. For the rest I was lost, could not remember anything except him. Time and day and night slipped away.

Sometime towards dawn, I crossed the carpet in our bedroom and slipped under the bedcovers. Jake would be lying on his back, awake, waiting.

He tried to talk to me. He cried. I was deaf, blind.

With sleep came the same dream: the bike's saddle slipping from between finger and thumb, my hand stretching, Adam shouting. Words. Falling.

And after that, the silence.

I dreamt of a bike as big as a house, a car the size of

a palace. The doctor telling me he would recover, I would have my boy back again.

I tiptoed around his train set, pulled out his box of drawings, tore down those on the wall, threw them in a heap on the floor. Jake put them back up.

I waited for his small arms around my legs, his voice. 'Will I live with you always?'

Nightmares. I awoke screaming. 'Adam, Adam.'

Jake rolled over and pulled me to him. 'Talk to me,' he urged, and tried to kiss me.

'I can't.' Turned away.

'You won't look at me anymore,' he said. 'I know I should have been with you. That bike…'

'He looked like you. I see him in you every time.'

He held me tight. 'We've lost him. I can't lose you too.'

I was stiff, ungiving.

I dreamt I was flying and woke crying. Mostly I was in that cold clinical room with Adam and the white sheet. Once I woke smiling, with Adam in my arms. It was Rabby. In the mornings I waited to hear his footsteps, running to me, calling MumMum…

I checked his hiding places.

I walked the streets searching, not believing, hate-filled, hate for everyone and everything. Stuttered and stumbled over the simplest words.

I refused to give way to others coming toward me, made it into a contest that I had to win. I stood on the left on escalators, confusing those in a hurry, trying to pass; let doors slam in the faces of those following, knocked into people.

A madwoman.

Some saw me, hesitated, took a second look: horror or pity. Or was it blame?

The fridge was stacked full of out-of-date food. I opened the door and closed it again. I had no idea what Jake ate.

Jake grew a beard. I wasn't sure he even noticed; odd for a man so careful about his appearance. It didn't suit him; he looked unwashed. I was unwashed, scantily clothed.

I couldn't help him, didn't want to. He hovered, offering comfort, tea, asking for comfort. I was neither giver nor taker.

I cursed the bike and that became Jake.

He went back to work.

I did not.

The post-mortem revealed fatal head injuries. There were to be no charges against Rosamund Beresford. The PC came to tell us, could not wait to leave.

More cards arrived. The doorbell rang and rang. I didn't move from my chair.

25

A firm bang on the door. Beth.

Go away, I screamed inside my head. *Go away*.

I opened the door and she flung herself at me, bawling like a kid, the way I wanted to and couldn't.

'Oh, Alice,' she cried.

I was smothered by her breasts, her signature small square cardboard box beating recklessly on my back.

'My darling Alice. Adam, oh Adam, your beautiful boy.' She disentangled herself, still holding me by the shoulders. Tears streamed, not mine.

It was me that offered solace. She took it for bravery, didn't see that I was dead.

'I'm so sorry.' She drew out a lace-edged handkerchief. 'That bitch who ran him down.'

That brought me alive, a little. I nodded.

She led me down the passage to the kitchen, placed the parcel on the table, offered me my tea or my coffee. I wanted neither. She ran the tap and poured herself a glass of water.

I pointed to the large green parcel with its yellow bow, unopened. Her present to Adam. I had intended to bin it.

She glanced at it and away.

'There are hundreds of bouquets and cards outside the school gate,' she said.

I didn't care. I was never going back there. I slumped on one of the kitchen chairs. 'The bike, he'd never seen anything so wonderful.' I put my face in my hands. She put her arm round my shoulders. 'Had it been a star he couldn't have been more excited.' I stopped, then, 'He thought he was flying.'

I could say no more.

'Brave little boy,' she murmured.

'It was stupid, too big. That's Jake, had to be the biggest and the best if it was for Adam.' I turned away from her so she couldn't see my eyes.

She was silent a time. Then said, 'That's love.' She sat back down opposite me, close enough to touch. 'Where is he? Jake.'

'Where he always is. Somewhere else,' I said. 'Work. He couldn't stand it here any longer.'

She flushed, drank a few mouthfuls.

'We can't talk to each other.'

She put down her water. 'Let's go out.'

I shook my head. 'People say the same thing, time. That won't change anything. He's gone.'

Beth started on the kitchen. It was a tip. I sat and watched. Could I tell her about the ride through the park? I opened my mouth. Nothing came.

She couldn't speak of her boys now. There was some desultory chatter about her work, her miserable boss, an exciting new find.

What did I care?

She pulled off the yellow gloves and picked up a stack of post from the table. 'Shall I?'

I shrugged.

She opened the cards and read each one out. Some of the names meant nothing.

Others: friends, work and neighbours. And one from Mr Williams with a dozen signatures.

Beth stood, had given up on me at last. 'A lot of people love you,' she said.

I laughed, a loud, ugly thing, then spoke. 'He said he was going to the moon, not to the sun, too hot.' (Memories. They worked like that: random, unexpected.) 'He said he would lift off like a rocket, put out his arms and fly. "Daddy too big to fly," he said. Just him and Rabby. "More stars than Adam can count. Stars are balls of gas and explode. Adam is afraid he might explode."'

He had rattled this off in his excited high-pitched voice.

'That's my clever boy,' Beth said.

My head shot up. He was not hers. 'Jake always said he was clever.'

'Of course he was,' Beth said, so quietly, so gently, so lovingly.

At the front door she took me in her arms. It must have been like hugging a long-dead fish.

'Anything I can do, phone me,' she said, taking me in her arms again. 'I'll be back, soon.'

I chucked the unopened present in the garbage, and the cards.

No tears. I belonged in space. Tears cannot flow there.

I woke each morning and went to the boy's room to check. Sometimes I got out his special cereal for breakfast, left it on the table, waiting. Jake put it away.

Anne left parcels of books on the doorstep. They built into crooked piles.

26

28th February 1991

The school closed for the day. The Head telephoned to tell me. I listened, said little. A thank-you perhaps. Unlikely.

I wanted it over quickly, a burial, not a cremation, not his body burning. Yet I didn't want him in the ground, rotting.

'No church service,' I said to Jake. 'And no hymns.'

Jake arranged it all.

On the day, he dressed me, choosing my clothes, pulling up my tights, kneeling at my feet to slip on my shoes. I lightly touched his hair.

We walked to the cemetery, side by side, holding hands like any happy couple out for a stroll. A clear, cold day with wisps of pale blue sky.

'It might snow,' Jake said.

I didn't look up.

The boy was already there, in his box, waiting for us. My son is dead, I told myself. Not out loud, didn't trust words, could not get my tongue round them.

We took the main road, avoiding the school, down two more streets to large iron gates. A man in black stepped forward, shook our hands, murmured words and guided us down a path, perhaps fifty yards. Interminable. I was in a hurry.

A large room, warm, stuffy and crowded.

People pressed in. I opened my coat and looked down at my clothes. Jake had chosen well: my black wool dress, long-sleeved and warm.

Beth was soon beside me, arm around me, a hug for Jake. She pointed at her crimson dress. 'I thought Adam would like this.'

Her boys were there, with Pete. They hovered, some distance away.

Anne and the staff from the library. And Mr Williams.

The Head of the school, Mrs Robinson, took my hand. Jake had murmured her name as she approached.

'A remarkable little boy, Mrs Oldfield. I'm so sorry.' She had kind eyes.

I was touched, hugged, my name spoken, softly, as if loud noise might break me, as indeed it might. Words of consolation, grief and love.

No blame.

Jake gently bent his head and murmured his thanks. I stood, silent, absent.

I wanted to be with my boy, just the two of us.

The man in black directed us to a small white box on a stand, waist-high. Adam had thought himself small enough to creep into a mousehole and tall enough to reach the stars.

I held Rabby, head down, dangling, in my left hand. Had I been an onlooker, I might have laughed to see it.

Jake cleared his throat. Silence fell.

'Thank you for coming. Alice and I are here to bury our son, Adam.'

He put his shoulders back and took a deep breath.

'Adam had his favourite star. I could never pick it out. That made him cross. "There, Daddy, there, can't you see it?" He stamped his little foot. So I pretended. Parents are good at that.'

My laugh almost escaped me. What did it matter?

'We found the star, Sirius, the Dog Star, the brightest of all, sometimes known as the Big Dog. Adam searched for it with his telescope, night after night. Sometimes he couldn't find it.' Jake smiled. 'That could make bedtime difficult.'

He paused, looked around. 'He knew all these things far better than me, our clever, wonderful boy. And the planets. He could list them in order. I can too, now.' He smiled, again. 'I'll spare you that.'

I put my head down.

'He was going to be an astronaut. His quest was to get to the moon. Alice taught him about quests.' He paused and took my hand. 'One day, when I have more courage than I have today, I will look into the night sky and find the Dog Star. Our son will be there. Our wonderful son.'

I put my hand on the white box, lightly. I didn't want to frighten him.

Jake let his head drop.

MumMum, I heard my boy whisper, taking my hand. *Will I live with you forever?*

Forever, I whispered back.

142

We were at the bottom of the garden. He had been hiding in the bushes, giggling.

Four men lifted the coffin, oh, so easily, and Jake and I and everyone else followed. The room transposed itself to a giant huddle in the cold, cold air outside.

Not much later, the thud of a sod. I almost cried out, for the noise and my boy in there.

I took the orange flower from my hair, leant down and placed it on the box. I wanted to spread myself over it, keep him warm.

Beth bent and placed a small piece of moss on the edge of the coffin. I heard her whisper, 'From one grubby-knees to another.'

Mourners began to leave. We were embraced, heard the same words again: sorry, loss; time, the cure-all. I wanted to scream back at them, tell them he was not theirs.

'You okay?' Jake said in his softest, gentlest voice. 'Soon.' He gripped my hand.

Nicola, his nursery teacher, murmured, 'He was special, your Adam.'

Mr Donovan, his schoolteacher, and half a dozen boys in school uniform gathered round us. The boys shuffled their feet and looked down when Mr Donovan said, softly, 'He was a remarkable boy. I shall miss him.'

I heard my boy's voice: *The best, the best*, he sang. *Mr Donovan says Adam could be a mathematician one day, but Adam is going to be an astronaut or a space walker. The other kids don't know about the stars, just Daddy and Adam.*

Where was I in that?

Beth was the last to leave, held me long. I refused to share my pain.

'I will come and see you. Soon,' she said.

A woman whose image was burned into my brain stood some distance away.

We caught each other's eyes. She took a step towards me, stopped, turned and walked slowly away.

The devil had bound us together, for all eternity.

27

Jake and I circled each other. He was waiting, waiting for me to speak. That's what I believed.

Night after night, in the wishing chair, or curled, foetus-like in the boy's bed under his starship cover, I listened to my own broken weeping.

Hours ticked by, so the kitchen clock told, pinging on the hour. I had once liked that, thought it a friend, sometimes a taskmaster. It had notched out my life. I took it off the wall, leaving a nasty mark, marched outside and flung it in the rubbish bin.

I took down the photograph of the boy and me from the mantelpiece, removed it from its frame and carried it everywhere.

'You're a vandal,' Jake said, a tremble in his voice, his hands made into fists.

I was a little frightened. We were both becoming other people.

'Where is it?' he demanded.

I pointed to my pocket.

'He was my son too.'

I walked away.

'You have to talk to me, Alice,' Jake said to my back, his voice hard. 'He was my son too.'

I stonewalled.

I had loved Jake once more than I had loved myself. Our love for each other had grown in wonder with our love for the boy and ourselves as a family.

I had forgotten that love. Love had become a twisted thing.

That day, 17th February 1991, was on video repeat. His birthday.

I sat on buses, on the top deck, sometimes almost the whole day, turning unread pages of books. Not getting off at stops.

The boy was hiding behind a large oak, peeping out, his chuckle giving him away; then he was running, laughing. I chased after him, fell, tights tearing, knee bloody. I looked up. He was gone. I was the grey heron, tried to stand on one leg, imagined myself tall and elegant. (When had I been either of those?) My balance too had deserted me.

I picked at my thumbnail, the flesh beneath, raw and angry, me in miniature.

I went through my wardrobe, threw out most of my clothes, kept all of my earrings.

The library gave me indefinite leave.

Jake was losing his hair. His father had died with a full head of hair. That had been Jake's only inheritance.

He came home late from work then walked, from his armchair to the sideboard, to the bottle of brown liquid, the silence filled with the clink of glass on glass. And back again, mumbling, 'Adam, my son,' intermingled with other words: stars, bike, fault.

He chain-smoked, lighting one cigarette off another, holding his cigarette between finger and thumb, close to his lips, a mannerism I once found so endearing. Often he slept on the sofa. He was too long for it.

It was a Sunday lunchtime, except we no longer had real mealtimes, long after we had heard the church bells call the believers. I used my fingers, my lips moving in sync, to count the days since… I failed, didn't know the date, except it must be Sunday.

We sat at the table, pretending. Jake had a chunk of cheese and a couple of water biscuits. I played with an apple.

'You were never here when we needed you.' I spat out my pain.

Jake's face twisted; fury was in his voice. 'I believed we would have him forever. I should have been with him every second of the day.' He banged his glass down on the table. 'You think I don't regret that? Every minute?' He paused, then, 'My son, dead, gone. I'd planned everything in my head: camping; bigger, better telescopes; the beach.' His hands, locking and unlocking.

He'd lost weight, his face was drawn; he was no longer the gentle man I'd met eight years ago. I was not the woman of eight years back, either.

His eyes grew soft. 'I was going to take him to San Francisco, show him the bridge, the Rockies. We would

147

walk, for days. And at night there would be stars and our tent. Star-man, that's what he called me.'

Where was I in all that?

A huge sob broke from him. 'Where have you gone, my Alice? I can't go on like this.'

I stood. 'Then go.' Even as the words left me, I knew I didn't mean them.

Each day I put on old clothes: the same grey skirt and a worn sweater. Mostly my feet were bare, despite the cold. Always the same earrings: stars. The powder compact lay fallow with the lipsticks and the other things I once couldn't do without.

Sometimes, before dawn, I crept up to the common. If I was feeling extra brave, I took his kite and flew it. That might have amused bystanders, a lone middle-aged woman flying a kite as the sun rose, had it not been too early, except for the occasional dog walker, and they, like lovers, had eyes only for their paramours. Or I left the windy open ground and hurried through the woods, past the big pond and another to his pond. He was always there, the grey heron.

I listened for the sound of the boy's feet, his chuckle, his cry of *MumMum*. I listened to the silence of ghosts. Yet he was everywhere. I never went back to that mound of earth.

I was afraid of the school bell, hid inside the house when the children were walking to school or back, with their mothers.

I had become fearful of so much. Once I had been ready for anything. That was gifted to me by Tom, my father, to be afraid of nothing. Although it turned out he was very afraid.

28

'I'm taking you out for coffee.' The volume of Beth's voice was higher than usual, the vowels more clipped. She must be a real tyrant in that lab of hers.

'You need to get out.' She was moving around the kitchen, tidying.

A fidget, my mother would have called her. Why was she in my head? Well, there was plenty of room there.

'Look at me, Beth, look hard. Do you want to be seen on the street with me?'

'Of course, my lovely one. You look a bit of a wreck, but so what?'

I looked away from her and back into the kitchen.

She dug into her bag and produced a white cardboard box, tore it open: two chocolate éclairs.

I stared at them, then away, felt sick.

She put the box down on the kitchen table and turned to me with a hug, a suffocating Beth hug.

'I love you, Alice. I'm here if you want to talk.' She stepped back. 'Sorry, but you need a shower.'

She led me upstairs and into the bathroom, undressed me, turned on the shower, handed me soap and a flannel and gently shoved me under the running water.

She returned a few minutes later with clean bra and pants, tee-shirt and trousers, and socks, placing them on the chair. 'I'll be downstairs when you're ready.' She left, leaving the door a little ajar.

A very small smile stretched the corners of my mouth. She hadn't selected randomly; the pants and top matched perfectly.

'How's Jake?'

I pointed to the empty whisky bottle near the draining board. Lazy bitch that I was, and such a lying shit. I didn't mention my vodka, had no idea where the bottle was. There was more than one. And I had never been a drinker.

'He's hurting too. You can see it in his face,' she said.

Her tone sounded loving. When had she seen him?

'He looked drained at the funeral. I know how it would be for Pete.'

'The bike,' I said, leaving out my part, the blame for the careless mother that I'd seen in strangers' eyes, although not in Beth's.

'My boys had bikes. It was that awful road. Something should be done about it.'

That's what the newspapers said, as usual missing the point.

'You can't blame yourself, or Jake.' There were tears in her eyes. 'I'm sorry. I promised myself I wouldn't cry. Oh, Alice.' She pulled me to her again.

'It was her,' I said into her shoulder. 'The barrister, she killed him.' I closed my lips tight.

We separated.

I saw her holding words back. Not like Beth.

'Perhaps you need help, Alice, professional help. I could find someone good you can talk to.'

I let her go on, couldn't find the strength to tell her she was wasting her time. I had to go away, be on my own. Sometime soon.

She looked at her watch.

'Sorry, work,' she said.

'Just a minute.' I left the room and returned a few minutes later with the small pack with its magnifying glass and spray bottle.

'For you. He would want you to have it.'

Beth stared at the pack then threw herself around me.

29

Jake was leaving for San Francisco. His eyes, with dark bags beneath, told me before the words, and the locking and unlocking of his fingers.

I no longer looked in the mirror.

'Are you coming back?' I asked, although, in truth, had little interest in his answer.

'Of course I'm coming back.' Anger in his voice, a flicker of denial in his eyes.

'Although it beats me what for.'

We had already parted, our hearts no longer reached out, the one for the other. Mine reached out only for the boy's, and his had stopped.

'We can't go on like this, Alice. Your silence, your blame. I would do anything…'

His voice startled, its harshness. He would find it easier away from me. Nothing, no one to remind him.

I shook my head. Blame? Whose?

'I don't know when I will be back,' he said.

I sat on a kitchen chair and watched him pick up his case and briefcase, put on his coat. He looked smart, work-smart.

'He was our son, our boy. I want to talk about him, remember.'

I said nothing.

He walked out of the front door.

I crouched in a corner of my bedroom. The phone rang, the front doorbell shouted. Beth tapped, then banged, over and over, shouting: 'Open the door, Alice. You can't hide away.'

I could, I would.

'Fucking humanity.' I strung the word out: fu u u ck ing. It felt good in my head. Humanity was something I had forgot. And fucking.

Empties were piling up. I mixed the vodka with any juice I could find.

On the top deck of the buses, I held tight to the front rail, leaning forward, my nose almost on the glass.

The lines in the middle of the road flashed messages, mostly telling me that there was no coming back from this. Or perhaps he was waiting for me at home, that I must hurry back.

The world grew too brightly coloured, and everyday objects lost their meaning.

One day I couldn't find my street. They all looked the same. I stopped and asked. And asked again. And again.

Jake phoned and must have heard the slur in my words. He had been away two weeks.

I found the box of photographs. I sat on the carpet in the sitting room and scrabbled through them. Mostly Adam, plenty of me, almost none of Jake. The first I plucked out was Adam standing barefoot in the sand, Rabby dangling.

The beach had been dotted with sun umbrellas, children, running dogs, buckets and spades. The clamour of children, murmurs of adults and occasional shouts.

Barefoot, Adam had run across the sand. 'Sand, MumMum, sand,' he shouted, then tumbled and lay flat on his tummy, giggling. He scrambled up and ran to the water, squelching over the wet sand. 'Sea, sea.' Then he stopped, fear in his voice. 'Poisonous snakes, Daddy.'

Jake drew a line in the wet sand, where the wave had retreated.

'The water is going out, son, no snakes here. A magic line.'

I pondered over the word *son*, decided it was a man thing. Girls were not called daughter by their fathers. Or their mothers.

'Magic, magic.' Adam nodded.

'A sandcastle, son, we'll build a sandcastle.'

'Sandcastle, sandcastle.'

Just above the tideline, Jake, using one of the green buckets and spades, started digging. Adam copied, his shorts damp from the wet sand. Jake wore a long-sleeved work shirt and knee-length khaki shorts. Adam ignored me, his tongue running across his lips, his eyes on the sand and his bucket and spade. Each spadeful was dug, and carefully poured into the bucket. Then another. And another. When full, Adam pounded the mound of sand flat with his spade the way Jake had shown him, and staggered a few yards to their incomplete sandcastle, his chubby legs struggling in the soft sand.

Always afraid for him. The waves felt over-big, their noisy sucking back into the blue-green mass a little threatening.

Yet their susurration was somehow calming.

I was content to sit in my short sleeveless dress on a towel, cardigan nearby, and watch or wander along the beach collecting a few sea-moulded stones.

Adam was a different boy when he was with Jake, more grown-up somehow, and perhaps more of a baby with me. He had two personalities, one for each of us.

A gull swooped, splitting the air with its raucous cry. Adam threw himself at the sand, screaming. Heads turned towards us.

I stood, almost falling, rushed to him, arms out. I held him, Jake hovered. I whispered in Adam's ear, 'Just a bird, little man, a bird. You are safe.' A seagull was a small thing compared to my nightmares.

Later, my two men went out in a small boat. 'Don't go out too far,' I shouted as they pulled away from the shore, Adam seated at the bow in a bright orange life jacket, his eyes wide, Rabby dangling from his wet, sandy left hand.

'Careful, Adam, careful,' I called out as he tried to stand.

'Careful, MumMum, careful,' he shouted back, his cheeky smile spreading across his face. He sat back down with a bump.

I scrabbled through the rest of the photos and picked out another. Adam and his snowman, both in dark glasses in the white land. My clever, funny boy. I placed the photograph in a drawer.

I was choking in London, had to get away. From everyone. From small boys.

I would flee north, further than The Street, further than I'd ever been, until I reached the sea. Then, perhaps, I would wade into it. My legs were not very long.

I could pack up my life in a suitcase and drag it behind me. Somewhere, anywhere.

I picked up his train set, tried to twist the track. Found a hammer. Smashed it and the trains.

I left a note for Jake: *I need time, I'm sorry. I don't know when I will be back. One day. Please don't try to find me. Alice*

I took from my precious-things-drawer Jake's first letter to me. Jake, the man who had made me real.

And a drawing. The photograph from the frame on the mantelpiece, as always, was in my pocket.

I held *Mrs. Dalloway* in my hands. Beth's copy from years back. I had never returned it. A day of preparation for a party, Clarissa with her troubled past, her depression. Septimius dead, stabbed by the railings. And the kiss, the Sally Seaton kiss of thirty-four years past.

I put it down again. It was somehow too frivolous.

I selected a picture from the box of photographs, taken not long ago. He was in school uniform. I shoved it in a drawer. I screwed up newspaper and put a pile of it in the sink. I threw the photographs on top and lit the newspaper.

Spring was slow in coming and it would be cold in the far north.

I left wearing trousers, blouse, sweater and coat and trainers and carrying a few toiletries and spare clothes in a small backpack. And Rabby.

I took enough money to last a long time.
It was late March.

30

At King's Cross ticket office, I asked for a ticket north.

'North where?' the man asked, his face screwed up with irritation.

'The furthest.'

He turned away and spoke to a woman.

'Thurso,' he said to me.

I nodded and handed over a lot of money.

'You'll have to change…'

I didn't listen.

It took two days to get there: train, train, bus, bus. I spent a night in a train station, curled up, out of sight. What was in my head during all those hours? Nothing much.

I got off the bus where the road ended, at a small cluster of cottages and a red phone box. The road had wound past small lochs among giant mountains, some with islands speckled with tiny trees, and a narrow track led up the mountainside.

My father slipped into my head, his easy grin, his arms outstretched, his voice murmuring, 'Come here, Princess.' Or perhaps it was the mountains.

'How far, Daddy, how far?' I heard my eleven-year-old voice; high, excited. For a moment, I was that girl, about to start at the Grammar, on her first hunting trip: *Run Rabbit Run*.

'You'll always come back, won't you, Daddy?'

'Promise, Princess.' His hand tousled my hair. 'Promise.'

He had lied. About much.

I was no one's princess now.

I passed clumps of Scots pines. Water ran down stone gullies. Sheer rock walls towered over me and brown heather swathed the slopes. Purple mountains in the distance opened out in a fan. Spiders, a dragon, in the sky, their doubles blackly etched onto the mountainsides.

Below, the death of a forest.

A whitewashed stone cottage, slate roof and a thin spiral of smoke from the chimney.

I trudged on, up, turned the corner. The primitive track faded.

Another cottage: peeling, cracked paint on the walls, small grimed windows, moss on the roof.

I peered in, pushed at the porch door. It surrendered, protesting with a groan of rusted hinges. A pair of Wellingtons on their side on the floor, old and cracked, and a plaid jacket hung on a hook. The inside door wasn't fully closed. I pushed at it, stepped in, drew back from the cold, stinking air.

It would do. I had reached not the sea, but the end.

I walked out of the porch and back down the hill to the mean spiral of smoke. I had no real idea where I was.

I knocked on the solid wooden door, waited, knocked again, not too hard, walked a few feet back to a small rock, slumped down on it, felt the wet through my trousers. I let my bag fall.

A small movement of a white muslin curtain to the left of the front door, then the rasp of heavy bolts being drawn back. An old woman, with knotted grey hair loose on her shoulders, pulled back the door and thrust her head forward. A ragged floral dress hung, baggy, down to her unsocked ankles and black laced shoes, a worn sweater over it. She was tall, thin, gnarled.

She did not ask, in words, why I was there; her eyes did.

I stood and walked towards her. 'That cottage, up there,' I turned and pointed up the hill, 'is it yours? I'd like to rent it for a while.' I put out my hand. 'Alice.' She went to take it but dropped her hand back to her side.

'It's not for rent.'

'Just a few days,' I pleaded. 'I've nowhere else to go.' I heard a man's voice in the background, anger lacing it.

The woman shifted from foot to foot, glanced over her shoulder. 'It's not heated. My grandson stays there sometimes. It's unsuitable.' She stopped, her eyes asking: What is someone like you doing in these mountains?

She looked around, up. I followed her gaze. Giants in all directions.

'Please,' I said, and heard the words from inside: 'Shut the door.'

I fumbled in my bag, pulled out my purse.

Her hands were thin, as worn as her face. She shook her head, took a couple of steps towards me and spoke very softly. 'You look troubled. There's wood in the yard. Use as much as you like. It's not locked.' She paused. 'There is pain in your eyes.'

She half motioned behind and her thin body scurried back through the door.

It slammed shut.

I opened the door leading inside from the porch and shivered. It was warmer outside.

The cottage had one bedroom with an iron bedstead, a lumpy, stained mattress and a stink that suffocated.

'Shit.' I stuffed my hand over my mouth and backed out of the room, slamming the door behind me.

Another door led into a small, dark room, then into an even smaller kitchen, and a bathroom where mould covered most of the surfaces. I ran a tap at the washbasin. Cold brown water gushed. I pressed the light switch. Nothing.

The sitting room had an open fireplace, the ashes long dead, and a rug in front of the hearth was spotted with burn marks. Pulled up close to the fire was a battered, sagging sofa, with a couple of blankets thrown over the back. Whoever stayed here before me did most of their living in this room. I would do the same, sleep on the sofa, try to keep the fire going all night.

Near the back door I found a hessian bag, and in the overgrown backyard, the woodshed. I overfilled the bag and dragged it over the ground and into the house. After that, it was feeble armloads, hugging the wood to my chest. I stacked the logs on both sides of the hearth.

There were matches and some paper on the mantelpiece. The fire flickered, spat its indifference. I knelt down and fed it.

In the kitchen on a worn, stained pine table I found two candles, stuck with wax to saucers, more in a drawer, and stale cereal in a jar on the table. God knows how long it had been there but I poured out a fistful, shoved it into my mouth and choked. I unearthed a jar with about an inch of instant coffee, unscrewed the lid. The coffee was rock solid. I chipped away enough to make one cup then I remembered. No power.

I built up the fire, too many logs but I didn't care.

Outside, a dark copse of trees, bowed down, suppliants to the wind. Mostly Scots pines but also an oak and a couple of alders. No sign of life in them. Not even birds.

Behind them, the giants.

Was I drowning in a child's dream?

I placed the plaid jacket from the porch over my shoulders, covered myself with the two blankets and fell asleep on the sofa.

The next morning, I found a tin of condensed milk in a cupboard with the door hanging partially off. I balanced a saucepan of water on logs in the fire, punched a hole in the top of the can with a rusty can opener and boiled the tin. I let it cool then ate it, spoonful by spoonful.

For the remainder of the day, I moved only to throw more logs on the fire. And in the flames I saw again the sink at home and the sacrifice of the photographs. The cold drifted away. I grew accustomed to the stench.

I heard clicking Lego pieces, watched the flames flicker, slept, my dreams fevered. He was in the ground. Never mind, he never did feel the cold.

I found freshly baked bread and a bag of potatoes just inside the porch door when I got up the next morning. I ate most of the bread at once, tearing chunks from the loaf.

Outside, only trees and mountains. And a light covering of snow.

Silence. I opened my arms and breathed it in.

31

On the third day, I dressed in most of the clothes I'd brought with me. And the plaid jacket from the porch. It came down to my knees. The snow outside was almost gone.

It had snowed the day he was born.

And…

I hovered in the porch. I had never been among mountains so huge, so desolate, so cold. Perhaps I should have run to the sea, wrapped myself in the soothing music of the waves. I had fled London with its memories, yet carried them, silk-wrapped, in my head. I heard his voice, "Adventure, MumMum, 'venture."

And Jake. What had I done? The short answer was destroy, run. Was it his love I feared? And the truth about that day. He too had been abandoned when almost the same age as me, his brother James. I had once thought of myself as a kind person.

I took a deep breath and stepped outside.

Not far from the cottage I found a narrow path through the stand of trees. That was the easy bit. The other side, I stopped, stared upwards, wondered. Why had I come? I could not spend the days in that cottage. The mountain tops beckoned, although they were beyond my reach. I started up through the heather, zigzagging, searching out lower growth, stumbling on the hidden rocks beneath, Rabby in my left hand, water in a small pack on my back.

Stumbling, cursing, breathless. Always up.

The boy's short legs climbed beside me, his slightly absent smile, slipping sunglasses, face reddening. I put out my hand to pull him.

I put it away, empty.

No gloves, niggardly sun barely lifting the frost from the air.

Shadows on the steep sides above told of dark stories.

'Sit,' I said to the boy, 'and I'll tell you a story.'

He sat. Then he was gone.

Just as well. My stories were not for him. Not now.

Jake would have different stories. His would be of the stars. I envied him that.

Sometime in the first days I threw my watch away, down a steep gully; watched it bounce, protest. I was afraid of the moving hand.

The light guided me after that.

Returning from the mountain one evening, I found a warm jacket in the porch with a note: *This will fit you, keep out the cold. It was hers.*

I set off each morning when it was barely light, shivering in the bitter cold, despite the jacket. The climb took me well into the morning. There was no one else on my mountain. I would have liked to fly into the sky, into the sun, another Icarus.

I didn't believe in heaven or I might have wanted to land at the feet of St Peter, holding the little man in my arms.

Stones in my pocket carried up the mountain, collected for him on that half sand/half shingle beach, each stone slightly different, rounded, smoothed by the sea.

I stood on the edge of a steep drop, swayed a little, closed my eyes. 'It would be easy,' a voice murmured. 'Easy as pie.' Street words.

I'd loved life. Once. Such fun, those at the library had said of me. Was I really fun? I tried. I existed to be the best. His fault, my father's. Love. I had not believed in that after him. A simulacrum perhaps.

I turned off the words in my head, inched forward. I did not want to die. I was not a believer so I would not find him in death.

I felt rather than heard a movement behind me. Almost toppled.

I turned.

A stag.

His eyes were big, brown, his coat dark brown with hints of red. On his head, three small stumps. I didn't know on that first day that I would see those stumps grow.

He stood, watching me.

I stepped back from the edge.

There was a broad, flat rock fifty yards away. I stumbled to it and sat. He followed.

On days to come, seated on the same rock, I would, in my head, walk the other peaks I could see stretching into the horizon. Many snow-clad still.

The mountains. I tried to make creatures, friends, of them; found a whale, beside it another mountain, not gentle, with jagged teeth. I had seen pictures of it, was sure it bore a girl's name: Holly? Polly? I would have liked to spread myself along its teeth, feel the spikes puncture my flesh, little of it now, spread sparsely over my belly, my ribs, my once-suckled, now dry, sagging breasts.

The other mountains resisted, insisting on their individual geometric shapes, especially triangles with their pointed tops. Bare, sheer rock walls, ridges, flat, needlepoints, all shapes.

Rothko might have loved them.

Purple-grey sky.

Cloud caressed and sheathed the whale, now revealing only its tail.

The mountains ignored me. I was insect-puny.

The glens below were wide, sprawling. Sheep wandered the slopes further down, and twisted limbs of birch trees and lichen painted the rocks, and the valleys were littered with stumps of pines. In the far distance, islands dotted the loch.

Snow in the high mountain gullies.

The mountains had their secrets, and the wind carried them from top to top. If I knew those secrets, they might save me. Nothing else would.

Silence. Not the absence of sound, although the mountains had that too, but full-bodied silence with its own character.

I sat, ignoring the cold stone under my bum. The stag snorted, lowered his head into the brown heather.

I didn't name the stag. To name is to own. We were both free, although my freedom was not his.

Each day, the stubs of his incipient antlers grew a little more.

We two, phantoms on a Scottish mountain.

I told him my stories, editing as I went. I used to be methodical, valued logic and order. Perhaps that was one of my many delusions. Sometimes I didn't use words, was too tired, let him read my thoughts, as jagged as the mountains: loss, boy, blame. I never spoke aloud his last words.

Stories of a small boy, his face, untouched by the world, puzzlement in his eyes.

'MumMum,' I said aloud.

Questions for Daddy: Why do you have such long legs; why don't the stars fall out of the sky; why can't we fly, Daddy; why can't spiders fly?

The stag looked puzzled.

'Look, MumMum, look.' The boy pointed to the stag.

'A stag,' I whispered. 'A friend.'

The boy put out his hand and the stag dropped his head.

I made up stories for the boy from the shapes of the clouds in the sky, the shadows on the hills: giant dogs, horses, birds, even a scarecrow. That is what good mothers do. Tell stories to their loved ones. Happy stories about a wonderful small boy. Never a snake. I didn't want to frighten him.

'Nephelococcygia,' I said to him. 'Shapes in clouds.'

'More, MumMum,' he said. 'More.'

His legs wriggled. He was always a wriggler, never still.

'MumMum,' he said, 'let's do sums.'

He was missing Mr Donovan.

And he might have made a snowman in the high gullies.

He had been happy, joyful. Himself, always himself.

Me? I didn't know. Deep inside, we are all incomplete. The Street started the process of me until I shrugged it off. What did growing up mean? Forgetting my father. I hadn't guessed that it had to be love, had given myself up as unlovable. Until Jake. Then the boy.

Blood slipped from my right nostril, unannounced, velvety. I let it drip, was familiar with its habits.

I changed. Love did that. I would like to be a poet but did not have that way with words.

And I had changed again.

The boy was leaping from top to top, whispering to the stag, running, shouting over his shoulder, 'Catch, MumMum, catch.' I was afraid he might fall, hurt himself.

Sometimes he sat beside me. The stag moved away, to eavesdrop from a distance. He was a good friend. His mouth twisted into his smile if he liked what he had heard.

My boy, flying higher, higher, screaming, or was it the birds wheeling overhead? His face, his words. The silence of the crumpled thing on the road, the wheels turning, turning. The bed, white sheet up to his chin, head bandaged, small arms outside the white, inert. His spinning done.

He was sitting there, rock still.

'Look away. I am your mother. You shouldn't be seeing this.'

I dug into my pocket and carefully unwrapped the cotton wool. Nestled inside, like a baby bird, was an exquisitely sharp razor blade.

I took a deep breath, raised my right hand with the blade between forefinger and thumb, selected a fleshy part of my left forearm, and cut, not too deep, the blade slipping through the unresisting skin, a line one inch, two. The blood slow, a few small blobs at first, perhaps checking its new territory. Then a trickle as the blobs multiplied, joined up and ran down my arm in an exultant small stream.

I watched, breathed deep.

The pain lifted me, carried me, a searing light, somewhere else, into nothingness. I breathed long and hard, tried to hang onto the elsewhere, a second or two more, a lifetime.

I gasped, bent over.

What had my life been? My mother had called hers a waste. Had mine been that?

Except for the boy. And the other in my life, Jake, who had become my life. Once I would have run down the mountain to him.

Could not. Would not.

I sat up, took a bandage from my pack and, with the aid of my teeth, wrapped my arm while the sun, sly thing, slid from behind a cloud, sending shards of itself to the brown heather at my feet, lighting it up, giving it hints of purple.

Back in the cottage, I made a small cup of coffee. I had to ration what was in the jar, and tore the loaf into chunks.

One day, I was late leaving for the mountain. A robin perched on a bush in the wilderness that was the back garden, sitting, his small head cocked while I stood. I heard the boy say, 'my robin', imagined it had followed me here. Each morning, I put out a few crumbs of my bread for his robin.

The climbing of the mountain and what followed became my daily routine.

After what must have been a couple of weeks, I found the old woman outside the porch as I returned from the mountain at dusk. The cat, paws neatly tucked in, sat beside her on the cold ground.

'Is there no one…?' she asked.

I turned away, then back, bent to stroke the cat. It ran from me, terror in its stride, yet cats, big and small, are the terrorists of the animal world. It read my anger, my despair, in my touch. It despised such an easy victory.

She and the cat limped back down the mountain.

Rain set in, days of it. Darkness, fear. I burned the wood. Got out the razor.

The nights were deadly. I waited through them for daylight and the climb. He only came to me on the mountain.

A storm hammered the mountain, the cottage. The wind howled, shook the windows. It was the punishing god of the careless mother coming for me. I huddled in front of the fire, hands over ears. At night, the room was lit up with flashes of lightning, followed by roiling thunder.

The old woman staggered through the storm, in through the porch and into the sitting room.

'It has set in, will pass in a day or two. Don't be afraid. Have you enough food?'

I nodded, thought of my mother.

Then the wind ceased and the mist blanked everything out, the tops of the mountains and far below.

Until the storm ended I rarely moved from the fire, except for more wood and bread and some water.

32

Longer days, shorter nights, and on the mountain, the sun more generous.

I sat on my broad, flat rock, the stag nearby, putting his head down when my words became too painful, pretending to eat.

His antlers grew. I longed to touch their velvet tips. He did not permit it.

He looked away when I took out the blade.

I picked up the water bottle, unscrewed the lid and took a small sip. Big things were beyond me. I pulled a piece of paper from my pocket, a drawing of a stick figure with two stars for eyes. Underneath, one word, his word: *MumMum.* I gazed at it, taking care not to let the blood defile it.

Sometimes I whispered to the boy, simple things like, 'How are you today?' I had never asked him that in life. And I was not a whisperer.

'Good, MumMum.' I had to lean towards him to hear.

I was fading, head and body.

I fell asleep, watched over by the stag.

I awoke, chilled, looked around at the mountains, darkened. I was etiolated, a nothing, something a stranger might pass through and not notice.

The blood had dried, the flesh either side of the cut risen to small mounds, red and angry, a criss-cross of scars.

I packed away the blade, wiping it first on a clean piece of gauze. Perversely, I was careful of infection. It was a long walk down the mountain to the cottage. I was shivering with cold.

I felt in my pocket for the newspaper cutting I'd brought with me from London, took it out, smoothed it and read: *Barrister not to be prosecuted.* There was a picture of Rosamund Beresford, soon to be a Silk, so the article predicted.

She had a six-year-old son, at the primary school, my boy's school.

I folded and replaced the cutting, stretched and bent to take Rabby from the rock where he was perched, waiting. I held him by his left leg, dangling head-down. He was dirty and tattered, bald on the top of his head from being dragged along the pavement and through the schoolyard. The lower part of his left leg had lost its fake fur where a small hand had clutched him.

I struggled back down the dusk-smothered mountainside.

I needed to be inside before the stars were out. I was in hiding from them.

The bright yellow of the gorse was beginning to stain the hillsides, and the heather would be out sometime soon. The youthful lime green of the larches dotted the lower slopes, growing fast.

The darkness was now brief, a mere cipher, the dawn not that long after the evening light had faded. Others would come to the mountains and I would have to leave. There was nowhere further to run.

Eight years back, a tall man had held out a book to me.

'John Clare,' I said. I spoke aloud often.

The mountains were reflected in *Four Darks in Red*.

I had been ready for him, for his grace and his passion.

After more than a month, I sent Jake a note, writing that I was all right, that I would be back, but not yet.

The old woman took the letter to post.

I ransacked the cupboards and found no more food so lived off the old woman's bread and potatoes, left on the doorstep every other day.

Daily, I left the cottage to climb the mountain. After a time, I ceased to carry the blade up the mountain. I had little strength and what I had the mountain took.

A slow killer.

Occasionally, I returned to find the old woman sitting in front of the fire, her black cat sprawled on the rug. He didn't move when I came in. The smoke curling into the sky, seen from far off, told me she would be there. She sometimes wore a housecoat just like my mother.

She would get up and leave as I came through the door, saying, 'It's warm for you.' The cat followed her out. I wanted him to stay.

33

Dusk, the time between the dog and the wolf.

The mountains were cracking. Lightning played with the peaks, ran down the bare rock faces. A kid's game.

The stag ran down the mountain, leaping from boulder to boulder, balletic.

I followed; slow, stumbling.

Someone moved among the pines near the cottage. I stopped, afraid.

Jake stepped out of the gloom.

I had dreamt about him the night before, my two men, leaping from top to top, short legs, long legs, shouts, laughter. I had screamed, 'Wait, wait.'

We stood, a foot or two apart, staring at each other. He put out his hand and eased Rabby from my grasp.

I hated him for that. I stepped back, my mind in turmoil. How I wanted to touch him, have him hold me. And yet… His smile wasn't the one I remembered. There was anger in his eyes, eyes I had always remembered as gentle. His face thin to the point of gauntness.

He had taken part of me. I'd given willingly.

He followed me inside. I hadn't cleaned the cottage since I arrived, filth on filth. I saw, with his eyes, the dirt-encrusted windows, the dust everywhere, and soot. A broom that I had never before noticed, propped in a corner.

His corduroys were grubby, as were the parts of his shirt I could see. He was unshaven, his hair unbrushed. An old man.

He had run from me, from us. Too often. We had fought, or I had fought. A fighter me, always had been, mostly mistaken.

I had driven him away and fled. A wasteland, my life.

Jake put down a small bag, balanced Rabby on the arm of the sofa and walked to the fireplace. He knelt, scraped out the old ashes into the box on the hearth, carefully laid the fire and picked up the matches.

'More wood?' His first words.

I pointed to the back door.

He carried in load after load, throwing logs on the fire. Sparks flew and some settled on the rug. He stamped them out.

I sat on the sofa and watched.

'How did you find me?'

'The address on the back of the envelope. It wasn't in your handwriting.'

Ha, interfering old bitch. Then I remembered the bread, the potatoes, and her eyes.

Jake stood and brushed the dirt from his knees, walked to the door and picked up his bag.

'A bed of sorts there.' I pointed to the door leading to the bedroom. 'I sleep on the couch.'

He strode into the bedroom, carried this bag, his body stiff, not the loose-jointed Jake of old. I hadn't been in that room since the day I arrived.

I stood (marionettes, we two) and walked to the sink, filled the blackened saucepan, settled it on the fire. 'No electricity,' I said, over my shoulder. I was running short of candles, despite the few I found from time to time in the porch.

I made two black coffees.

He came back into the room with two plastic-wrapped sandwiches and some apples. 'All I could get at the service station. Not much of a feast.' He tried out a smile, and put the food on the small table then stood, awkward. He dug into his jacket pocket and brought out a small box.

He held it out, my favourites: Peppermint Creams. Too rich. Just to look at them made me want to throw up. I turned away.

The fire was blazing, throwing out malign shadows: small boys. Yet giving off little heat, its flames twisting and curling with promise and disappointment. Jake tore open one of the sandwiches and pushed the other towards me.

'Thanks.' I left it where it was.

He sat beside me.

He chewed, the way he always did, with vigour and no haste, then put the half-eaten sandwich down and looked at my hair. It had grown but still had the look of a haircut done by a half-blind idiot with a razor blade. Not too far from the truth. The only mirror here, in the bathroom, was small and tarnished. He put out his hand and took it back before touching me. He picked up the sandwich.

'You should eat something.' It was an instruction, as he held out the other sandwich.

I shook my head.

I listened to his chewing, wanted to shout at him to be quiet.

'They've given me time off from work,' he said. 'I made a mess of it in San Francisco. No one wanted to talk, not to a sad old man.' He threw the packaging into the fire. 'I didn't know where you were, thought you were dead.' His voice told anger.

I looked at him. I was forty-five; he must have been fifty-two.

We sat, our bodies not touching.

'Why did you come? I asked you not to.'

He picked up a bottle of whisky from beside himself, took a large mouthful and held it out to me. I shook my head. His movements were clumsy. He took another slug.

'I'm back in Hampstead,' he said. 'There's nothing for me in Wimbledon.'

I understood what he meant.

He stared at the fire. 'I've taken the Rothkos.'

I might have missed them once.

'My son is dead.' Huge sobs shook him. He raised his head. 'You are right to blame me. The bike. It was not her that killed him. It was me.'

'I don't blame you.' I did. And myself.

'Then why won't you help me? Why won't you tell me what happened?'

'I can't.' My heart was in my ears, my rasping breath competing with his sobs.

He looked at me. 'What has happened to us? I can't go on like this. Without you, without him. He was my son too, my son.' Anger, despair in his voice, lips tight.

Flames flared in the fireplace, taunting us both.

'I found your bonfire, the photographs, what was left of them. Did you have to take all of him from me?'

Shame stopped my mouth.

'Come back with me, Alice. We have to live. This is not living. We have to find that joy in each other again. He would want that.' He looked out of the window. 'What are you doing up here?'

I pointed towards the tops.

'You?' There was scorn in his voice.

My head shot up. Fury in my eyes. 'I can't go back,' I said, putting my hand out for the bottle. It was half empty. I put it to my lips and took several big swallows.

'You can. I'll help you,' he said.

'I can't. I've gone.'

'Where?'

How would I know? I was warming up, or perhaps it was the whisky. Jake was already in shirtsleeves. I started to pull the sweater over my head. It got stuck at the neck. I tugged my arms out.

Jake dragged it over my head, roughly, and grabbed my wrist. My arm, the cuts, some barely healed, others scabbed, the more recent ones red, angry. A couple began to bleed.

I winced.

'Alice.'

I was surprised to hear my name. She'd gone, no longer existed.

His voice was loud. 'Why? For God's sake. How could you?'

'God?' I looked at him. His face quivered. His teeth were bare.

'Don't play that game, Alice. If you don't talk to me, how can I help you?'

I didn't want his help. If I understood, I might be able to stop. Somehow it cleansed me.

'Why? Why?'

I shook my head. I couldn't speak of the rage, the guilt, the emptiness. The razor between my fingers, just there, no planning; and the calm that came with the pain.

I pulled the crumpled piece of newspaper from my pocket and slapped it on his knee, picked up the bottle from the seat and took another large mouthful. I hadn't eaten since this morning, was light-headed, a little hysterical.

He let go of my wrist, picked up the cutting, took a few seconds to read it, screwed it up and threw it into the fire. Flames, taunting.

I clenched my fist. For the first time ever I wanted to hit him. 'She killed him.'

'There's nothing we can do about that. We have to talk, Alice.'

'What about?'

'Our son. That day. Look at me, Alice. We have to get through this, together.' His eyes were as hard as the rock I sat on up the mountain. 'The bike. I wish I'd bought the bloody thing. I'm a fool.'

I moved away, as far as the sofa allowed.

'I don't understand.' His voice was loud, harsh. 'Where am I in all of this, Alice? I love you.'

I had never before heard this rage. Not from him.

'You ran,' I said.

'I've told them I won't go to the US anymore.' His voice was hoarse. His hands clenched. 'Come back with me, to Wimbledon.' He pulled out his cigarette case and lit up. 'You need feeding up. You've lost weight.'

I watched him smoking. I had teased him once, told him he looked like Rowan Atkinson. That was when we watched *Not the Nine O'Clock News* together.

I wanted him gone.

'We have to talk about that day. We will lose him if we don't. I came all this way.'

'I didn't ask you to. I asked you not to try to find me.'

'Alice, who are you now? I don't know you.'

I didn't know, either.

'I've never stopped loving you,' he said. 'Do you still love me Alice?'

Love. There was only room for the one.

His monk-grey eyes steel-hard, his fists clenched. I was a little afraid of this man who I had taken into my heart, made myself over for and adored for his generosity, his understanding and his love.

'We can start again. It's not too late.'

He paused then said, each word separated by a second or two, 'Adam is dead.'

The name reverberated through the room, flew out, into the dark. The black mountains outside bounced the name among themselves. The stag lifted its head and listened. Surprised.

'Don't,' I shouted.

'Don't what?'

'Say his name.'

He threw his cigarette into the fire. I shifted away from him, stared out through the window. It was utterly black, mirroring our anger.

'Adam,' he said. 'He was mine too.'

I pointed to the starlit sky outside. 'You and your stars.'

'This isn't you. Where have you gone?'

'With him, I suppose.'

'You can't.'

I could.

'It's too late.' I hadn't meant to shout. 'For us.' I turned back, saw his face, twisted, a stranger. I stood, quickly.

He grabbed me from behind, his hands on me, hard, angry fingers dragging me down onto the settee. A scream welled in my throat, died. I tried to get my hands on his face, claw at his eyes. He pressed down on top of me, tore at my tracksuit bottoms, then his own trousers, pushed himself roughly into me, fucked me hard, fast, as if he had never done it before. No love. Punishment.

Punishment I understood. I turned my head, watched the flames flicker and turn to ash.

We were some other couple.

He rolled off me, pulled himself up to sit at the far end of the settee, head in his arms. 'Adam,' he sobbed.

I didn't stir. What seemed many minutes later, he stood and picked up the almost empty bottle. The sink sucked the liquid down the plughole.

He took one of the blankets and walked into the cold bedroom, shutting the door behind him.

I lay awake, watching the fire, tracking its spurts, its quiescence and its dying. Much, much later, I heard short, sharp snores from the next room. Oh, for this evening to have never taken place. We could no longer read the dreams or pain in each other's eyes. They were oblique, veiled. We were each in our own purdah.

The man who had held out John Clare: "I am – yet what I am none cares or knows."

Words, weapons.

The rules of my life. What were they? I had no idea anymore. To be strong, to never give up, to be the best, never to be afraid. But the man who had insisted on those rules, my father, had abandoned me.

I woke, stiff and cold, and lay, staring at the dead fire and the open bedroom door.

On the arm of the sofa, a note:

My love (you are that, despite the awful thing I did), my Alice,

Forgive me, I beg you. I cannot explain what I did. Despair perhaps. Forgive me.

Do you recall my first letter? I am unreal without you.

I can't be in that empty house without you and our son. I cannot.

I am a father even though he's dead. And a husband. Yours. If you want me.

I have rented a flat in Hampstead where I can walk on the heath, holding your two fingers.

I've missed you, Alice. Life is unbearable without you. I'm lost, and angry. I will not lose you. Yet you

have to want to be with me. More than that, love me.
Do you love me? That love we once had. We said we
would never part.

Let me know when you leave here and I will be in
Wimbledon, waiting for you. Please let it be soon.

I will always love you and look after you. There
will never be anyone else.

Forgive me.
Your Jakey

Below his note was a Hampstead address.

I put my hands between my legs, felt the soreness, yet the real pain was the despair, the fury in his eyes, and anger, self-blame, bewilderment. He came for my help and I refused him.

I knew myself to be often careless and the opposite, caring. I hoped that outweighed the other.

I pulled the rug tight around me.

I thought of death not love. Love is life.

A spark flew out, settled comfortably on the rug and burned a small territory around itself.

I was too old, too barren for another small life. Just as well. The boy, his death, never imagined, not for a second. No mother contemplates that. My life had once cleaved in two: before and after Jake. It had broken again. Perhaps finally.

I did not leave the cottage, and a few days later the old lady left a letter for me in the porch. It was short.

If you don't come home, I will come to you. Beth

It was dated 1st June 1991.

The sky was too big, suffocating, squeezing my breath from me.

34

Dusk. The porch door was open, smoke rising from the chimney.

I stopped at the open door into the sitting room. The old lady was there, seated on the sofa, the back of her head to me, the cat on her lap.

'It's nice and warm for you,' she said, in a strong, different voice to the almost-whispers of other encounters. She pointed at the fire, didn't turn around.

I walked in, flung my hat on the easy chair, walked to the tap and filled a saucepan of water and placed it on the fire.

She chuckled. And stood, dislodging the cat.

'Don't go,' I said.

I picked up my mug, stained and unwashed from yesterday, and bent to find another in the cupboard.

'Nothing for me,' she said.

There was a hot, glowing bed of coals and the room was

warmer than it had been since I arrived. I wondered how long she had been there.

The cat strode off.

She sat. 'She would be about your age now. She left when she was sixteen.'

She was staring into the fire. I could only see the side of her face. Oddly, it was young, almost unwrinkled, hopeful.

'I left home at sixteen too,' I said.

She didn't hear me.

'He took her up the mountains, away from me. She came back happy. He said he loved her.' The old woman pulled her grey plait round to sit on her flat chest. 'Said he stayed for her. It was only him she wanted to be with.' She sounded far away. 'She looked like him, not me, with her beautiful red hair that he would never let me cut. I loved her.'

'I've loved you, always,' my mother had said to me, and pulled the ashtray closer. 'But he was the only one that mattered to you.' Her voice was soft and low, her face flushed. I looked away.

'When she wasn't with him, it was the books.' The old woman blinked, once, twice. 'He got them for her. She stopped school early, didn't see the point,' she said. 'He wanted that.'

She got out a large white handkerchief. 'He hasn't left the house since she disappeared. She never came back. He just waits. She won't come back, not now, but she comes to me sometimes in my dreams, tells me she misses the hills. She doesn't mention him.'

The old woman swung her plait behind her back and stood.

'My boy comes to me, walks with me up the mountain,' I said, and stepped towards her.

35

My last day. Spring was giving way to summer: the green of the budding trees, different greens – olive, lime, sage, emerald. Primroses dotted the sides of the track.

I climbed the mountain higher than ever before, searching for my friend, the stag. He had gone. I sat on my broad stone slab and wept. Much later I looked up. A golden eagle hovered. Perhaps it was my stag in another life. It stayed long, using the thermals and its broad wings. I stood, stretched upward, an etiolated version of myself.

Then he swooped down. Close. Danced. His hooked bill, golden tinge on his head and neck, and wings wide enough to frighten. He could pluck me up and carry me high into the sky, into the sun. To burn, not a phoenix. I would not rise again.

Then he was in free fall, swooping far below, to the fields and the newborn lambs.

Perhaps I imagined him.

The sky was pale violet. I would carry that away with me.

Near the cottage, clusters of daffodils had appeared and rhododendrons and azaleas. The trees were in leaf.

I was going back. Home, a simulacrum.

I spent the next day cleaning the cottage, every surface, every dust mote, every crack and corner. It sparkled its thanks. If the old woman's grandson had really existed (which I doubted), he would be here soon.

I had a plan. I could think of nothing else. If I was a Catholic, I might have found a priest and confessed in advance. Absolution.

I burnt the clothes I wouldn't be wearing and put Rabby in my bag with the photograph. I hadn't looked at it while in the mountains. It was the first one Jake had taken of me and the boy. He must have been only three days old. The drawing was in my pocket.

I would miss the giants.

I was scarred and pitted like the rock face.

I waited outside the woman's cottage, seated on the rock.

The curtain moved and I heard the bolts of the heavy door being drawn back.

I took out my purse and again she shook her head. I offered the Peppermint Creams. She looked over her shoulder and slipped them in her apron.

'Thank you.'

She placed a bunch of daffodils in my hands.

I held out my arms.

I carried the daffodils down the mountainside to the bus. They did not survive the three-day journey back to Wimbledon. She never did call me Alice, and I never knew her name.

36

Exhausted, numb, I opened the front door, dumped my bag in the hall and climbed the stairs. I shook off my shoes and fell into bed, fully clothed.

An empty house.

Downstairs, the next morning, I gathered what remained of the strewn Lego, the train set, everything that was his and slung them into his hiding box.

I cleared him out.

Except for the telescope. I left that, staring blindly at the sky.

I had become a fishwife, someone, Jenny said, who shouted all the time. I wanted to shout, at everyone.

I cleaned the house. The more menial the task, the better. I vacuumed needlessly, its raucous voice blanking my mind. Or I switched on the television, sat in the chair, neither watching nor listening, letting it wrap me in a meaningless cocoon.

Sometimes, before dawn, I crept out of the house and up to the common. I was no longer news yet feared people. I hurried through the windy open ground to the woods, past the big pond and another, to the grey heron. He cocked his head and asked me where the boy was.

One night, I lost myself in the woods, somewhere near the heron. I knew those woods, as they say, like the back of my hand. I wandered. A stranger passed and I hid. When it was dark, I curled up in some bracken, and in the morning, I woke utterly bewildered. I heard a voice calling, 'Alice' and wondered.

A Saturday, about a week after I got back from Scotland, I walked down strange streets, searching, past large houses. There was heat in the sun and a bright blue sky. I came across a park, not particularly large, mostly grass with a small selection of swings and a slide at one end.

Two people: a woman and a boy.

I stumbled a little, blood rushing to my head.

I made it, trembling, unnoticed, to a nearby seat.

The woman's long black hair was pulled back from her face, looked to have been done in a hurry or by someone who didn't much care. Her black slacks hugged thin hips, her blouse sleeves were rolled up above the wrists. Her clothes looked surprisingly tatty in contrast to the pearls around her neck, hanging down over her full breasts.

The woman, standing a little way off at his funeral. The photograph in the newspaper.

She was watching the boy on the swing, in his pressed shorts and shirt and bright trainers. His innocent face was framed by brown curly hair.

Her eyes were entirely for him.

The boy jumped off, ran towards her, too fast, and toppled, shrieking, 'Mummy.' She hurried to him and knelt, taking his grazed knee in both her hands, kissing it, and his face. He stopped crying.

There was a dog, running with them, or rather round and round the boy. It was big, floppy.

I glanced round as often as I dared. My breathing had steadied.

When they left, I followed.

She walked out of the park, turning left, holding his hand. He was looking up at her, talking, excited.

For a moment, I wanted his hand in mine.

They turned into two more streets, the houses becoming larger.

They were about fifty yards ahead, hadn't looked back once. The dog ran ahead of them. She stopped. Moments later, the groan of metal gates opening.

I slowed my steps, dawdled. The street was deserted.

High gates and a laurel hedge.

Parkside: a large, gracious house, cream brick facade and generous windows in both storeys. A Virginia creeper covered the roof of the front porch and made its way up the wall. All the gardens on that side of the street stretched far back behind the houses, a mix of trees and lawn and well-maintained borders, south-facing and perfect for long summer days.

I had found her.

37

You needed to be a little deranged to want to peer into another's life.

In a central London library I pored over newspapers, law journals.

Rosamund Jane Beresford, an Oxford scholarship girl. I envied her that. First-class degree, Law, Lincoln's Inn.

Her name in the List of Benchers. Her nickname at the Inn: Pearls.

Not yet a QC, a good reputation as a barrister, described as "passionate" in her defence.

Younger than me, thirty-nine. She had been absent from the Inn for over three months. Her husband, Edmund, was an architect, a good-looking man, I knew, for some mornings I crept from my bed early, to walk, casually, down their street, to loiter just a few moments.

Edmund, dressed in sports coat and corduroys, carrying a brown leather briefcase, drove the boy to school in that car. Most of the other children in the street left, in different uniforms, for the nearby private school.

Henry Beresford, born 26th April 1985, a few months younger than my boy. I imagined her dressing Henry in his school uniform (the same as my boy's), watching him eat his breakfast, checking he had his lunch, his school bag, all those motherly things.

I walked down the hill to the station and took the Underground to High Holborn, wearing my best clothes, to Lincoln's Inn, to her chambers.

A middle-aged woman demanded to know my name (I lied) and my business. That was more difficult and it is unlikely she believed I was a solicitor's clerk. Mrs Beresford wouldn't be in her chambers for some time.

I found my way to the Great Hall and Library. I would have liked to work in the shade of these wonderful buildings and their history: Wilkie Collins, and fifteen prime ministers, Pitt to Blair, had practised law here.

And the Chapel and John Donne. "No man is an island, entire of itself; … never send to know for whom the bells tolls; it tolls for thee."

The Chapel bell tolled when a bencher died.

Back home, I struggled with the lock of the front door, a first, and raced down the hall into the kitchen and, from a large bottom drawer, dug out an out-of-date *Yellow Pages*, thumbed through it and picked up the phone. Messaging services dripped out their dreary, formulaic responses, until Dave. I liked the sound of his voice.

I could start driving lessons the next day.

'How many?' he asked.

'Enough to pass.' How would I know?

'Have you driven at all?'

I took a deep breath. 'No, that's what I want you to teach me.'

'Got a provisional licence?'

'Of course,' I lied.

'Okay, love, we'll see how you get on tomorrow. I'll know after the first lesson. Everyone is different.'

He offered a discount for ten lessons. I agreed, although the total cost sounded way more than I'd imagined. I gave him my address.

'Tomorrow then, love,' he repeated, '10am.'

Back to the *Yellow Pages*. I telephoned a few garages to enquire about second-hand cars, nothing fancy. I didn't really understand what they were talking about: mileage, brands, condition. My father had, after all, taught me nothing about cars.

Dave was a small, compact man, a little cocky, but over the days I grew to like him, trust him. "*U Pass With Dave*" was plastered all over the yellow car in bright red letters.

'What's the hurry?' he'd asked when I demanded daily lessons, and that included weekends. He was firm about the weekend bit. 'I've two kids, they need their dad.' His voice softened. 'Their dad needs them. Two boys.'

I panicked, told myself I could do it. Had to.

He didn't ask if I had children and after the first lesson he never mentioned his boys.

It was immediately clear I didn't have a clue about driving. I lacked coordination, and even I winced at the grinding of the gears. 'Have you had worse learners than me?' I was forced to ask on the second day.

'Oh, much worse,' he said with a laugh, and told me yet again that I was in the wrong gear. Gears are stupid things.

He didn't bully, and we might have become friends.

He was patient and I improved, almost looked forward to the doorbell, prompt at 10am.

Two weeks and ten lessons later, he said he was going away for a week. I needed a few more lessons, and we needed to drive the test route. He would contact me on his return.

Dave shook my hand as he said goodbye. He had eyes a little like Jake's.

I had a few days to find a car. I went back to the list of dealers I'd made and visited the closer ones. By Monday, I had a two-year-old Ford Fiesta delivered to my house, 19,000 miles on the clock. Grey. I didn't haggle over the price.

38

13th July 1991

I sat in the wishing chair, the boy's photograph in my hand: he and the snowman both in dark glasses. Neither Jake nor I were much good with a camera.

I took off my star earrings and my rings: a diamond ring that had been Jake's mother's, and my gold wedding band. I opened the box with my mother's pearls and slipped them in. The lid clicked shut.

I scrabbled in the kitchen drawer for the photograph, the survivor from the pyre. I turned it over, wrote on the back: *Never send to know for whom the bells tolls*, and slipped it into an envelope.

A cloudy early July evening. I was dressed in brown cotton trousers, a blouse and a dark-coloured sweater.

I set off on the long walk to her house, turning right from the common, carrying on down the High Street, then left. Another long street and then right. I passed no one.

I fingered the envelope in my pocket.

Parkside.

Inside the gate, two cars, one of them an old Range Rover with a small dent on the front.

Her house had a privet hedge a couple of feet taller than me, but through the black painted metal I saw lights on in a downstairs room. I pushed gently at the gate. It eased itself open. Some magic hand aided me. I stepped inside, keeping in the shadow of the hedge, well back from the lit windows.

She was sitting at the dining table, at the end of a long side, leaving room for at least another six, Edmund opposite her. In the subdued light, the table looked to be mahogany, as did the chairs. Edmund, with his back to me, was in shirtsleeves. She was wearing what looked like the same tee-shirt I'd seen in the park, her hair still tied back in a ponytail. Loose wisps straggled over the sides of her face.

He was eating. She held a half-full glass of wine in her hand, sat silent, I sensed almost absent.

The boy, Henry, ran into the room. I turned away, then dragged my eyes back. He was in his pyjamas, pale blue. I clenched my fist, stuck one hand in my mouth to stop myself crying out.

He kissed his father then threw his thin arms round his mother's neck. She dropped her head onto his brown curls and kept it there, murmuring something to him.

I wrapped my arms round myself. My tears fell. For a moment I doubted.

She lifted her head, his father spoke, and the boy, smiling, scampered from the room.

I crept further round the house. All the other windows were shuttered.

Back at the gate, I eased it open, just far enough to squeeze through, shoved the envelope into the letterbox and hurried back down the street.

39

At the pond I walked quickly over the grass towards the woods. Hurrying, for what I knew not. I bade farewell to the heron, a hunched grey old man, dipping his head in and out of the water, paying me little heed.

A plane passed overhead. I looked up, watched the tight line blur and fatten.

'Contrails,' I murmured. That's what my father had told me.

Rabbits put up their heads and fled.

I sank to the wet grass.

*

Thirty-four years ago, aged eleven, in the wood: witches, wolves, bears, and Mr Badger and stoats and weasels. Deep in its heart there would be a small cottage and a princess.

My father started to sing, softly at first. "*Run rabbit, run rabbit, run, run, run.*" Then a little louder, "*Run Adolf, run! Run! Run!*"

All the kids in The Street knew about Adolf.

'Princess,' Daddy said, so softly I barely heard.

I swung round. He had his fingers to his lips.

He lifted me onto the still-warm car bonnet. 'Quiet now,' he whispered. 'You're my spotter.' A weak shaft of sun lit up his big silver watch with its stretchy metal band. I wanted a watch like that.

The rabbits wandered out of the shadows, none of them white. I was disappointed.

They put their heads down to the still-wet grass.

I held my breath, watched him raise the gun to his shoulder. His eyes shone, looked strange, made me a little afraid.

'No, Daddy, no,' I wanted to cry out. Instead, I shut my eyes.

He half smiled. "'*Run rabbit, run, run, run,*'" he whispered.

I slid off the bonnet and fell. I sat there, on the ground, arms around my knees, hands over my ears, eyes screwed tight shut.

Another bang. I looked up. The rabbits had gone. There were two bundles of fur on the ground under the trees.

'Off you go,' he said in his "don't make a fuss" voice, and pointed.

I didn't move.

He prodded me with the toe of his shoe. 'Princess.'

I sat.

His shoe again.

I scrambled up and saw dirt on my dress. I wiped it and scrubbed at my knees. There was blood on them. I didn't cry. That was for babies.

'Princess.'

I took one step and stopped. *You have to*, a voice inside me said. *He'll think you're a coward, not the best.*

He smiled and I hated him. Then I walked, counting slow steps, towards the wood.

It was dark at its edge. A bundle of fur lay on its side at the tip of my black patent leather Sunday-best shoes. Blood matted its long ears; one eye stared up at me, empty. The back legs quivered then were still. I must not cry yet my lip trembled and I blinked.

Except for the blood and the eye, I might have wanted to cuddle it.

I looked back at him. He had a cigarette in one hand and the other, mid-air, was raising a small silver flask to his lips. The gun was leaning against the front of the car like an errant stick fallen from one of the trees. I wanted to go home.

He lowered the flask and smiled. The sun flickered over the trees, laggardly in its rising.

'Come on, Princess,' he called, his voice soft, as if not to disturb the dead.

The rabbit's eye was somehow empty. Would I look like that when I was dead? I bent down and picked it up by the neck, holding it as far away as I could, shut my eyes, opened them and saw the blood on its head. 'Crybaby,' I hissed out loud but not so loud that he could hear.

I ran back to the car and dropped it at his feet. A laugh and I turned and ran back to the edge of the wood. Not much later, two rabbits lay at his feet like discarded toys: dirty, dishevelled, ragged.

'That's my best girl,' he said.

'There isn't another girl,' I cheeked back.

He tousled my hair. 'Princess.'

I grabbed his hand. 'Stop it, Daddy,' I said, pretending.

He lifted me onto the bonnet and pulled out a pack of Camels, struck a match, cupped the cigarette in his hands and lit it.

Soon rabbits crept out again, into the faltering light. I sat, pointing a fist with the first finger stuck out: pow, pow, but put my hands over my ears as soon as he raised his gun to his shoulder.

He laughed at me.

I ran to the edge of the woods again and again until eight rabbits were laid out in a neat line.

'Good girl,' he said, and walked round the car, opened the boot and took out a large knife. He picked up the rabbit nearest my feet, sliced down its belly through its fur. He inserted his fingers and dark, smelly stuff flew into the grass.

'Innards,' he said. 'Something will get a good feed.'

I put my hand over my mouth and nose, retched, tried to look away, could not, from the quick, sharp knife.

He cut round the legs and peeled off the skin like taking off a jumper. Then he cut off the head and threw it and the skin into the undergrowth. He held up the naked rabbit.

I ran away, towards the field.

He smiled and went on skinning, placing each one in the newspaper-lined box.

I watched him while pretending not to, couldn't wait to get home to tell Jenny and Billy.

The sun was climbing in the sky, warm, at last.

My dress was splashed with blood.

'We'll go to America one day. Bears. To the Rocky Mountains,' he said, cleaning his hands on a handkerchief and walking over to me.

I turned to him. 'Will we shoot them, Daddy?'

'Perhaps. They're big.'

'I know that.' I wondered if I would be brave enough. 'Promise, Daddy.'

'Cross my heart and hope to die.' He threw his head back and laughed.

I loved him then.

'Can I hold it, Daddy?'

'I suppose so, if you are careful.' He dug in his pocket and unwrapped a small bear, made from a bit of aircraft, and handed it to her. His good luck charm.

'The war, Daddy, for luck,' I said, running my fingers over it. 'I want a bear like this.'

He took it back, wrapped it carefully and put it in his pocket.

I did a short run then a handstand.

I held out my dirty hands.

He took out a clean white handkerchief, spat on it and wiped them clean.

40

14th July 1991

The night measured out its short self. I roamed back through my life to The Street, heard my father say, 'You can do anything, Princess, if you really want to,' and recalled the same man at my mother's funeral, a lost old man who had run from his shame.

Sometime in night's blackness, I got up, sat in the boy's chair downstairs, could feel him leaning against my legs.

'Story, MumMum,' he said, so I read him *The Little Prince*. He put a small finger on the drawing that many took for a hat.

'Elephant inside snake, MumMum,' he said. 'Bite. Prince go back to his star after bite. Adam not let snake bite, go to star another way.'

He stood and started to spin, shouting. Then stopped. 'Adam order sun to set, like the king in the story, but at weird times, like when school bell rings.'

I felt his smile.

'Adam never be grown up.'

When the first light forced its way through the carelessly closed curtains, I crawled out of bed, checked the time and went downstairs. I opened a drawer in the kitchen and took out the put-them-backs, the boy's name for the secateurs. In my nightdress, in the fresh, early morning, I walked around the garden cutting the few flowers, imagining I was hand in hand with Jake. He took the scissors from me, cut some white buds and handed them to me. We were doing this for him, for our boy.

I rocked my boy in my arms, newborn, no idea of how I might care for him. I would, somehow, forever. I took my right hand and wrapped it round the forefinger of my other hand, held it just as the baby boy had held it.

And then I took the first two fingers, the way Jake always held my hand. I had been loved, and one had been taken from me and the other I had thrust away.

Back in the kitchen, I searched for a vase. Defeated, I found a slightly dirty tall glass, filled it with water and shoved in the flowers.

I sat in the wishing chair but it was just a chair.

I counted the days since… As if that day was the start of life, not the end.

I went back upstairs.

The newspaper slapped through the front door: 14th July 1991.

I glanced at the headlines: yet another minister leaving the government, associated with crooks. One time, I might have cheered. I kicked it into a corner. Newspapers reminded

208

me of Jake, reading them from cover to cover and over breakfast listening to Radio Four, a news junky. I couldn't stand the radio first thing in the morning, tended to shout at the commentators and let rip at the politicians.

In the sitting room, the bottle of vodka leered from the sideboard, a not-very-clean glass beside it. I picked up the glass and put it down again. My hands shook.

An hour and seven minutes to go.

I dressed with care, pulling my favourite blouse from its hanger, its aqua long-sleeved cotton soft against my skin. I chose slacks over a skirt, and a newish pair of court shoes. I reached for my make-up, ignoring the lately hatched wrinkles round the eyes and mouth. I gazed deep into my own eyes. Hard eyes stared back at me, with a hint of fear in them.

In my pocket, his drawing, the photograph of him and his snowman and the metal bear.

I took out the bear and put it back in the drawer. Luck had no place in my life now.

I would go to prison. No matter. What did I know of prisons?

I found a notepad and wrote:

Dearest Jake,

I will be leaving you for somewhere you can't follow me. You must make another life for yourself.

I have loved you.
Alice

I slipped it, with the battered photograph of me and the baby boy, into an envelope and wrote on it the Hampstead address he had left on the kitchen table. I placed a first class stamp in the top right corner.

I picked up my keys, nothing else, and walked down the stairs and out of the front door, not bothering to lock it behind me.

School holidays would start soon.

I climbed into the driving seat.

The car wouldn't start. I tried again. It screamed back at me.

I sat still, tried to remember the lessons. They'd gone, no trace. I lifted my left leg too high and hit the steering wheel.

The clutch beneath my foot surrendered. I was sweating.

I backed out onto the street and crawled up the hill. Someone waved, looking surprised. I waved back.

I pulled up at a post box.

The car stalled as I turned right alongside the common. I restarted. Traffic built up behind me. Cars overtook, one driver giving me the two fingers, horn blaring. I resettled, concentrated, my hands gripping the steering wheel as I leant forward.

I took a right turn into the school road, the park on my right, the school on the left, the gates a little further on. Breathing hard, I pulled over, switched off the engine. I hadn't been here since that day, hadn't seen so many children, so many small boys.

Mothers and children streamed down the footpath, the children skipping, running, shouting, looking up at their mothers.

I sat, looked around. What was I doing?

I pulled out, started to do a u-turn, made a mess of it.

To the left, in the distance, I saw the Range Rover pull up, facing me. A few moments later, a small boy with brown curly hair got out, said something to the driver, slammed the door, stepped back and onto the pavement. Cars were no longer permitted to park on the road opposite the school. The boy waited for the Range Rover to drive off.

I swung back onto the road.

The car passed me, Edmund driving.

I pushed hard on the accelerator, my knuckles white on the steering wheel.

The boy stood on the pavement, hesitating, his violin case slung across one shoulder, his school bag in his other hand. The violin case dwarfed him.

He looked both ways, put his head down and stepped off the kerb.

I was back in that northern wood, with the sombre pines, the white-trunked birches, the wild blackberries, white bobbing rabbit tails. I closed three fingers with my thumb and pointed my forefinger and started to sing: '"*Run rabbit, run, run, run*".'

I changed up through the gears. My foot pressed down hard. I touched the steering wheel, lightly, an expert, leant forward, eyes narrowed.

I was somewhere else, somewhere totally silent, a star perhaps, circling the moon, singing.

On the road, a small brown-haired boy; he too, in another world, a six-year-old's world.

I accelerated. '"*Run rabbit, run, run, run*".'

Movement in the seat beside me, small legs and feet swinging. A voice: 'Careful, MumMum, careful.'

Tears coursed down my face. I gasped. My foot pressed down hard.

The swinging feet had gone.

I swung the wheel away from the figure on the road.

The same squeal as on that dark morning. A small thud. The car shuddered and stopped, the wheels ceasing their lament.

A violin fled its case and lay crushed and broken on the road, alongside the boy.

I slumped over the steering wheel, tasted blood.

What had I done?

Yet, in my head, a cacophony of cymbals. Of singing.

41

Sirens, shouts, screams.

I reached into my pocket for the stones, fingered them. "And yet I am and live with shadows lost." Jake and that first day in the library.

An ambulance pulled up, the road was blocked off, traffic diverted. More police.

I sat, head down, trembling, behind the steering wheel.

My door opened and I was led to a police car.

At the police station, I was stripped of my watch. My pockets were emptied of the stones and one overused handkerchief, the photograph and his drawing.

'Are those keys to your house?'

Whose did he think? I just smiled.

Outside the room, people hurried past.

The policewoman put out her hand to press a button.

'14th July 1991, 10.47am,' Detective Sergeant Michael Morris said out loud. I looked up.

'Your full name and date of birth, please,' the MM detective said.

'Alice Oldfield, 4th January, 1946.' My voice was clear, sounded so like someone else's that I looked around for the other woman. It was a small, dull room; table and chairs and little else.

I was cautioned. The bit about the right to remain silent '…if you don't mention something now…' made me want to laugh, felt like a bad TV drama.

Photographs were taken, and fingerprints. I moved when instructed, put out my hands, said nothing. Questions.

I didn't listen, answer.

The man asked the questions; the woman wrote on a pad. She didn't look at me often.

The sergeant asked if there was anyone I wanted to contact. I began to shake my head, and stopped. My shell was cracking, shadows pressing in.

'My husband,' I said. I had never been good at asking, for anything.

I was led to a telephone. I dialled and gave my name to the woman who answered. He was away, wouldn't be back for some weeks. I asked her to give him a message.

'The message?' she said crisply.

'I need help,' I said, and gave her a telephone number.

I was taken down a grubby corridor and locked in a cell. A solid metal door with a viewing slot high up, a small single bed and, tucked away, a washbasin and toilet.

Later that same day, I was escorted to a room and pointed

to a chair on the far side of a table. Opposite me sat a man, smartly dressed: navy suit, white shirt and mid-blue tie. He had a strong chin, receding hairline. His ears fanned out from the sides of his head.

He stood, put out his hand.

'David Penryn-Jones,' he said. 'Of Penryn-Jones and Robinson. Your husband asked me to represent you.'

His voice was surprisingly deep and strong for a slim man. Public school accent.

He took back his hand. 'We went to school together. Jake was a few years ahead of me. He asked me to contact you urgently. We don't have a lot of time, so forgive me if this sounds abrupt.' He used his right hand to tug down his left shirtsleeve.

Jake. I almost smiled. Did they learn that tugging thing at their posh school?

'The police believe they have enough evidence to charge you with grievous bodily harm.' He enunciated the last three words slowly, weightily.

They didn't mean much.

'The boy, Henry Edmund Beresford, I believe his injuries are not life-threatening.'

My head shot up. An eye for an eye. Yet part of me was glad.

I denied myself a shrug and said, 'I want to plead guilty.'

He looked startled. 'That's a bit hasty, Mrs Oldfield.' He tugged at both shirt cuffs, one after the other, pulling them below his jacket sleeves.

'Can you tell me what happened?' He paused. 'You got into your car and…' He gave me what I supposed he thought an encouraging look.

'Haven't they told you?' I jerked my head towards the door.

'They have told me something but I need to hear your side. From the beginning.'

He waited, then a small sigh. 'I'll know more tomorrow. The police are interviewing witnesses, collecting statements, building their case as we speak. They can only hold you twenty-four hours without charge.' He put his blank piece of paper in a briefcase made of exquisite leather. I wanted to stroke it. He slipped his pen into his inside jacket pocket. 'I'm here to help you.' He sounded a little irritated. 'I'll request bail, of course.'

'No.'

I slept badly in the hard, narrow bed. Picked at the food.

Penryn-Jones, PJ, I called him in my head, was back the next morning, early.

'Adam,' he said, 'your son, Mrs Oldfield.'

I stared at him, hoping my contempt would clatter out like the noise from my mother's old typewriter.

'I know my son's name,' I snarled back.

He was unmoved. Jake was paying him to be polite.

'The boy you knocked down, Henry Beresford, is the son of Mrs Rosamund Beresford who—'

I interrupted. 'Killed my son, yes.'

For a second, he looked uncomfortable, tugged.

'If I am going to defend you, I need to know all the facts. What happened outside the school? Why were you there?'

I was silent.

'Witnesses say you deliberately drove at the boy, that your car was on the wrong side of the road.'

He waited a minute.

'Did you intend to hurt Henry Beresford? The police say you were not driving at speed.'

Silence.

He sighed, asked me to go through my movements that morning and the night before. I knew what he was after. My arms were crossed on the table, my head resting on them. I could sleep. Forever.

The suit hauled me back, tethering me. 'Mrs Oldfield, are you all right?'

I lifted my head and really looked at him. He had lovely eyes: sea blue.

'I'm fine.'

He sighed and fiddled with his pen, looking at some notes on a piece of paper on the table. 'There is one more thing.'

I sat up.

'Mrs Beresford claims someone put a photograph of your son in her letterbox the night before the accident.' He paused. 'Was that you?'

'Yes.' I spoke clearly. He wore the same aftershave as Jake. I hummed, '"*Run rabbit, run, run, run*".'

He stared at me. 'The police said you were singing that when arrested.'

Was it compassion in his eyes? I didn't want it. For the mad.

PJ looked at his watch. 'Mrs Oldfield, you are likely to be charged with grievous bodily harm with intent. That is serious. If you would like me to act for you, I will prepare your case. There will be mitigating circumstances, things such as good standing, occupation, no previous convictions. These will all help.'

He didn't state the obvious: I was as mad as a hatter. I smiled again. I liked that expression.

'Do you insist on pleading guilty?'

'I do.' Was I marrying the man? I didn't offer words of remorse. It was a curious sort of indifference that I felt. I was too tired to work it out.

He was silent some time then looked at me. I admired his blue orbs.

'If you insist on pleading guilty, there will be a brief hearing at the Magistrate's Court tomorrow, and you are likely to be placed on remand to await a date for the Crown Court sentencing hearing before a judge.'

He took one long, slow breath.

'Do you understand all this, the seriousness of it?'

'How long?' I asked.

'Two to three months, shouldn't be more than that. The intent is the problem, the photograph.'

'Sentence?' I said.

'Three to five years.'

It sounded a bit of a lottery.

He stood and paced the few steps the room allowed, keeping to his side of the table. We each had our territories. He stopped and turned to me. 'I would like you to see a forensic psychiatrist. It will help your case.'

'No.' He had my full attention. 'Never.'

He sat. 'Please think about it.'

I laughed, a strange, hollow sound. '*Lovers and madmen have such seething brains/Such shaping fantasies that apprehend/ More than cool reason ever comprehends.*' He looked at me, blankness in his eyes.

'*Midsummer Night's Dream,*' I said. I hadn't read that

play since I was at school. What curious things we treasure and offer up.

I was cautioned and asked more questions, which I failed to answer. As PJ had predicted, I was charged with GBH with intent.

They were just words.

PJ told me later that a driving instructor had come forward claiming I told him I'd only wanted to drive once, that I was in a hurry to learn. All true, yet I was disappointed. Dave, I'd thought of him as a friend. He had two sons.

I was kept in the police station and, as PJ had predicted, was taken before a magistrate the next day, pleaded guilty and was remanded in custody. I think that is what happened. In my head I was elsewhere.

After the hearing, I was handcuffed to a prison guard and walked from the court to a large white van with tiny windows high up. My cuffs were taken off and I was shoved into a small compartment, one of several that lined each side. I wondered how the obese managed. There was someone else in the van, more than one. Someone was sobbing, and a different voice shouted, 'Shut up, bitch.'

The drive was slow, noisy, uncomfortable.

Then the slamming of a gate. High prison walls decorated with baby curls of razor wire. Placed in what they referred to as a holding room. Cattle, pigs.

I repeated my name and address many times, a parcel handed from uniform to uniform. Stripped and searched, too intimately, hands on my body, large hands. My clothes were taken from me and replaced with prison issue tee-shirt, tracksuit bottoms, socks, shoes. I could have my own clothes brought in to me. I would be some time in prison issue. I was handed blankets, plastic cup, plate and cutlery.

I had become a number. I filled in forms, was given information that meant little and asked if I had any questions: thousands, none.

So many uniforms.

A cell, then moved to another, given a special number for the phone in the corridor, open to any curious ears. I could only call people on their list. I gave them PJ's, and as an afterthought, Jake's. I was to learn that there were always queues for the phone, always someone behind, waiting.

I stayed in bed until the screws made me get up. Other prisoners worked, I didn't. I heard the noise and talk in the corridor outside. I wanted them gone. Everything reverberated.

I didn't have to share, was grateful for that. The cell walls were filthy, and the floor. It had a narrow iron bed along one wall, a small table and chair opposite, and at the far end, an aperture masquerading as a barred window high up. I calculated that it faced east so would get little sun, and below it, a stainless steel washbasin with a toilet attached to its side.

I sat on the bed, put a finger in one ear and rubbed vigorously, then repeated it in the other. I looked at my little fingernail: yellow/orange success.

A piece of paper was shoved under my door. The canteen order form. I didn't yet understand that it would become a life-saver of sorts, the highlight of my week, vital for phone cards, stamps, cheap chocolate bars and toiletries. I would stuff myself with the chocolate. But that was in the future. I spent almost two months waiting, a model prisoner: quiet, obedient. Empty.

I left my cell for meals only, would have missed them had they allowed it. I had become an automaton. Anonymous. The dining hall was huge, noisy. I kept my eyes down, avoided the ones I thought dangerous, aggressive; had always considered myself a good judge of people. I was to learn that I was not. And time. I began to understand why it was called "doing time".

Some days later – how many, I had no idea – I was given a bag filled with my own clothes. Jake. I held them to my face, breathed in my own fragrance, put the photograph of my boy in my pocket and his drawing on the bed.

It was the noise I found most trying: banging, metal on metal, keys jangling, shouting. Yet I seemed to adjust quickly, shut away my other life, closed down.

42

'A visitor this afternoon,' the screw said.

I didn't want to see him.

I did what I could, mourning the absence of my star earrings. Beth had instructed me to put her lipstick in her coffin for when she met St Peter should she die first. For me it would be the star earrings. St Peter was pretty unlikely now.

Corridors, gates, keys, the music of a prison; an open yard, one gate closed before the other opened. I walked, slouched, hands in pockets, head down. Searched then brought into a large room and told to sit at a low table. It had a number fixed to it, table fourteen. It had the novelty of being somewhere new. The other women were dressed more smartly. I knew none of them, had no friends.

There was a rush of visitors, children running to their mothers, who took them in their arms, some weeping. Then, within minutes, the children were away to the toys set up in a corner of the room. Social workers brought babies and placed them in their mothers' arms. I looked away.

The rush became a trickle. My back was to the door. Every time it opened, I turned my head. We were not permitted to move from our chairs except for a hug with visitors on arrival and on departure. Some held the hug long, others were quick, embarrassed; some sat silent with their visitors, others seemed to be spilling out a lifetime's talk. Children ran around, paying too little attention to their mothers fixed to their chairs. The noise ratcheted up.

Two of us still waited.

Some visitors had already left, others had run out of conversation. One well-dressed mother was crying, as was her daughter.

Jake stood, looked around, was dressed, as usual, in his navy suit. He hurried towards me, almost tripped. He was part of me, had been, once. I longed to look into his eyes, his gentle monk-grey eyes, fall into them like a trapeze artist plunging from a high wire and finding the net. And yet…

He tried to hold me. I was stiff, stranger stiff, didn't fit into the shape of his body the way I had once. He murmured into my shoulder, 'Oh, Alice.'

He stepped back, looking exhausted. He was changed utterly, reminded me of the anxious boy in the photograph, about to go to boarding school. His suit was a little crumpled.

He sat and stared around, at the officers, the other prisoners and their visitors.

'Alice, what have you done?' It was almost a shout. Heads turned to us.

I smiled, one of the silly, false variety.

'Another child, Alice, a boy like ours. You might have killed him.' His fists were tight.

I didn't speak. PJ will have told him all, old public school buddies.

'I shouldn't have left you,' he said. 'I might have stopped you.'

Pigs might fly. My mother again. 'You have forgotten the cottage.' That was a cheap crack.

'Never,' he said.

'I did it for my boy.'

'Are you mad?' His voice was raised now, hard. 'Do you understand what will happen? You could be in prison a long time.'

I smiled, this time probably that of the deranged.

His voice hardened. 'You are being stupid.'

That brought me up, sharp. Stupid. I'd never been called that, although much of my past life probably contained many elements of stupidity.

Visitors and a couple of nearby prisoners turned to watch us. Two officers moved closer.

'I know I was wrong… in the cottage, but not this, not this.' He put his head in his hands. 'I came back as soon as I heard.' He looked around. 'How can you bear it?'

'I'm putting on weight.' I was. 'You said I was too thin. The food is awful.' I almost giggled. I admired his long, slender fingers. Once, I'd longed for their touch.

'Losing Adam, then you. PJ—'

'Ah.' I leant back. 'One of your old school buddies.'

'He says you have pleaded guilty. That was rash.'

'But true.'

'Please talk to me, Alice.'

'She killed our son.' On the mountain, I made the decision, knew what I had to do.

He sighed, deeply. 'We can't keep going over that.' He put his head in his hands. 'I don't know what to do, how to help you.' He got out his handkerchief. 'Help myself. You're the only one that can help me.'

For a moment, I was tempted to reach out to him, hold his hand, wipe the tears from his eyes. It passed. I had to be strong.

Jake crossed his legs, sat up straight. 'PJ will keep in touch with me. Perhaps I'll write, I don't know. He'll let me know when you go to court. I'll come back for that.'

'I thought you weren't going to the US anymore.'

'What is there to keep me here? I can't be in Wimbledon. There have been letters, my car damaged. It's not a good place right now.' He sounded angry. He looked away then back. 'You need help.'

I snorted. I'd sent PJ a message agreeing to see his shrink. I didn't really care.

We sat. I looked at the clock. Visiting would soon be over. I didn't want him to stay.

'Alice, please. We should have worked this out together. How could we…?'

He meant the fights, the hostility, the lacerating of our love.

'Every day since we met, I thanked fate for bringing you to me until…'

I looked down. 'And the boy, Henry, he is recovering well, I believe. Oh, Alice.'

He stood. 'It will be a while before I can come again. I love you, Alice.'

We didn't hug.

Jake walked quickly away, didn't look back or wave.

43

I was escorted down unfamiliar corridors until, finally, a door was opened, my cuffs taken off and the officer spoke to someone in the room. 'I'll just be outside.'

A square, older man walked round from behind a desk. He was wearing slacks and an open neck shirt.

'Welcome, Mrs Oldfield.' He held out his hand. 'I'm Doctor Jackson, please take a seat.' His face and voice were soft, his eyes a faded green. He pointed to a comfortable-looking chair.

The prison wall with its crown of razor wire was not far away, yet sun streamed in through a large window. I sat, breathed deeply and stared out, my chin tilted upwards.

The doctor pulled up a chair. He had a pad on his knee and a pen in his hand. He smiled, a kind, open smile. He had teeth just like Jake's and my fingers itched to touch them. 'Mrs Oldfield, I'd like to get to know you a little. May I call you Alice?'

I didn't answer. He had some white powder round his mouth, residue, a sweetie probably.

The boy whispered something to me. Probably asking could he have one.

'Mrs Oldfield then. Would you like to tell me something about yourself?' He looked down. There was a typed sheet interleaved in his pad. He pulled it out, glanced at it.

'Perhaps we could start with where you were brought up?'

The Street: Jenny, Billy, my go-cart, the fastest in The Street. There, everything, anything was possible. I could tell him about that.

I smiled then remembered where I was and wiped it.

'Would you like to talk a little about that time?'

I said nothing, lifted my head and stared out of the window. What was The Street to him?

He waited. Wrote something on the pad, the pen scratching.

'Any brothers and sisters?'

I shook my head. It was a sort of truth.

'Can you tell me something about your mother and father?'

I stared at his shoes. 'He had shoes just like yours. You could see your face in them.'

He gave a deep chuckle.

'The war, it changed him.'

'How did it change him?'

'That's what my mother said.'

I had spoken so few words these last weeks that I felt a little giddy, on a roll.

He looked at me, steady brown eyes.

I wanted to take out my hanky and wipe the powder from his mouth.

'He left us, for good.'

Me, was what I wanted to say. I picked at my left thumb.

'How old were you?'

'Fourteen.' I added, 'Ariel, I was Ariel.' I would not mention Princess.

'Ah, *The Tempest*. What was he like, your father?'

My father. Which version did he want?

'You could come with me,' my father had said in a faraway voice. 'We could have fun.' That was when I'd last seen him, at my mother's funeral.

A small part of me had been tempted to take his hand and run with him across the sea to the land where films were made, where dreams came true, where Marilyn Monroe lived and died.

'I waited for him, always, believed he would come home,' I told the man.

'And he didn't. That must have hurt.' He crossed his legs.

You're the expert, I wanted to shout at him, you work it out. I made do with an angry nod. 'He was a fake,' I said, 'like the pearls.'

'The pearls?'

'That he gave to my mother and to the other woman. My mother's were fake. I expect the other woman's weren't.'

I sometimes wondered why I'd kept them. The jeweller had examined them for a few minutes. I guessed, from the embarrassment in his face, what he was going to say.

'Why do you think that?' The sweetie powder moved with his lips.

'He was with us from Tuesdays to Saturdays. The rest of the week he was with his other family. He was a shit.'

'And your mother?'

I took a deep breath. 'I didn't notice her.'

He wrote something on his pad, probably describing my beautiful eyes, writing me a love letter, or perhaps a shopping list. There was black hair on his knuckles.

'How do you feel about that?'

He waited.

'What do you mean when you say you didn't notice her? Why was that, do you think?'

'Just him. I just wanted him. Then he left us.' I picked at my thumb. 'Too late.' I said, 'When she got sick, she told me.' I did most things too late.

'What did she tell you?'

'About my father, the other woman. She still loved him. More fool her.' I spat out the last words.

That caught him out. He took a breath, hesitated.

'Princess, that's what he called me.' Surreptitiously, I slipped my right hand up my left sleeve, then quickly I pulled my hand out and crossed my arms over my chest. 'I called him Captain, but he wasn't really. I was his Princess. Once.' I was no one's princess now.

I had forgotten the doctor's name. Things like that didn't stick anymore.

He wrote something on his pad.

I looked away, suddenly tired. I couldn't tell him about waiting every Tuesday on the stoop, sick with excitement, wearing my best dress. Too tired to tell this man that my father was fun, my life, and no one else mattered back then.

Until Jake and then…

We sat in silence. I'd get up and leave soon.

Shelves of books lined one wall. I would have liked to look at them, perhaps pick one or two out, hold them.

'You like books,' he said.

'I was a librarian.' I filled my voice with scorn and shifted in my seat.

'What was he like, your boy?'

He couldn't say his name, either. 'A boy,' I said. I could have filled the rest of the day with my words, my wonder.

'Adam,' he said.

I half stood, wanted to shout, then sat, rocking back and forth, forgetting the man for a time.

He cleared his throat.

'Could you tell me a little about him?' He looked down, 'Adam.'

'A genius, his teacher said. Loved the stars.'

He waited.

'And his daddy? The stars. They had a telescope, looked at the sky every night.'

'How did you feel about that?'

Star-man and Star-boy. I shrugged.

The man handed me a box of tissues.

'I'd like to talk a little about the day of your son's accident.' He looked down at his notes. '17th February.'

I blew my nose, too noisily. 'It was his birthday, his sixth.' I had to be careful, too many words.

The man was writing something on his pad. He stopped and said, 'He was riding the bike to school.'

I leant forward. 'I told him it was too big.'

'Who did you tell?'

'He gave it to him.'

'Who did?'

'Jake.'

I shifted in my seat. I had had enough.

'Could your son ride it?'

'Of course.' I picked at my left thumb. 'Too fast, too fast.'

'You went through the park, the two of you.'

I kept my head down. There were other things I wanted to say, couldn't. 'My fault,' I said, so quietly I hoped he wouldn't hear.

'How was it your fault?'

'Just was.'

'I don't think I understand. I need you to help me.'

'I can't.' I sounded like a sulky child. 'I fell. He was angry.'

'Who was?'

'My boy.'

'What was he angry about? How did you know he was angry?'

'What he said.'

'Can you tell me what he said?'

I shook my head.

I slipped my hand up my sleeve, scratched as hard as I could. The scars were too old.

'Is that why you are angry now?'

'I'm not.'

'That's how it seems.'

I took a deep breath. 'Once upon a time.'

He waited then said, 'A story.'

I looked at him. He looked straight back.

'He took me hunting.'

'Who took you hunting?'

'My father.'

'So he took you hunting. How old were you?'

I looked away, trying to remember if I'd put on deodorant that morning.

'Eleven.'

'How did you find that, the hunting?'

'I was frightened at first. I was a kid.' I hummed, '"*Run, rabbit, run.*"'

I was in the woods. Blood on my hands from the first rabbit, held out at arm's length, away from my dress, its blank eye. I wanted to cry. And him, leaning against the bonnet, laughing, flask in his hand.

'Rabbits,' I said. I hummed a little – '"*Run rabbit, run, run, run.*"' I wanted to get up and do a handstand.

He listened to my song, put his pad and pen down on the desk, moved closer to me and asked me to roll up my left sleeve.

He held my arm below the cuts and bent to look. 'Some look sore, recent. Others,' he pointed to some very faint scars, 'long ago.'

I didn't confirm the obvious.

He took his hand from my arm.

'How does it make you feel?'

Silence.

'Better about your son?'

232

I didn't know how to answer. I rolled down my sleeve.

'Trapped,' I muttered. I was locked in some dark tunnel, the walls and ceiling closing in, no escape and I didn't care.

'How trapped?'

I blew my nose.

'Just trapped.'

I heard him take a long, slow breath, guessed what was to come.

'Could we talk a little about the other boy, Henry Beresford? Can you tell me about the day?'

The boy in the beautifully pressed shorts. And her. Pearls, I called her.

'Got up, got dressed, drove the car.'

'Can you remember what you were thinking?'

Was I thinking? I doubted it. 'Driving the car.'

'Anything else?

My boy, of course, but I didn't say that.

'You were singing that song when the police found you?'

I'd had enough, wanted to go back to my cell.

'The Prosecution say you left a photograph at Mrs Beresford's house the night before.'

Silence.

'Can you remember what you wrote on the back?'

Of course I could. I was not an idiot. 'Ask not for whom the bell tolls,' I said.

'What did you mean by that?'

'John Donne.' Then I added, 'Her.'

He looked at me, right into my eyes. Then nodded.

'The day of Henry Beresford's accident, can you tell me some more, perhaps about the car and the drive?'

'He was with me?'

'Who was?'

I flushed and stared at him. 'His little legs were swinging. It was his first time in the front seat, he was excited.'

'And when your car hit the other boy?'

I looked away and hummed, clenching my fists, my right foot hitting the carpet. I was driving towards the boy. I hummed, loudly: *"Run, rabbit, run, run, run."*

'The violin,' I said. 'Broken.'

44

Beth Cuthbert requested a visit. I refused to add her to my visiting list. And I refused to see Jake.

Anne wrote bright, cheery letters, full of news, keeping me up to date as if I would be back there next week. Words, nothing more.

The weather mostly disappeared in prison. It was the time of year I had once hated most: neither summer nor winter, just the auguries of the rain and cold to come, the sun lazy and the leaves turning. Not that I could see them, but my imagination usually ran in tandem with the seasons.

I spent much of my time queueing: for meals, for the shower, for medication. I didn't see the man with the sweetie powder again.

Then all my belongings were shoved in three plastic bags. I wouldn't be returning to that prison. None of the other prisoners noticed me go.

'Good luck, Oldfield,' the officer said as she walked me,

handcuffed, up the stairs from the underground car park and handed me over.

It was early, not yet 8am, everywhere silent except for the jangle of keys and thud of footsteps. We were in the basement below the court.

I tugged at my jacket sleeves, thinking of PJ, felt for the collar of my blouse, fingered my ears, looked down at my skirt. PJ insisted I wear something formal. In that, at least, I had gone along with him. Jake had sent the clothes and a short note, saying he loved me. He didn't wish me luck. That wasn't in the equation.

The cell was small, airless; no windows, bare floor, a bench. I had two hours to wait. I had dreamt last night of the boy, not my boy, the one with the violin. I had smiled at him as he stood on the kerb.

On a late September day, just before 10am, dressed in a navy suit, white blouse and navy court shoes, remnants of my library days, I climbed the stairs, step for step with the officer beside me. He was a little fat, unfit. I stepped from the gloom into the courtroom.

The officer pointed to a chair in the dock. I blinked in the over-bright light.

Those seated below stared up.

I shrank back into the chair. The officer sat a little behind and to my left.

At the opposite side of the courtroom was the judge's bench, high above the rest, and behind it the royal coat of arms: *Dieu et Mon Droit*. I was indifferent to God and possibly to my rights. The remainder of the court was splayed out between us.

Below, men chatted quietly. I recognised my bewigged barrister and PJ behind him with a stack of folders and papers. The wigs were whitish, ridiculously curled with short pigtails at the back.

A low murmur of voices. Waiting, all.

I sat up straight and looked to the front, my barrister's instructions. I'd met him briefly, not a man I had much liked. The court seemed full except for the seats where I assumed the jury usually sat.

A small wave. I leant forward a little, swivelled my eyes to the left. Beth, not in her trademark red but in a smart grey suit with a touch of red in her blouse. She caught my eyes, placed her hands on the railing in front of her to show the crossed fingers and arms. Beside her, Jake. He too was watching me. Passive. I couldn't read him.

There was a time when I could not have imagined the distance between us now. I was not thinking of him on that day. Was not thinking, although the detail was carefully planned.

I swivelled my eyes. Rosamund Beresford and a man holding her hand, the fingers of her other hand curled into a fist. Her dark brown hair was back in some sort of bun and she was wearing a silk blouse and pearls, black jacket and skirt, had a black handbag on her lap. Her eyes were fixed on the judge.

Her son was out of hospital, the boy with his mother at the dining table, her head on his brown curls, a portrait of love.

PJ had got straight to the point. 'The Prosecution may argue that you intended to commit more serious harm than actually happened, that you deliberately targeted a child, a vulnerable victim.' He paused, then said, 'With

237

the photograph, they can contend a significant degree of premeditation.' He smiled, the only one I recall, and said, 'But we have a good defence.'

The psychiatrist's report would carry weight, although what the weight was PJ didn't say.

I could expect three to five years if the Prosecution could show intent.

Like a child at the circus for the first time, I stared around, but eyes only, no head turning, no smiling.

Someone barked, 'All rise.'

I flicked my eyes back to the front. The officer behind me stood and moved towards me but I was already on my feet. A clatter as everyone got to their feet.

The judge walked in through a side door to his bench, wearing a red robe and a greyish wig that was flat on top. He looked older than me and I had become Methuselah. He was good-looking, for a judge.

He bowed to those in the benches below him and looked briefly at me.

We all sat.

The case of the Queen against Alice Oldfield.

'Will the defendant please rise.'

I stood.

The charge was read out: grievous bodily harm with intent.

'How do you plead?' the judge asked.

'Guilty.' My voice was strong.

Murmurs in the courtroom and some movement. Rosamund Beresford was on her feet. I saw her husband's lips move and his hand go out to pull her back down to her seat. Jake's head was in his hands.

I sat.

The Prosecutor was on his feet.

He expressed sympathy – that is what he called it – for the loss of my son, a tragic accident, and moved quickly on: the defendant's attempt on a young boy's life.

Separate words and bits of sentences floated up: Your Honour, six-year-old child deliberately knocked down by the defendant... Your Honour... wrong side of the road, act of premeditation... Evidence of driving lessons for that express purpose and a photograph left in the letterbox at the parents' house the night before to show her clear intent... Your Honour ...The child suffered three breaks in one leg and was severely traumatised; indeed, it is remarkable that he escaped more serious injury... Defendant shown no remorse.

The tone of the apparent conversation was polite, considered; no raised voices. I only half listened to the evidence against me.

Your Honour (I began to count the number of times I heard those two words), deliberate and cold-hearted...

The barristers and clerks were busy, passing papers to each other, and to the clerk, to be given to the judge.

I was almost incidental to the process.

Witnesses were called. I recognised a mother of one of the children from the school. She stared in my direction, hatred in her face.

Police officers gave evidence; dry, factual.

The Prosecution made much of the offender's planning, especially the driving lessons and Dave's evidence; and the photograph. He wrapped up the case for grievous bodily harm with intent.

Jake appeared to listen intently. Beth glanced at me whenever voices were raised.

Rosamund Beresford never took her eyes off the judge. I supposed that she too was weighing up the evidence.

I picked at my thumb. I wanted it over; some seemed to be enjoying themselves.

I looked at my watch. Almost 12.30pm.

My barrister stood, adjusted his black robe and called Dr Jackson to the stand.

I almost smiled. The powder was gone from around his mouth, and he wore a dark suit. He didn't look at me but his calm voice carried. The judge's gaze flickered from him to me. A couple of times he spoke to Dr Jackson, questions I assumed, for I saw Dr Jackson nod. The judge turned over pages on the bench before him.

I winced at some of the words: abandoned aged fourteen by her father whom she adored, carried that loss through life. Dominant emotion: anger. Debilitating grief. Guilt for death of son; flashbacks, depression. He made much of my disturbed mind, PTSD.

I didn't like that label.

Many in the court looked up at me, some with anger, contempt; one woman with sadness in her eyes.

Dr Jackson left the stand without looking at me, which disappointed me a little.

My barrister spoke, in measured tones. I listened at first: the boy's full recovery, defendant unable to return to work after death of her own child, changed by that death; accepted some of the details of the prosecution case. Then he turned to the issue of intent and the forensic psychiatrist's report and post-traumatic stress disorder.

The judge glanced up at me.

I slipped my right hand up my left sleeve and scratched.

There was some discussion between my barrister and the judge, inaudible until, 'My client accepts full responsibility.'

He spoke more clearly then. 'We don't deny evidence of intent; however,' his pause was lengthy, 'in mitigation, Dr Jackson's opinion is that Mrs Oldfield was suffering from clinical depression over the death of her son and was not in a position to form intent. Rather, it was a psychotic fantasy. She lost touch with reality. She had witnessed her son's death, a brutal accident. Her grief unhinged her and destroyed what had been, until then, an exemplary life. A disturbed mind.'

I pondered the last three words. He meant mad.

He asked for my madness to be taken into account in sentencing. And my previous upstanding character.

He had much more to say, speaking directly to the judge, who was making notes. I sat back, put my hands in my lap and dreamt of my boy.

A different voice brought me back, the judge's voice; low, considered, sombre: evidence of a pre-meditated act of revenge... *mens rea*, the defendant's state of mind... Guilty plea taken into account.

He gifted me a four-year custodial sentence, time on remand to be taken into account.

Jake's head was in his hands. Beth looked up at me, mascara rivulets down her face.

'Be upstanding in court.'

I stood, leant forward and turned my head to stare at Rosamund. Our eyes met. Was it anger or triumph, or...?

45

Alice Oldfield. Prisoner No. A45306. Category B prison, somewhere in the Midlands.

The word was out: the intent, the planning made much of, and the song. Some called me Rabbit. Young mothers hated me. The prison was replete with mothers and grandmothers.

I had lost my son so a few looked at me with sad, curious eyes.

I had no friends, spoke as little as I could. My silence was mocked with talk of cat and tongues. Tempers were quick to flare.

Mad Madge, a foot taller than me, a prison rule-maker, all muscle and proud of her name, was in the accuser camp. I tried to steer clear of her. She was quick with her fists, slow with her tongue. She had murdered her husband, forgetting he was a policeman. She was the trading queen, anything you could want. Fags the biggest earner.

It was midday, our main meal of the day. I queued, and I was, as my father might have said, "away with the birds". Why had he come back to me in this place of shame, of horror? Mealtimes were usually rushed, lingering not encouraged.

I shuffled, letting a gap open between me and the woman in front. She cast me a hostile backward look, then returned to her conversation. I was searching for a safe table but knew few, no friends, knew I was vulnerable. Another woman walked towards me, carrying a plate of food, not on a tray. There were rules for all the minutiae of our days and nights, and food on trays was one of them. That should have alerted me.

I turned away, towards a noise the other side of the room. Something hot poured over my head. I put up my hands, ran them over my head, my face. My eyes were shut, stuck shut. I dragged them open, looked at my hands: beans and red sauce.

The woman was strolling away, an empty plate hanging from one hand, leaving a small blood-like trail following.

I wanted to go after her, couldn't, was rooted.

The noise in the dining room faltered, then a few giggles.

An officer sauntered over to me. 'Get used to it, Oldfield,' she said.

I stood, stupid, the titters increasing.

A woman, Mary, for that is what she was called, was by my side and handing me some paper serviettes, helping me wipe the stew from my clothes, hair and face.

'Come,' she said, 'come and sit with me. Silly bitch,' she said, over her shoulder. 'The place is full of them.'

I followed her.

The empty walls of my cell closed in on me. I was afraid, asked for something to help me sleep, was refused. The meds here were arbitrary. I didn't yet know that, like tobacco and much else, they were traded, probably by Mad Madge.

Often, I longed for the razor and the sharp peace of the pain.

I begged some Sellotape from a screw and stuck the boy's drawing on the wall above the table where I could see it from my bed. It was roughly torn across the top, ripped from his special notebook, tatty now, having travelled to Scotland and up the mountainside with me. Below the stars, in his awful handwriting, the word, "MumMum". Oh, for his touch, his arms wrapped round my legs.

'Big boy, MumMum, big boy,' he'd said, standing on tiptoe, arms stretched high. 'Big boy.' I had worried how he would manage the world when I was not there.

My dreams were of a bicycle and a violin and sometimes I woke, sure that woman was standing beside my bed.

Sad Sal had the cell opposite mine. Her eyes told how she got her name. Yet she was a talker, going on about the child she was carrying, a girl. She was certain she would be moved to a mother and baby unit, could keep this one. Two children had been taken from her and she had five more years to serve.

She must have hung there, in her cell, for some time. Prison gossip spoke of a dawn death. At 8am, her door was unlocked, her name called. Lockdown, running feet, shouting for a medic. We all knew, even a novice like me.

I had seen her belly grow. The baby came early, her daughter. After two days, she was back from hospital, alone. She expressed milk and was taken away to feed her daughter.

Her smile was even wider, full of love. The next day, the baby had gone to another mother. Two days later, Sal was dead.

Midday. The dining room was noisy; shouting, talking, laughing. Carol, one of the few whose name I knew, manoeuvred her wheelchair to my table, smiling. Her flesh folded downwards, her belly resting on her knees like a contented oversized pet. She was sixty-one, looked much more than that, the gift of a jail term. She couldn't work so no pay, paltry as it was. Her hair was cut short. 'Stopped bothering,' she'd said, when she saw me looking at it. 'Easier, it was down to my waist once.'

We often sat together at meals.

'I get on with them,' she said of the officers. 'Some are miserable buggers, like anywhere, but if you don't give them trouble, they're okay. They'll even help you on a good day. Some of them.' She pulled a plate of chips towards herself.

'My old man, I stabbed him, should have done it sooner. He drowned my cats. I didn't have any kids, just the cats,' she said and laughed, and her broad face shifted into one of the loveliest smiles I'd ever seen, her eyes alight. 'And my mum.'

I laughed with her. An odd sound in my head.

'What's she like, your mum?' I asked.

'You'd like her. She's kind. I'm an only one. She'd visit if I let her. I don't want her to see me here. I write to her, a lot. She sends me photos of her cats. We both love them.'

She manoeuvred her chair around to face me. 'It's hard on the mothers here.' She pointed to a woman who looked to be in her thirties, scraggy, hunched over herself. 'Four kids,' Carol said. 'She's in for a long time. They never come and don't live that far away. She never sees her grandkids.'

Carol never complained. Some never stopped.

'What would I do outside, like this? I've gotten used to life in here.' She pointed to the wheelchair. 'I eat too much, too greedy. There's not much else to do, stuck in this thing. You get used to the food. Just need to stay away from the crazies.' She turned her head to where Mad Madge sat.

'Rumour is that they are moving her soon. Mind you, you don't get much notice when it happens. Me, I've been here from the beginning. She doesn't stay anywhere long. She's been in the Block a week. Drugs, the word is. A place to stay away from, the Block. Solitary, food is crap. Would drive me insane in half a day. Chatterbox, me. I wasn't made for me own company.'

I looked over at Madge. She was busy talking to someone. She had an angry raw mark down the side of her neck and face.

'It's worse over her shoulder and tits. She keeps it covered. Boiling sugar. They meant to get all her face. You could have heard the screams miles away. It burns deep,' Carol said. 'Don't let anyone's kettle too near you.' She laughed. 'Come on, let's get a cuppa.' She tossed her head in the way she might have done had she still had the long hair. 'How long you got?'

'Four.'

'Behave yourself and you'll be out in half that. If I get out, I expect I'll just come right back.'

She'd been inside for almost eight years, another four at least to go, didn't expect ever to leave. 'I'll come back, find a way, if they throw me out. It's not too bad here, once you get used to it.'

I looked away.

She smiled. 'No, I know, not you. You'll be out in a couple of years back to your man. Don't let here get to you.' She smiled. 'Mind you, I'd like to get out just once more, to see my mum. Just for a weekend.' She pointed to her sweater. 'She knits me all this stuff. I've got a cell full if you want one.' The colours were bright, happy, garish. I shook my head. I saw disappointment flit through her eyes. 'Perhaps when I've been here a while and got sick of my own clothes,' I said.

My mother had knitted me a hat, her parting present, something I was supposed to treasure. As the train pulled into King's Cross Station, I placed it on the luggage rack and walked away.

Carol touched my hand. 'You should come to Association. It's okay. It passes the time.'

'Perhaps,' I equivocated.

'Your boy,' she said, and held my hand. 'You don't want to talk about him.' I shook my head and let her hand rest on mine.

Beth sent me a card with exquisite flowers on the front, an old lady's card. They were usually outrageous, fun; semi-naked men or women, crazy people.

She was busy at work but would come soon.

Nothing from Jake. The helplessness of being in love had dropped away, been replaced by... what? Nothing.

A new inmate in the next cell shouted through the nights. It would have been entertainment of sorts had I been able to understand what she was saying. Shouting through the cell windows went on long after lights out most nights.

46

Beth wouldn't give up. She didn't, as a rule.

I laid my black trousers and green blouse on the bed, unworn since I'd arrived. We were severely limited with the clothes we could have but it wasn't that. I hadn't bothered. In truth, there was little I bothered with.

I did my best with make-up.

The noise in the visiting hall was ferocious. Some of the women, unable to move from their seats, shouted across the visiting hall to each other. It was large with three glass walls so the voices reverberated, amplified.

Two young women were feeding their babies. They had been brought in by social workers. I couldn't bear to look at them, hoped not to be still there when the babies were taken back from their mothers.

Beth's footsteps signalled her: quick and determined. She was dressed sombrely, for her: black trousers, a deep blue sweater over a white blouse and carrying a jacket over her arm. She walked across the visitors' hall, her heels drumming on the hard floor.

Prisoners' and visitors' eyes followed her.

She knelt at my feet, put her head in my lap before I had time to stand. The officers must have been mesmerised for they left us alone.

She sat back on her heels. 'Alice, I could not bear it, that day, when you were led away, Alice. I hate seeing you here. How will you survive?'

Her words rushed out.

'You'll have to sit on the chair.' I pointed to a screw watching us.

'Oh, screw them,' she said, tossing her head.

We both giggled.

She sat for a moment head down, hands folded tight.

'Oh, Alice, how could you? Why didn't you let me help you? I'd understand had it been her, but the boy. Help me, Alice, I'm lost.' There was an undertone of anger in her words.

I bridled, tightened my lips, looked hard into her eyes, really into them, unflinching, then away. What did she know?

'This is not my Alice.' Her words trembled, reverberated.

I couldn't help her.

She sat, wiping her eyes and cheeks with her hand, smudging her mascara.

For a second, I considered telling her about the baked beans, decided against it.

She turned her head around in the direction of the small kiosk run by volunteers. 'Chocolate? We need it.' She stood, walked past half a dozen tables with inmates and visitors, mostly chatting and laughing. She returned a few minutes later with four chocolate bars and two coffees.

'Best I could do.' She smiled. 'Not French, I'm afraid.'

I tore open the Mars bar, hoping she would stay long enough for me to pig out. I couldn't take anything out of the visiting room, despite the search I would go through.

'I'm getting fat,' I said.

'You are, my lovely. I expect the food's not good. And what have you done with your hair?'

I kept on eating. Finally, with a full mouth, I said, 'Nail clippers, not allowed scissors. It took me all day.'

She laughed. Or was she crying?

'Do you need any books?'

I did but shook my head.

'I have to understand. She's a mother too. It was an accident, your lovely boy.'

I shrugged. I wasn't going to argue. She was supposed to be my friend. And she still had her boys. For once, she was not talking about them.

'I would have helped you. Anything.' She took a deep breath. I could almost hear the voice inside her head, telling her to change the subject. 'Oh, Alice,' she said. 'I want to help you.'

I took that as code for Jake.

'Jake,' she said, 'he telephoned me.' She put out her hand.

Ah, I thought, that's why she's here, his messenger girl. Yet I had to admit I'd always found her honest, perhaps too much so, not one to hold back.

'He loves you, Alice, but…'

I could have told her about that night in the cottage, yet couldn't be bothered. I was here in this place, would be for a long time. I had already begun to switch off from outside.

'He's coming next week,' I said. A lie, a stupid one. She'd know he wasn't, but he would come soon, my gut told me that. I shifted in my seat and reached out for the second chocolate bar and tore off the wrapper. I looked around as I chewed. I hadn't made many friends, knew none of the other prisoners in the room. All of them had heaps of chocolates, crisps, sandwiches stacked on the tables in front of them. Pay for our work didn't go far at the canteen, especially if you smoked. I'd taken it up in a half-hearted way, although recently I'd run out before my weekly canteen order. I had a job cleaning the wing. I hankered after a job in the garden, hard work but it got you out.

Beth sat with her head down, quiet.

She looked up. 'I don't know,' she said. 'It does this.'

'What does?' I threw at her, not bothering to keep my voice down.

'The death of a child,' she said, in an un-Beth-like quiet way. 'It can tear couples apart.' She looked hard at me. 'The blame.'

'Oh, so it's my fault,' I sneered and sat back. 'My fucking fault.'

'I didn't say that. He loves you. You love him, although you might not think it right now. You have to find a way.'

She looked around, shifted in her chair. 'He blames himself.'

I wanted her to go. I wanted everyone to go, leave me here. She saw it in my face.

'Work is not good for him right now,' she murmured.

My head shot up. Well, he was certainly spilling the

251

beans. I looked hard at her. Beth and Jake, no way. A little voice said, *Why not? You don't want him.* There was only one I wanted and he was gone.

'I don't really understand what he does, not my thing,' she said. 'He says he can't concentrate, can't really hear what his group are really saying. Says he's lost the words.'

I sat in silence. My Mr Alice.

She gave up. 'How can you bear it here?'

'You get used to it.' That lie swam out so easily. I didn't tell her how I looked over my shoulder every minute when out of my cell.

I told her about Sad Sal. Tears came to her eyes and she turned to look at the two mothers with their babies.

I kept on eating.

She talked about her work: new boss, tougher targets, nothing exciting. She still didn't mention her boys.

'Do you need anything?' she asked, again, sadness and helplessness competing in her voice.

My son.

I couldn't wind back time and relive that day, 17th February, his birthday. Or that other day about five months later, a day that was insinuating itself into my head more, demanding attention.

I smiled and said, 'I could do with you for company.'

She shuddered. 'Not in this place.' She finished her coffee, hadn't touched the chocolates. 'Promise me you'll try. With Jake.'

I promised nothing.

'Be brave,' she said, and reached out to touch my hand. She looked at her watch. 'A long drive. I'll be back soon.'

She was the first visitor to leave.

47

Mad Madge was sent to another prison. That was my best Christmas present. I no longer had to suffer her standing beside me, close, staring, always staring.

A card from Jake. On the front a Christmas tree and inside he had written, *Happy Christmas. Love, Jake.* Pretty low-key but he received no card from me.

Christmas. Excitement and laughter clattered down the corridors; homemade hooch did the rounds, and the kitchen made a feeble attempt at Christmas food: turkey, roast potatoes and cabbage and a tasteless Christmas pudding. The prisoners decorated the dining room and their cells. There were none in mine. Early lockdown to let the screws go home, time for their Christmas.

I wondered how Jake was spending his.

My boy spent some of the day with me, running round in excitement, shouting, 'Christmas, MumMum, Christmas.' For the rest, I slept.

I left my cell to work, clean and to eat. Little else. In a weird sort of way, I enjoyed my job cleaning the wing. I had become accustomed to the life: dull, repetitive food, anything filling – pasta, potatoes, curries; the endless counts, lockdowns, weekly change of clothes and bedding, strip searches and boredom. I still didn't go to Association.

For many, ruined lives and long shadows from family outside.

Life was inside. Lonely.

Shortly before 6pm, no one else was around. I'd eaten and faced a long evening. It was early in the new year, 1992. My 46th birthday had passed uncelebrated except for a card from faithful Jake. I was missing him, thought of writing. What could I say?

Footsteps outside, from the cell to the right of mine, then a knock.

I got up from the bed and opened the cell door.

Mary. I hadn't seen her since the incident with the beans. Prison was like that.

People just disappeared.

She was taller than me, and thinner, with large staring eyes and long black hair which she wore in a plait down her back. She had thin lips; a strong face with an almost perfect Roman nose.

We stood for a minute looking at each other.

'I'm your new neighbour,' she said, smiling.

I stepped back so she could pass. She pulled the chair out from my small table, her brown eyes level with his drawing, and sat.

'MumMum,' she said. 'That's good, a double Mum.'

I loved her for that. I sat on my bed and waited.

She turned back to me. 'I don't go often, either,' she said. 'Association.'

We talked a bit, nothing big, about the food, pretty bad, although Mary didn't mind it all that much.

Mary had been here years, knew her way around.

'I can get you stuff. Whatever you want. Not drugs. Someone else will get you them. Then you can be off your head too,' she said, a slight sneer in her voice.

I wasn't going there again, although I had only been playing at it, years back. I shook my head. Tobacco and cannabis were the most traded items here; pills of any sort almost. Coffee, tea, tobacco were borrowed or traded, often at two-for-one rates. Canteen time was the highlight of the week, especially for the smokers. Some were always on the scrounge. I was generous with my surplus sugar and tea. That was easy.

'I don't do them,' she said. 'Not now, not here. Mind you, nothing will ever be as good as my first H. That's why you keep going, seeking that ultimate.' She stood.

'See you again,' she said.

She stopped at the door. 'You'll need friends to get you through.'

So I was marked out as a loner.

Easter Sunday, 19th April, 1992. Many had gone to church. It was just an extra meet-up and chat for some. Seven months gone. I was drying up, a barren brown field that I couldn't green with my tears. I was destroying myself.

Of course I would get out sometime, but for what?

Mary's cell was a mess, the surfaces littered with

cosmetics and clothes. Different smells competed. One wall had a swathe of photographs, mostly of a boy; smiling, happy, cheeky-looking.

'Have a look,' she said.

I walked over to them. The light was lousy and the pictures were old and a little faded. In one, Mary was standing with her arms on his shoulders.

'Beautiful, isn't he?' she said, and patted the bed beside her.

I sat down, Mary and me, hip-to-hip, both a little hunched over.

'I could do with a soft pillow like yours.'

'I bet you could. I can get that for you.'

There were a few moments of silence, then Mary's voice a murmur.

'Lot of us are here 'cos of our kids. Stealing, drugs, anything to keep the kids going. Me, I were the opposite, my boy were called Darren.' Her voice softened at his name, like caressing a favourite pet.

Shock coursed through me at the past tense. I turned to look at her face. I was good with guessing age: early to mid-thirties, I was sure.

'My Doug, he were handsome, we were sweethearts at school. He were just like my dad, carried on where my dad left off. A young thug were better than an old one, I suppose. Thought I'd never have kids, been too battered down there.'

She was silent, had left me, was back there, wherever that was.

'What happened?'

'The usual: booze, dope and finally H. Then Doug legged it. I didn't much notice he'd done a runner. My boy were enough.'

'They took me back there, the police,' she said, staring at the wall, her face set, her voice hard. 'Afterwards. The house were two storeys once, but now you could see the sky from the ground floor. My boy, Darren, died in that fire. I should have died instead of him. Gave him something to make him sleep, locked his door, didn't want him to see his mum out of it, don't remember the fire. Coke and fags. Neighbour pulled me out.'

She let out a high-pitched squeak. 'Keeping him safe, from me. He couldn't get out. They found his body the other side of the locked door. The draught sucked the smoke up the stairs and under it. That's what they said. How would I know? Never let me see him.' Her voice was trembling. 'Manslaughter, that's what I were done for.'

She turned to me. 'Not much of a mother, me. He were all I had.'

'He was lovely,' I said, and put my arm around her shoulders.

'It eats you up.' She dug in her pocket, took out tobacco and papers and slowly, with trembling hands, rolled a cigarette, then another. I took the matches from her. She had spilt tobacco on the floor. I lit hers, then mine from the same match. For a minute or two, we sat, each watching our own curls of smoke in the stuffy room.

A sort of snort mingled with her smoke and pushed itself out between her thin lips. 'I'm all right here, you get used to it. No one else killed Darren. I miss him. Gotta live with it.'

I put my head down, shut my eyes. Manslaughter, of her son. That day in the park rushed through me, as fast as the bike.

A bell rang. We stubbed out our cigarettes in the washbasin.

'I never went to school much, not book learned, my dad

saw to that, but I know life, too much. It destroys you, the blame. I seen it, here.'

Mary's words found a small crevice in my brain, worked on me.

The tabloids had named me a monster.

A few days later, I tapped on Mary's door. The flushing of her toilet told me she was there. I pushed it open.

'Alice.'

Her smile drew me in.

She patted the bed beside her. I sat, and the hard bed gave a little.

'What were your boy like? Tell me about him.'

I was utterly still.

'What were his name?'

I didn't answer.

'Say it,' she said, 'move your lips, whisper it in my ear.'

I stood, walked towards the door.

'Adam,' she called after me.

I turned, wanted to hit her; my heart raced, I couldn't breathe.

'Don't go. Bet he were beautiful, your boy.'

I walked back to the bed, three long steps. I had on what my father had called my tiger face: lips pursed, eyes narrowed to slits.

'Adam,' I said, his name reverberating in my head and heart. My stomach lurched and I eased down onto the bed and bent over my knees. Minutes later, I pulled the photograph from my pocket, his eyes unknowable behind dark sunglasses. I passed the photograph to her.

'My Darren built a snowman, wouldn't let me help. We didn't have money for much, except my habit.'

'Adam,' I said, and rolled the word round and round in my mouth, a short word, only two syllables. Jake had wanted a name that couldn't be shortened. For me, it was Adam, the first man and his name began with A like mine. For a moment then I believed him alive, just somewhere else.

'You were his MumMum.'

I shook my head so hard it hurt. 'Not anymore,' I whispered.

'You'll always be his MumMum,' she said. 'Kids, never knew what went on in their heads, did we?'

'She killed him, ran him down in her car,' I said slowly, giving each word weight. I flushed, my heart churned.

'A barrister. In the papers,' Mary murmured.

We sat, unmoving, unspeaking, our sons with each of us.

Mary sighed. 'She's a snooty bitch but the other boy, her son, had his own small life, like my Darren. Lucky you didn't kill him.'

I moved away from her. It was this place. Inside. Unreal. A place I would leave one day and never return to, I hoped. Or had the routine, the mindlessness, taken me over?

Lucky?

She wriggled after me and placed one arm round my shoulders, pulled me to her, then removed her arm and took my face between her two hands, kissed me on the lips.

I pulled back.

'You've never done this before with a woman, I can tell. Plenty here do, it's all right.'

I turned back to her arms.

We lay together on the hard, narrow bed. I started to sob, brutal gasps. Mary held me tight, breast-to-breast. My tears, the first since that day in court, ran down my neck, snot joining them, into her hair. She moved away a little, held my breasts. I shut my eyes as she whispered, 'We loved our boys.'

Her hands moved over my body and I knew again its softness, its curves and its wetness.

'Take these off,' she murmured, tugging at my trousers.

We sat up and undressed. I didn't look at her.

We kissed again.

Mary took me in her arms, her soft lips surprising. It was stealthy, the sex, a touch at a time: finger to finger, a stroke of an arm; lips, soft, gentle, like the kiss of a child. I longed for touch, anyone's, so I could feel alive, and yet I drew back.

'It's good,' she murmured.

Then the urgency, the inevitability took over. Our hands found each other; our bodies whispered acquiescence, joy. I was somewhere else, an isolated beach hidden deep in the dunes, felt the sand beneath us, a little gritty, heard the susurration of the waves, closed my eyes and saw the water's blue-green stir. A deep sigh inside me. No one, not even Mary, heard.

Our tenderness transported me from the grubby cell and the high ramparts with their razor wire. These 25-foot walls held us in thrall, as fearful fairytales do a child. We couldn't escape our little lives. Our families and friends were elsewhere. All we hoped to do was survive.

For a short time, I left it all behind.

We moved apart, our bodies sticky.

'Jake,' I said.

She rested on her elbow, placed the first finger of her right hand on my lips. 'Shush,' she said. 'You will tell him, one day. He loves you, he will understand.' She laughed. 'They call him the toff,' she said.

I was silent so long she lay back down, distance between us despite our touching naked hips.

Finally, I said, 'Jake.' I paused. 'I found myself when we met. We became part of each other. I've lost that now.'

Mary kissed me on the forehead. 'I'm sure your Jake is lovely, lucky sod.' She laughed; a small, bitter sound.

She rolled a cigarette, lit it and placed it between my lips. I took a puff, passed it back, pushed myself onto my elbow and turned to face her. She lay down on her back, her face soft, smiling, a tin ashtray rested on her belly.

I trusted her, had not trusted anyone for a very long time.

'He was going too fast, his strong little legs were turning, he kept screaming at me, "Let go, MumMum, let go."'

Mary grabbed the ashtray, spilling some of the ash, placed it on the floor and turned to me. She wriggled a bit and rested a hand on my hip.

'He were a little boy. They're like that, don't know what they want. That's how it were with my Darren. His rages were terrifying. Your Adam loved you.'

I shook my head, tried to get my tongue round the words. He was turned back, his face a couple of feet from mine, a screwed-up, furious face; his sunglasses had fallen off. His words, those I had tried to bury deeper than anything else in my life?

'I ran after him but it was too late.' Through the trees, and the space opening up to the light and the road. Adam flying across the road, the squealing of brakes and the noise that tore out my heart.

'He loved you,' Mary said again. 'Kids say stuff they don't mean. You never meant to hurt him, never would. Not you. Some here, not you.'

Was that true? I didn't know. 'I lost it after Adam, really lost it.'

She passed the cigarette. 'Here.'

I couldn't stop trembling.

Mary pulled herself back, took the cigarette from me, placing it in the ashtray, and kissed me, long and tenderly then raised herself on her elbow, her face now inches from mine. 'It took me years to find my Darren again and it was me that killed him. You never killed your Adam. You loved him like I loved my Darren. He loved me, I know it.'

She paused, looked deep into my eyes. 'You have to find him again, your Adam. I'll never forgive myself, not completely, but I've moved on, got him back, the good things. You weren't to blame like me, what I done. I promised myself I'd never do drugs again and I don't, and won't. Promised him.'

I couldn't speak, took her hand in mine and kissed it.

'That's why you did that thing to her boy.'

I let go of her hand, turned away.

'Not a good idea, not the boy. Her, that were different.'

I dressed and left while Mary rolled another fag.

Back in my cell, I buried my head in the pillow and bawled, smothering the sounds as best I could. I cried half the night, whispering, in between sobs, 'Adam, my Adam.'

I thought of Jake, tried to recall the detail of our early days of love, the joy, the excitement. I made up my mind to write to him. Mistakes, accidents, deliberation, revenge and the one I kept out, forgiveness. I had chosen a deadly tool for revenge, an easy target. I knew that now.

And I had to find a way back to that earlier me, hear myself reading *Peter Rabbit* to Adam, hear his chuckle, ''scape, MumMum, 'scape.' And those moments of wonder – snowman, sandcastle, and when I first held him in my arms, saw my daughter was my son. I had to hear him, see him with Jake, looking at the stars, the three of us together.

Two boys' names danced in a weird circle through my brain: Adam, Henry. One still lived.

48

We stood a moment, apart, searching each other's faces. I had been his friend, his lover, his life, these years.

Then he held me, here in the din of the visiting room, his cheek rough. I relaxed a little. For a moment I was back in his Hampstead flat, in front of the Rothkos, puzzled, trying to flee them, then swimming in their intensity.

We parted and sat, looking at each other across a small low table.

I had so much to say to him yet was mute. I picked at the skin below my left thumb nail as I had done ten years back when he took it upon himself to help me stop. He failed in that.

He tried to settle in the hard chair, gave up and sprawled, his long legs finding little room. His hand rested on the table. I stared at his long white fingers.

'You've stayed away a long time,' I said.

'Missed me.'

It wasn't a question. He sounded bitter but then he smiled, the old Jake smile.

'Oh, Alice.' He leant towards me, his monk-grey eyes anxious.

'I haven't been ready to see anyone. Beth came but we had little to say to each other.' That was a first. It was Beth's silences that dampened us. I recognised the doubt in her eyes. 'She said she'd seen you, that things were not good.'

He nodded.

'She said you were troubled.' I put my hand out, touched his. 'You're here now. Tell me what you are doing.' I sounded odd, formal, a well-intentioned stranger. I looked past him, to the empty exercise yard.

'Working.' His voice was soft with a hint of defensiveness.

I wanted to hold his hand.

'Is it tough?' he asked.

I didn't want to talk about it. 'It's getting better.'

Mary came into my head. I flushed but he didn't notice; he was staring around.

'So young, some of them,' he said, then added, somewhat oddly, 'Adam was a good boy—'

I cut him off. 'You think I don't know that?'

There was silence between us. I shifted in my chair.

'I have to go back to the US, Alice. My mind isn't in the right place to look for another job. My company is good to me. I've made a mess of my work since… I seem to have lost whatever it was I had. They don't open up to me anymore, the people we recruit.' He sighed. 'I suppose they see it.'

I touched his hand, quickly.

'Listen to me, Alice. When I found you, I believed my life was perfection, doubled. He called you MumMum,

265

another double. Our Adam. You were a wonderful mother and he and I had the stars. We must hold on to him together.'

'Not now,' I said. 'Not here, Jake. We will talk. I promise.' It surprised me, that promise. I had not expected it. 'Give me time.' Then I smiled. I had time in plenty.

It was not a good visit. We were both on edge, caught between love and recrimination.

Three weeks later, a letter.

I had written to him, saying I was missing him, wanted him to visit. And yet...

I walked the six steps up and down my cell, washed my face, sat back down, opened the envelope, took a deep breath.

20th April 1992

My darling girl,

It is too long since I called you that. Do you remember the first time? It was when we made love, strangers still, yet already in love. Falling in love with strangers, is that what love is? And the years after that when our love never faltered but opened itself up like those white flowers in the garden. Lushes, you call them. I don't know their names, never was much of a gardener. And the fun we had. I taught you to sing, although you are not very good, and you taught me to dance the tango, or rather we went and had lessons, me with my big feet.

You gave me VW and I gave you Mark Rothko.

Christmas has passed. I barely noticed it, and his birthday months ago. We should have been together. He would have been seven now.

I listen to our song almost every day now. That is all I have of you. I first sang it to you in the restaurant in Soho, softly, but it can't have been that soft, for the people at the nearby tables applauded: "Love me tender." Elvis, of course. We didn't need Elvis. I would always be true to you.

I put the piece of paper down carefully. We hadn't needed Elvis. It had been totally unexpected, our love. For me anyway. A girl from The Street and a toff. That's what Mary called him. My toff. Life with him had been so good that I began to dream of something I had always dismissed, a baby, and Adam had arrived. A wonder. Our little boy who was determined to fly to the moon, Rabby trailing from his left hand.

Do you remember our days, before Adam? I learned to know you, to understand your uncertainties, your unpredictability, and you learned mine. Then Adam came. We took our time, you and I, getting into the parenting thing, both late starters, me forty-six. We learned his ways and he loved us both utterly. Never doubt that.

He was going to be an astronaut.

I beg you to forgive me that night in Scotland. Your silence, your arm, defeated me. I wanted to both love and punish you, make you mine. It was shameful. Is that why I have stayed away so long?

I had almost forgotten it.

Let us not go back to that day outside the school. Let us remember the six wonderful years: his, ours. Let us banish the anger, the blame. But we have to talk.

Anger, blame: small words, giant conceits. They are softening a little inside me. There is much of both here and those who have banished them. Can I? Too soon, too soon, I cry out. There are things I have to say. My shame, not his.

Where now? You are in a dark place, the prison, yes, but that is not what I mean, and I have failed you, too wrapped up in my own pain. I may not be able to find the right words in your dreadful place. You have gone where I cannot follow. I don't mean the prison, but in your head.

I love you, Alice. Forever. Do you still love me? You will be out one day…

I want to tell you every day how much I love you. I am not the man I was. I need you to help me find that man again. Your smile gave me life.

Come home to me. There is a beautiful moon outside right now, a blue moon.

Remember our first?

I have bought you a dress. It is green, to match your eyes. I have never done that before.

I'm coming to see you soon.

Your Jake

I sat long, the letter in my hand.

I couldn't imagine going back to our house in Wimbledon, had forgotten the stuff of day-to-day living, didn't long for shops or neighbours, or even the library. I was out of the way of real conversation, grown to like my own company.

Of course I remembered the restaurant, the songs. My shy, brave Jake. We would talk, one day, but not here.

A dress. I smiled. He would have chosen well.

I reread the letter, then placed it carefully in a drawer with other letters and a few treasures.

A week later, a small parcel arrived. Half a dozen photos of Adam: at the seaside with his sandcastle, peering down the hose for snakes, and several baby snaps, including one of him in the bath. And one of me and him in the back garden. And a note: *I found the negatives. Love, Jake*

I showed them to Carol and Mary. Then to others.

It was followed by half a dozen postcards, arriving at brisk intervals, each of a different Rothko painting.

The prison officer who gave them to me (after opening each envelope and reading the contents) said, 'Funny pictures, Miss. Do they mean a lot? A bit dark, I'd say.'

I was beginning to trawl back, to life before that day in the park.

Mary and I were still friends, wandered in and out of each other's rooms, held each other at difficult times, but no longer the other thing, although I missed it.

'It's the toff, isn't it?' Mary said when I moved away from her embrace.

I nodded.

Adam was on the common, flying his kite, shouting, 'MumMum,' and the grey heron smiled at me.

I started going to Association. Carol was usually there. We had a laugh.

Mary didn't go.

Fourteenth of July 1992. A year since… I pleaded sick and spent the day in my cell. The boy Henry was with me, not Adam. And the broken violin. Mary's words came back to me: 'Not a good idea, the other boy.' And I felt his mother's eyes on me.

Not long before my second Christmas (by then, I was counting the months, less than seven to go if I served only half the term as PJ assured me I would), I received a short note from Jake. He was back in the London office.

My father wanted to visit.

I had wasted too many years believing he would come back. He didn't so I tried to forget him.

Jake had found his card; it had fallen out of a book. I knew exactly which one, *The Tempes*t. Jake wrote to him, told him, he said, just the bare bones.

I didn't want to see my father. Not here.

He telephoned Jake, was coming over from the US.

Back in my cell, I stretched out on my bed, a fag moving from my mouth to ashtray and back again. As a kid, I hadn't wasted time on where my father went the other nights. I knew I was best loved.

There was still a whisper of a foolish child's love in me.

'What's he like, your dad?' Mary asked.

'A dreamer and a liar,' I said.

'Men,' she said, and waited.

'He taught me to hunt, rabbits.'

'Ah,' she said. 'The song. In the papers.'

49

I lay on my bed, knees bent, hands behind my head.

My dad. A dreamer and a liar, I had told Mary. Yet he had been the heart of my universe. He had made me. Not my mother. I had wronged her. My mother died, eighteen years ago, June 1974.

*

'What are you talking about?' I spat out, the girl who was no longer a girl and had been living in London for almost twelve years. It was a bright northern May day in 1974.

The older woman, her grey hair tied back with a blue ribbon, shrank back in her armchair.

The room was hot, too hot. I had stripped off my jacket and sat in blouse and slacks, my handbag on the floor and my empty mug on the small table.

I had made us tea but my mother had drunk little.

The house had night storage heating and a two-bar radiator switched on, not far from my mother's legs so that their skin was red and blotched. She sat in her armchair in a pink flannelette nightie, a floral dressing gown buttoned up to the neck, fluffy slippers on her feet and a rug over her knees. My mother had left herself in The Street. Here nothing was her except for the two photographs on the mantelpiece: her wedding photograph and ten-year-old me. The house had a small kitchen, mostly taken up with a table. And two bedrooms.

I rarely stayed the night.

It was almost six months since I had seen my mother, and in that time, the flesh had leached from under her skin, skin now like dry autumn leaves, outlining the bones and blood vessels beneath. Her eyes, always one of her best features, were too large, lost in a shadowy cave above too prominent cheekbones. Furrows ran down her cheeks to her mouth then set off again down her chin.

'What are you talking about?' I repeated.

'His other family. He kept to our bargain: Tuesdays, Wednesdays, Thursdays and Friday nights with us.'

'I don't understand,' I said, too loudly for the hot, stuffy room.

'Her, his other family, where he went on Saturdays,' she said quietly, looking into my eyes.

'What family? You aren't making any sense.' I sat, rigid.

'Two boys, brothers. Another woman.'

She'd written saying there was something she wanted to tell me, so I had travelled north from London.

Brothers. I didn't want them, pushed them away. How had I been so stupid, so secure in his love? This woman, my

273

mother had kept this secret all these years and now she was dying… for she *was* dying.

What would I have done had I known?

'Some bargain, he was a bastard. Why did you let him get away with it?' Then it hit me, became real, almost. In truth, I would never entirely let it in. My father. I had adored him, thought he was mine alone, that is what he had led me to believe. Yet I had, unknowingly, shared him all those years, thought he was away working, when he was screwing some other woman and probably saying the same things to those boys as he said to me. Hunting, did he take them? I wanted to scream with rage and loss.

'I often asked myself that,' she said, weariness in her voice, putting out her hand to take mine. I tried to pull away. She gripped, surprisingly strongly, refusing to let go. 'What could I do? He loved you, remember that. And the war never gave him up, not his body, his mind. He had nothing left to give to me or to her.'

'The war. What's that got to do with anything?'

'It just does,' she said.

'Why haven't you told me?' I said, hard-voiced, full of mother-blame.

'Well, you haven't been around much, and when he left, you were so young, so bereft.' She sat up straight and snorted. 'Where do you think he was from Saturday to Tuesday? Working?'

'Yes,' I said, so quietly I almost missed my word. So stupid.

'Beggars can't be choosers.' Her smile thin, like my voice.

Her other much-worn saying was "once in a blue moon". I had loved the idea of a blue moon, had searched the sky for it until someone told me that it simply meant a second moon in a month.

I took a deep breath, heard her say, 'It was better than nothing and that way you had a father.' Then she gasped and the furrow across her brow deepened. She stubbed out the cigarette, breathed in deeply but softly.

I leapt up and tried to adjust the cushions behind her back. She waved me away.

'Stupid of me, I should have seen he was used to babies.' She tugged at the rug on her knee. '"My little girl," he said, "my Alice." We hadn't talked about names but he insisted.'

I turned away, and with that movement tried to banish my mythical brothers.

Minutes later, she murmured, 'He left us both at the same time,' and closed her eyes.

There was a stack of books on the table beside her, all by Georgette Heyer, and one on her lap. She loved the bounders and rakes and I knew then that she had loved one for real: my father.

I waited.

'She came to see me once.' A small laugh yet the pain in her eyes mocked the laughter. 'The other woman, she came to see me, and you know what?'

I didn't move, didn't look up. My breathing was as heavy as hers.

'The pearls she was wearing. They were the same as mine.'

She pulled the rug tight around herself. 'The pearls, over there, that drawer. They will be yours.'

She hadn't worn them often. Occasionally, I had found them in her drawer and carefully placed them round my neck to gaze at myself in the mirror. My mother's most treasured possession.

'What was she like?' I asked, hating myself.

She shook her head then said softly, 'Not even a husband. He'd already married her.'

'You lied to me.' Yet my anger was waning.

'We both did, we agreed it was best.'

I looked away. Then, 'Two boys,' I said, although I hadn't been sure I could say the words. I wanted to slap my mother, slap someone.

'Your half-brothers.'

'The photograph,' I said, half standing.

'Oh, it's real but there was no wedding, only a photograph and a ring. He had it all sorted. We had a wonderful week. I thought it would last me a lifetime. A moment or two later she added, 'I forgave too easily.' She stopped speaking and her laboured breathing swam through the room.

'He loved us both. He did his best, but you only had eyes for him.' She shifted in her chair, looked out of the window. 'He promised to take me to America, travel the world.'

No, he was taking me. He probably promised them as well.

She raised a weak hand, her smile twisting her face into a grimace. 'Are you happy?'

There was no account I could give that wouldn't disappoint.

'I have always loved you. I should have done better,' she said. There was a dreadful weariness in her voice. 'I loved him, but you were my life.'

I had not noticed and now it was too late. I leant forward and placed my lips on the dry frozen side of my mother's face and put my arms around her. Into her neck,

I murmured, 'I love you, Mum,' and pulled away, surprised.

She had whispered to me as I stood years ago, aged sixteen, on the station platform, waiting for the London train, 'Please don't go.'

Now she licked her crooked lips, a half smile. That was all her face permitted.

'My life's been a waste, Pet,' she said. 'A waste,' she repeated, 'except for you.'

Two months later she was dead.

The black box that sighed when opened, with its pearls inside, snug on their bed of silk, was one of the few things I took from Rose Avenue.

The house sold for a surprisingly large sum. In addition, there was her deposit book, my father's blood money.

'I never spent much,' she'd said, that time of my last visit. 'We were like that, the war generation, never knew where the next meal was coming from.'

50

The Funeral, 1974

What remained of my father's brown hair was combed across the top of his head from above his right ear over to the other side. Some sort of hair cream kept it fixed in place. I prayed for a strong breeze, a good puff from the right direction. I cursed him for a vain fool.

The same musky smell, overlaid with whisky.

'So where did you run to?' My voice was full of disdain. Or was it anger?

He stiffened, folded his arms across his chest then dropped his fisted hands to his side. 'America,' he said. 'A big country, you'd love it. We could find the bears.' He laughed, a small soft sound, not the guffaw I recalled. Hints of his adopted country in his voice.

'I learned it from you.'

'What?'

'To ignore her.' I pointed to the heap of earth, the abundance of flowers, the mourners now in the distance. 'What a fool I was.' I turned, my back to him.

'Please.' His voice was strained, pleading.

I turned around. His arms were out.

'Bullshit, that's what you are, all bullshit. You're a bastard, what about her?'

I meant what about me, of course.

He let his hand rest lightly on my arm. 'I've wanted to find you. That's why I'm here, Princess.'

'I'm not your princess. Did you ever love her?'

'Of course.'

I wanted to slap him and to have his arms around me.

'I've loved you from the first minute I saw you.' His voice was full. 'A beautiful baby.'

I pointed to the piled-up earth, to the flowers. 'She told me. Everything.'

*

The night of the school play, *The Tempest*, that was when he left us. Not long before my fourteenth birthday. I was Ariel. '*All hail, great master! Grave sir, hail! I come/To answer thy best pleasure; be't to fly. To swim, to dive into the fire, to ride/On the curled clouds. To thy strong bidding...*' At the end, my father had stood there in the third row, shouting, 'Ariel, Ariel.'

There was a party backstage but I left it early, wanting to throw myself into his arms, hear him tell me how wonderful I was. When I saw his car was not in its usual place, I ran my eyes up and down the street. Perhaps they had fought, but they didn't often, and she had replaced fighting with icy withdrawal. I ran through the door. Her face told me. 'He's gone,' she said.

279

On my bed, a note and his bear, a piece of metal in the shape of a bear made from an old aircraft. His good luck charm. All the airmen had them in the war. That enchanted isle with all my dreams had vanished.

Be lucky, Princess. Be the best. Dad, the note said.

Had I been lucky? How did we know? Alternate lives remained a mystery.

Life changed that night – the fork in my life road. I still waited for him, not believing he could desert me. I carried the bear with me everywhere. It would be my luck. He often stayed away an extra week, would return with excuses, presents, usually enormous boxes of chocolates or ribbons for my hair. He gave me a 2/6 postal order every week and I saved them for eight weeks until I had a pound. He'd never missed a birthday, until the one a few weeks after the play, so I knew then that he was really gone. Yet I still listened for his car Tuesdays, and every day.

'Why does he only live with us Tuesday to Friday?' I had asked my mother more than once.

'That is just how it is,' she said, or something like that. Sometimes she blushed; mostly it was anger I heard.

At first, after the play, I lied to Jenny and Billy. 'He's gone to America, to the Rockies to hunt bears.'

When I ran out of stories, I crept into my mother's room and looked in the wardrobe. His clothes were still there.

*

I pointed to the earth over my mother's coffin, and the flowers. 'She told me.'

My father examined his shoes.

280

I didn't move. 'Seen your sons yet?' I mocked, yet something inside me was twisting, burning, not all of it anger. 'She wasn't your wife. Poor Mum, what a sucker. Both of us.'

'I loved her.'

'Funny way of showing it.'

'And I loved you from the first minute I saw you.'

'What about the other woman, the one you married?'

He stopped and turned to me. He pushed one brown-flecked hand back towards the grave. 'Your mother understood,' he said.

'What?' although I knew perfectly well. 'What did she understand? What choice did she have?'

'I never let her want for anything.'

'That was it, was it? Weren't we enough for you? Do you know how hard it was for her?'

And me.

I held his gaze until he looked away. I had run too.

He studied the gravestones and then turned back to me. 'I left them too.'

I snorted. 'It must have been great. When you got tired of one family, you could run to the welcoming arms of the other.'

'It wasn't like that,' he said.

'Another woman over there, I suppose.'

'No.'

I believed him.

'All these years,' I said, 'and now you pop out of a rabbit hole.'

A blackbird sang in a nearby tree. I turned to look and saw a butterfly. It had red bands, brown/black wings, white spots near the tips of its forewings. A red admiral.

'Did you make the same promises to her as well? The other woman.'

'I did my best,' he said.

'Ah, the universal excuse. You married her and then Mum came along.' I didn't bother to keep my voice down. The blackbird was silent, sitting in a bush, his head slightly cocked.

'You thought you could get away with it and I suppose you did,' I said. 'And don't say it was the war.'

'We were in love. I had such dreams, once.'

What did he expect of me? I walked a few steps away. The brothers. I had done my best to expel them. Perhaps we might have had fun together. But they were not Street kids, didn't sound like it.

'You had a posh family and then us. The Street. Thought you could bugger off and we'd still be waiting for you. Not me,' I lied, voice too loud for the dead.

He took my arm and pulled me down the path.

'I had to.' He looked away. 'Selfish bastard, I know. I'll tell you. I did my best until…'

He stopped, turned to face me. 'The forecast was rubbish.' His voice was soft; he had gone somewhere else. 'I don't know where I was in my head, but it was a bad place, no excuse. My calculations were wrong, way out, and I navigated us straight into enemy fire. The Luftwaffe got us.'

I sat down on a headstone. He sat beside me. Close.

'The plane's nose fell and we started to plummet. We took a hit, a bad one, and Don, the rear gunner, my best mate, and Dave, the wireless operator, were trapped. I dived for the escape hatch. Utter cold and darkness, jumped, fumbled for my ripcord. The plane going down in a ball of fire. My last mission.'

His eyes were shut tight, his lips thin.

My mother had been right; the war still had him.

'When we were demobbed, we were told just one thing: "You have to look forward, not back." Nearly thirty years ago.'

He stood up and walked a few steps away.

With his back to me, he said, 'I almost managed to do that until one day, in the town, in the market square.'

He turned to face me. 'In a wheelchair, burnt, unrecognisable, except for his voice: Don. He got out of that plane, somehow.' Tom took a couple of deep breaths. 'He stopped in front of me. "Hoped I might find you, it's taken me a while," he sneered, pointing a twisted red hand at me. "The war hero," he shouted, in a half-human, throttled voice. People stopped, listened.'

I didn't speak. What could I say?

'"Look at him, look hard." Don waved that thing that was once a hand around to the crowd. "The war hero? Been killing any mates lately? Couldn't wait to jump, could you? Just left us there." The crowd began to break up.'

My father stared straight ahead. 'So I ran. From him, from you, from your mother.'

'Did you tell Mum this?' I asked.

'No. I couldn't. You know what was the worst? I wished him dead. It was the end for me here, and the drinking had got to me by then.'

His voice changed. 'I'm going to try and find him before I go back.'

'Why?'

'See if I can help him.'

'Good luck,' I said, a little ironically.

After a moment, he said, 'I left you something. Did you find it?'

'What?' I said, slipping my fingers into my handbag to feel the bear's sharp edges through the tissue.

'I left it on your bed. It brought me good luck for a long time.'

'I threw it away,' I lied. I took a deep breath. 'I ran too,' I said. 'You taught me.' Then after a minute, 'Mum had no one.' I raised my eyes to the yew trees and the now leaden sky. 'I didn't get back often enough. She was lonely. I just lived my own life, forgot her.'

'You were young, too young,' Tom murmured.

'Sixteen and a half,' I said. 'Didn't care, just wanted to get away. Daughter, like father.' I would not recount how I had searched London's streets for him.

My father put his arm round my shoulders. I didn't push him away.

'Alice in Wonderland. I named you for her: curious, brave and just.'

I moved a little closer.

'I haven't seen them, since I left,' he said, 'the boys, Robert and Alistair. She's gone, taken them with her.' His face told his sorrow.

I shrugged off his arm, tried not to believe in them. 'I don't want to hear about them. You lied. I'm twenty-eight, made nothing of myself.'

He touched my arm, lightly. 'You look good, not a kid anymore.' His eyes pleaded. He put his hand into his breast pocket and pulled out a small parcel, holding it out.

I stood, hands by my sides.

'And you were my part-time father. You kept us like mice in a cage, opened the door for a time, fed us and put us back. Especially her.' I waved, somewhere in the direction of another planet. 'Playthings at your disposal.'

He stood. 'It's getting cold, let's walk.' He took my arm and replaced the parcel in his pocket.

We were nearing the end of the graveyard now, the scruffy end, my mother had called it. Words, dormant for so long, had a way of creeping in.

We paused on the cobbled path in front of a headstone. The words, once chiselled into the stone, were now almost completely obliterated. I bent close and made out the date: *1837, Beloved mother*. Time had erased the rest.

'It's not too late,' he said.

'For what?'

'America.'

I stared at him.

Small tears gathered in the corners of his eyes. 'I'm a silly old fool, made a mess of things all my life. Mind you don't do the same.' And then the grin, almost lopsided, once more. 'Have you someone? You married?'

'No.'

Geese passed overhead, honking, their formation jagged. Father and daughter stretched their necks in unconscious mimicry.

I checked the time. 'Why didn't you write?'

'I wanted to. It wouldn't have been fair, clean break. I should have. I didn't want you to forget me.'

'Well, I did,' I lied.

'I could come to London,' he offered.

I shook my head. 'No,' I said and knew I hadn't really grown up, was the same stubborn Alice from The Street.

He straightened himself. 'I'll be off then,' he said. 'Things to do, a man to find.'

He stood a few moments then pulled out his wallet and extracted a card.

'Houses,' he said. 'A realtor, not half as much fun as cars.' There was a flash of the hunter.

I looked at him, briefly.

'I don't have your address so you'll have to write to me,' he said.

He placed the card in my hand. And then the small brown paper parcel.

The geese were now specks in the clear sky.

He walked away, slow steps, the muscles of his back telling defeat. I could run after him, tap him on the shoulder, take his arm, whisper softly, '"*Run rabbit, run, run, run*",' and he would swing around, that lopsided smile spreading, and would hold out his arms.

I sat for a time. It was over. The Street had died and all that went with it.

Hints of dusk multiplied.

Daughters are supposed to return with flowers, memories, love. I would not.

I unwrapped the parcel: *The Tempest*. I slipped his card inside.

51

A couple of kids were running wild in the visitors' room and one woman was nursing her baby girl, a bottle held to her lips. She had been taken from her shortly after birth and redelivered to her mother in weekly snatches. Both were oblivious to the noise around them.

'Curious, brave, and just,' he had called me, named after *Alice in Wonderland*. The first, I had mostly been.

His footsteps were slow, no longer bouncing off the soles of his feet.

I looked down at a pair of mirror-polished black shoes, could almost see my face in them. My eyes travelled up: grey trousers, a check shirt, tucked in at the waist, a tweed jacket and green and yellow tie.

He stood, his smile huge, his arms outstretched.

He was almost completely bald.

I was that small girl again. I stood, stepped towards him. We hugged. I buried my face in his shirt, in his familiar, time-warping scent.

He lifted his leg, thrust out a shoe and laughed.

'Alice', he said. 'My Alice,' and sat, his smile wide but his eyes anxious.

I was too afraid to speak. Blood rushed to my face. 'Too late,' I wanted to cry at him, yet wanted another hug, a special Alice hug.

'I've come back. Your man, he wrote to me.'

'So I see,' but my voice was soft, whispers of love threaded through. I sat, straightened my back, pulled in my burgeoning tummy.

'I'm buying a house, in London. Your man, Jake, says you'll be out soon. We can see each other, have fun.'

He made it sound as if it was only a month or two since we last met, not over twenty years, and that I wasn't locked up.

'I've got a lot to make up for, if you'll let me. I want to try.'

'I've spent my life waiting for you, ever since I can remember,' I spat out. 'For Tuesdays. When I was fourteen you ran, the night of the play. You were gone when I got home. I was sure you'd come back, sure you hadn't abandoned me.' I couldn't stop myself. 'I even searched for you in London. What a fool. I trusted you.'

I swung my arm to take in the other prisoners and their visitors. 'I don't care if I'm in a place like this, what makes you think you can turn up as if it's just been a week or two?'

He looked around, saw respite. 'A drink, chocolate, a treat?' He half rose.

'No,' I snapped.

I didn't know what to say so started with the banal. 'So how's the real estate market?'

He looked puzzled. 'Stocks, the financial market, it's big, I've made lots of dough,' he said. Somehow his voice lacked verisimilitude.

His cars were real but it turned out the company wasn't.

'So did you find him?' I asked.

'Who?'

'The burnt man.'

'Don. I tried. He didn't want to see me.'

A silly laugh dribbled out. 'What did you expect? Still playing the hero.'

His face crumpled.

What a bitch. Where was my moral high ground? I looked more closely at his clothes, cared for and well worn. His strut had gone. How old was he? Mid-seventies surely. He was careless, Tom was, my father, a Gatsby of a man. My damaged hopeful father. Perhaps I was his mirror image.

The volume of noise ratcheted up.

'You look a lot like your mother,' he said.

That surprised me. What surprised me more was that I was pleased.

'I loved your mother,' he said. His eyes wet. 'She was a stunner, your mother.'

'You already had a wife.'

He clasped his hands and looked down. 'A dreamer, me. Nothing's lasted. A pack of lies, me, except the war. That was good, in its way. Except...' He looked up. 'You were real. I always came back for you.'

'Not always,' I snapped.

'I ran because I couldn't bear for you to be ashamed of me,' he said.

He stopped talking a moment or two. 'I don't suppose I've got that many years left, and I'd like to spend some of them with you. If you'll have me?' His voice broke. 'I wanted to bring you flowers, a really big bunch.' He paused. 'Stupid, I know.'

'Not stupid,' I said, and touched his hand. 'And you can't, not in here.' Stupid giggle. 'You haven't asked me why I'm here.' I half-waved my hand around, offered up incarceration.

'I know.'

'How?'

'Oh, ways, and your Jake, he told me some. I found out the rest for myself.' He added, 'He's a good guy.'

I looked into my father's face, saw the hope in his eyes, remembered the laughter, the fun, the love.

'I tried to kill a child.' I'd never spoken those words, so unambiguous in their meaning.

'You had your reasons,' he offered.

A small boy ran past us. We both watched him.

'He must have been lovely, your boy. My grandson.'

'He looked a little like you,' I said, 'Adam. That determined expression, he had that too.' I had intended none of these words. 'He loved the stars, spent hours with Jake searching the sky through his telescope. He knew the names of lots, and the planets. He was going to be an astronaut.' My voice weakened. I took a deep breath. 'He wanted to fly to the moon. A bit of a dreamer, like you. He was a smart kid.' I laughed. 'Afraid of snakes, not much else.'

'I've missed out, on you and on him,' he said, and looked down.

Back in my cell, I took Adam's drawing off the wall and held it carefully.

His grandfather.

I slept well that night.

'So how did it go?' Mary asked.

'Good,' I said. That was the truth. A troubled man, but who was I to talk? And a man who had always loved me. Something inside was softening. I was a little fearful of where it might lead, to the stuff I still had to sort, at its heart, Rosamund Beresford.

A few days before Christmas, my second, I put some of Jake's cards on the wall, all Mark Rothko. And the last card he sent: VW's portrait, the same one I'd fallen in love with several lifetimes back. I stood back a minute, then moved Adam's drawing, added the photograph, smoothed as best I could, making the two the centrepiece.

Christmas Day, turkey with some of the trimmings and Christmas pudding and what passed for brandy butter. Association for the afternoon, then locked up until 8am on Boxing Day.

Mary gave me chocolates from the canteen; the same, it turned out, that I had bought for her.

Christmas cards: one from Jake and another from Beth. I arranged them on the table. Jake's card said he was in LA, that it was difficult to get back but he would manage it in the new year. As always, he wrote that he loved me. And a card from Anne, signed by her and half a dozen other staff.

No card from Carol. 'I don't do Christmas,' she said.

And a handmade one from Mary. She'd drawn a small boy and a Christmas tree.

52

I wandered into the library to read the newspapers, and loitered in front of the books. I imagined I was back, with Anne and Mr Williams and my friends.

Someone behind me spoke, softly.

I turned.

'Can you help me, please?' Her voice only a little louder than a whisper.

'Liz,' she said. She was taller than me but not much. Fizzy hair, generous mouth.

I didn't speak. Just looked at her. We stood, a foot or two apart.

'They say you were a librarian once.'

'Who does?'

'Gossip.'

'Different life,' I said.

'You've not been inside before.'

That was not the first time I had heard this. What did I

do that made it so obvious? You don't ask why someone is in here, and few volunteer the information. Some lie, brag.

'Me. I made a mistake,' she said. 'Were good most of my life. Lot like that here, not all, mind you. I don't see my daughter. She was given to someone else when I came here. She's a lovely girl, probably doesn't remember me.'

She rushed on as if determined to get it all out. 'I was a fool. A bloke, of course. We hurt a girl. No. Truth is, I did. I'm going to try and see my daughter when I get out. Vicky, she's called, couldn't walk when I got caught, my baby, the youngest.'

I wanted to hug her.

'Will you help me, please?'

'How?' I was puzzled, wary.

'I need to write a letter to a solicitor. A pal gave me a name, said she were good.'

That was my first letter. I never did find out if she got her daughter back.

Soon after, I left my cleaning job to work in the library. One of the officers finessed that for me. I loved being back among books, pathetic as the selection was. And my hands grew soft.

Word got around fast. It was like that, the grapevine for good and for bad.

At the library each day, women would be waiting, many new to prison life.

Sometimes it was comfort they needed, reassurance, hope, but mostly it was letter writing: to parents and children, lovers or husbands; to solicitors or other legal professionals. Letters of love, pain, rejection, misery, mistakes, sometimes malice. I was the scribe; I wrote what they told me to. If they wanted to talk, I listened.

Their stories were mostly to do with their children, too often abused, neglected, like their mothers. The women's crimes: low self-esteem, lack of education, confidence, manipulated on the outside (and often also the inside), full of love for those they had lost. And there was hate. I wrote those letters too, full of abuse. Who was I to judge?

Some were embarrassed at not being able to read, others almost boasting of it.

It was writing the letters to the children that I found hardest. The love the women poured into their words, the way they described their little ones to me.

Many were angry.

I heard admissions of guilt, saw the eyes of shame, and my own grew. The boy Henry in the park, at home, his mother's head resting on the top of his. And his small steps across the road, violin on his back. I offered myself excuses: madness, grief. Both true. And anger. I had grown up seeking to be the best and failed. Worst of all, perhaps I had failed my Adam. And yet there was another mother, Rosamund. Perhaps I was, after all, part monster.

I asked PJ to help a couple of the women, said I would pay him when I got out.

Then I asked him to help me. 'You know her.'

He nodded.

'Would you ask her to come and see me? Please.'

53

'Which is the biggest planet? How big is the sun? Which is the brightest star?'

I failed all the tests and Adam's solemn voice disintegrated into giggles. He moved on to the Greeks, that smirk on his lips. 'Who lives in the sky?' he asked.

'Zeus,' I replied.

And, 'Who is the mighty hunter?'

I procrastinated.

'Orion,' he shouted.

'Tell me our story, MumMum,' he urged, in my dream, daydream or night dream, what did it matter, 'of the boy who flew.' So I told of the boy who wanted to reach the sun and the moon and the stars. He grasped the handle of his star kite in his small, grubby hands and held tight as the wind lifted and carried him in wide curves far into the sky, higher than the birds, so he could no longer see the earth.

He flew faster, faster, shouting for joy, and laughing at his shadow trailing behind.

The bright, busy sun watched the boy and smiled, making the world below wonder at the brightness of the early day. It noted the boy's hair, and the small limbs, and the strange, dark shape behind.

The shadow didn't like being laughed at, so it picked up its feet and ran, past the boy, closer to the sun. The boy shouted in protest and the sun wanted to punish the dark thing, for he loved the boy. He sent down a flash of light that burnt up the shadow. The boy fell back to earth, landing on a pile of soft grass. He stood up and looked for his shadow. It was gone. He laughed. My brave boy.

And the other boy, Henry, came to me, that day in the park, playing with his mother.

'Rosamund Beresford,' I said, aloud.

Oddly, a few days later, a note arrived from PJ telling me that she was now a Silk, a Queen's Counsel, wore a special robe and a long wig.

She would visit.

My hands trembled as I read.

'Your Rosamund,' Mary said. 'She's part of the system, one of them, but you got nothing to lose. She can't hurt you now.'

'I'm afraid,' I said. We were sitting on my bed.

'What of? She's coming, ain't she?'

On the day, I wore the special lipstick I usually saved for Jake's visits and my only skirt and decent blouse. I did not look good, had not slept well the night before. I had become accustomed to the hard mattress but that night it was torture. It was as if this was my first night in prison. I was frightened in a way I had not been on the first real night here or at the other place. It was not a good omen.

Eighteen months since I had last seen Rosamund Beresford. In court. I had no idea what I would say to her and I was a little afraid of her, not just for what I had done but also her confidence, her success and, I suppose, her wealth.

If things went well, I had just under three months to serve. I was surviving, possibly well.

'Follow me, Miss,' said the officer, and led me to a separate room at the back of the visiting area, glass all round, reserved for solicitors and their clients. The officer motioned me to the chair with its back to the wall, facing into the big room, in front of me a table and a chair. It was strange to see other prisoners and their visitors the other side of the glass, sound muted.

The far door opened. Rosamund spoke briefly to an officer, smiled at him and walked the length of the visitors' room, confidence in every step and dressed much the same as when I had last seen her except that her silk shirt was pale blue, her hair tied back with a matching blue ribbon.

Another officer opened the door into my room for her, and words that I was too nervous to hear were exchanged. He left, shutting the door behind himself.

I pushed back my chair, stood, wanted to run.

My visitor stopped the other side of the table, exquisite perfume hovering, and put out her hand. I reached across the table and took her hand. I was pleased I no longer had cleaner's hands.

She sat, straight-backed. I copied her, shed my prison slouch. The sun flickered briefly on the glass wall of our room.

Two images were interwoven: a bike and a pool of blood on the tarmac and another, different boy, stepping off the kerb onto the same patch of road, young, innocent. I breathed hard.

'Your solicitor, Mr Penryn-Jones spoke to me. Thank you for asking me to come,' she said, her voice low, her speech clipped, a little like Jake's. 'Please call me Rosamund. May I call you Alice?'

I nodded.

We looked closely at each other, a few seconds only.

I had feared arrogance, accusation. What did my eyes show? I looked down.

'Are they treating you all right? It can be tough,' she said.

My head shot up. When she left here, she would go back to her big house, sit with her husband and son at her large dining room table.

'Yes,' I said, lips thin, tight.

She smiled. 'What would I know? I don't but I have visited many places like this.'

Not quite the same.

'You asked to see me,' she said.

I had been thinking about the other boy, Henry. The letters I wrote for others, the stories I listened to. I had written one that morning. *I love you*, I wrote for the young woman, in large print so her son could read it. *I will be home soon and will bake you a big cake and we will play in the park. Mummy loves you.* She had done a drawing for him of swings and a slide in a park. She hadn't seen her son for three years.

He was six now, lived with his grandmother. The woman would not be out for years yet.

Rosamund reached up and brushed a strand of hair from the side of her face. She looked tired and there was strain in her eyes. 'Sorry,' she said. 'I've been up late for a few nights. Difficult case in court.'

She paused and looked hard at me.

I hid my fists under the table.

'No,' she said as if speaking to herself, shook her head and the piece of hair fell back across the side of her face. 'I would like to tell you a little about myself, just a little. I am being selfish in this, imposing on you, trying to find my way through. Would you mind?'

'Please,' I said, trying to sound calm.

'Thank you.' She took a deep breath. 'My family wasn't well off and I had five brothers and sisters. I come from the North. Where do you come from, Alice? I think the North also.'

I nodded, unable to speak.

'We have that in common, although I have lived many years in London. I always wanted to be a lawyer, wanted to change the world. I'm no longer sure that the law does that but I keep trying, in a small way.' Her voice was becoming a little uncertain. 'I wanted to defend those who could not defend themselves. The sort of people I grew up with and loved.'

I might, right then, have told her to look around, see those behind her. Instead, I cut in. 'He was going to be an astronaut. His quest was to get to the moon. I taught him about quests.' Then I remembered that those were Jake's exact words at Adam's funeral. The woman sitting opposite me had been there, in the shadows.

'Angel Delight was Adam's favourite,' I carried on. 'He would have eaten nothing else had I let him. "Angels live in sky," he said when I refused to give it to him. He was going to the moon, would live on stardust.' I smiled, to myself. 'He and Rabby.' I studied the prisoners and visitors in the big room the other side of the glass wall. Children played in the games corner; couples, oblivious to anyone but themselves and one or two visitors staring around, silent.

She shifted in her seat. 'He is my only one, my Henry.' She paused. 'Did you know Henry and your son were friends?'

I shook my head, surprise and dismay coursing through me.

'Henry was a bit of a loner. Perhaps your Adam was too. He said your Adam was clever, liked sums.'

I started to speak but a small movement of her hand silenced me.

'He was there on that day, the day your Adam...' She swallowed. I could almost read her determination to go on.

Then she looked slightly away. 'Henry saw it all, the accident. He cried much of that day, sobbing, his body shaking. "You killed him," he cried. What could I say? It was the truth. He would not touch me for a long time, cried himself to sleep or in his father's arms. How could I explain? He is my joy, my boy, my Henry. Nothing else matters as much as he.'

Why didn't she shut up?

'Perhaps I should not be saying this but I want you to know what you did, what it did to me.' She turned her head back to look at me. 'That was many, many weeks ago. I don't think he has forgotten, but we are all right. He is my joy, my boy, my Henry. Nothing else matters as much as he.'

I wanted her to stop. She was stealing my words.

'I know that is how you must have felt about your boy. Yet you tried to take mine from me. That is why I have come. You have lost your son. I have asked myself over and over, gone back to that day, almost two years ago, every minute, second of it, outside the school.' Her voice was almost too quiet to hear, her eyes a little glazed. We were both back there, outside the school on that day. 'Although it was an accident, I have asked myself how it might have been different.'

She took a deep breath, folded one hand on top of the other.

'Suddenly he was there, flying across the road. I couldn't...' She paused. 'I'm sorry. I'm making it sound—'

'As if it was his fault,' I interrupted, voice too loud. The officer outside swung round to watch us. 'Or mine.' I said again, 'Or mine.'

'Oh, Alice, Mrs Oldfield, you mustn't think that. Your boy. I took him from you. That was why I had to see you.'

I shifted in my seat, tightened my lips.

The officer turned back to face the big room.

She turned around to look at the other room. Scenes of loss and separation. Then back again.

'After your boy...' She paused, twisting her wedding ring with her right hand, '...after that day I didn't work for a long time.' She laughed; a quick, almost disguised, thing. 'I sat on the garden bench all day, every day, unable to find a way forward...' She paused, '...to forgive myself for what happened.'

301

She breathed in and out, put her hand to her hair. I could almost hear her telling herself to be calm.

'Thank you for asking me to come. I've wanted to say I was sorry. What you did got in the way of that.' She lightly ran her fingers over her pearls. 'Please forgive me, Alice.' Her eyes closed for a brief minute.

Forgiveness, somehow different to "I am sorry", more biblical, less personal, yet a word I had heard much from the women in the library.

The piece of hair was tidied away again.

'My husband didn't want me to come here, didn't see the point, said it was the past. In truth, he is still angry. It isn't the past for me, Alice, could not be until I had seen you. But when you did that to Henry, he too an only child, and when I saw you that day in court, I wanted you locked away forever. The note in our letterbox, your planning of it all. Until that day I prided myself on my compassion.' The anger was there in her voice.

I half stood.

'Please don't go.'

I sat, hand covering my eyes. She passed me the box of tissues.

'I told Henry that I was coming to see you. "Will she be sad, Mummy, without Adam?" he asked.' She took a breath. 'I took Henry in my arms and said, "Yes, very, very sad. Do you think she is bad, Henry?" I asked him. His bottom lip was stuck out. He did that when he was thinking about something. "She was sad because of Adam."'

She sat back. 'That was the child you tried to kill. There, I have said it.' A hardness washed through her eyes.

I unclenched my hands, placed them on the table.

'You did that terrible thing. I understand that you wanted to hurt me, but not my son, Alice.'

I measured out my words. 'I wanted you to know what it was like to lose the person you loved more than anyone in the world. That was your son. Adam was mine.' The boy in the park, and in the dining room. Yet I was somehow pleased that he and Adam had been friends.

Rosamund pulled her chair round until she was almost beside me. Her voice trembled a little. 'I still have my boy. You and your husband do not.' She held out her hand again. 'Henry's words were right. We must move on together.'

I hesitated, took her hand and held it. I took in a breath, opened my mouth.

'Rosamund,' I said, 'I'm… your boy, I am sorry.'

Bad. Yes, I had been that. There were careless, greedy, women here, some innocent of intent but I had planned every detail of it. Those words I had said to my father echoed: I had tried to kill a child.

I reached for the tissues.

The officer swung round again, looked at us then turned away.

'He is fully recovered,' Rosamund said.

'I was more than a little mad after Adam,' I offered.

'I understand that,' she said.

Our hands separated, she looked at her watch and stood.

'Thank you,' I said.

'Your solicitor is good and will help you to get parole. You'll get out early.'

She smiled, touched my hand again, stood and walked through the door.

The crescendo of voices from those in the big room poured in. She walked away and even with her back to me, I could see a smile in her step.

At the far end of the visitors' room, she half turned, waved.

I waved back, then let my head fall into my hands.

I sat on my chair at my table; the cards, photograph and drawing close by.

My life, not like hers, serendipity, a broad, tumultuous sea dotted with small boats. I had stepped on any that came my way.

I had blamed. Everyone. Her, Jake, myself, had destroyed love, joy.

What had I done?

Another child.

I had allowed my own pain to take over, let it transform itself into the ogre of revenge and rage, let it become me.

My shame.

Children hate and love in the same instant. Perhaps we grown-ups are the same.

I shifted in my chair.

Jake. A generous-hearted man. I had tried to destroy us both.

We had to talk. He would laugh at Adam's words, "I want Daddy", perhaps find solace in them.

My words and what followed. Would he forgive that and still love me?

Adam and Henry. They were part of the same story. I could not change that.

I had to talk to Jake. What was I going to do? He had written to me that he was my husband, always would be. Would he be waiting the other side of the gates? Would he stay once I'd told him? I had to find a way.

He was in the States. I wrote him a brief note: *I have seen her. Adam and Henry were friends.*

54

Mary and I walked round the exercise yard, the sun high in the sky, taunting the gloomy walls. It was two days since I'd seen Rosamund.

'Tell us,' Mary said. 'The snooty bitch. How'd it go?'

'Good,' I said. 'I liked her.'

'Nothing more to tell me?' She sounded sharp.

How could I begin to explain?

I took Mary's hand, held it.

A week later, Mary was gone. It was like that; we were moved with twenty-four hours warning or less, like pawns in a chess game but without its rules.

Jake was back from the States.

'It was Rosamund Beresford, wasn't it? That is who you meant.' He smiled. 'A bit cryptic, your message.'

'Yes, it was Rosamund Beresford.'

His smile didn't falter.

'Adam and her boy, Henry, were friends,' I said, forgetting I had already told him. 'At school.'

He looked at me, tears in his eyes. 'They really were friends, our boy and hers?'

I nodded.

'And did she…?'

'Yes.'

'And you?'

I nodded, still finding the words hard. I got them out. 'I told her I was sorry, that I was a little mad.' I half smiled. 'As I'm sure you have noticed.' I looked around. 'I'm sorry Jake, for everything, for how I have hurt you…'

'Hush,' he said.

'When I get out of here, we will talk. I don't want to talk about him in here. Then it will be done and we'll grow old together, you and me. Adam will be with us.'

He smiled.

Tears ran down my face. I had become a crybaby.

He touched the wet with his fingers and put them to his mouth.

I would tell him everything.

'Miss, sir,' a voice behind me said.

'Sorry,' I said, without taking my eyes off Jake and heard the officer walk away.

'I love you, Jake.' The words felt odd but good. 'There are things I have to tell you. That day… You may not love me then.'

'My love, always,' Jake said. 'I have to go back to the States but I'll be here when you get out.'

Did I detect uncertainty in his voice or was it my rampant paranoia?

'I'll be out, Jake, soon. I'm being good,' I said, sounding like a toddler. 'I have things to tell you,' I said, a hint of fear in my voice.

That evening I sat down to write two letters.

In the mirror I saw wrinkles at the corners of my eyes. And hope. I was never the best. What did it matter?

I sat on the edge of my bed, a book on my knee and resting on it a blank piece of paper. I took out my pen.

25th March 1993

Dear Rosamund,

Thank you for coming to see me.

Your son was right in what he said. A wise little boy. It seems so right that he and Henry were friends.

I am no longer the person I was on that day. I punished myself and I tried to punish you, although in those last fatal moments I do not know where I was. Who I was.

I was wrong.

I am here in prison. I do not complain of that. I pass most of my days in the library, among books, my friends and among the other prisoners locked up here in this appalling place. Many of them are no danger to anyone but themselves.

I spend much of my time writing letters for the women: to lovers, husbands, children, lawyers. Ah, the children. What a brutal thing it is for a mother to be shut away from her child.

They are letters of love, anger, recrimination. Some beg forgiveness.

And I listen to their stories.

When I was at school, in the North, as you rightly guessed, I wanted to be a writer. Perhaps when I leave here, I'll try to tell the lives of the women who cannot speak for themselves.

You and I have moved on, together.

Thank you.

Best wishes,
Alice

I carefully folded the letter, placed it in an envelope and addressed it.

Then I sat for a very long time with a new blank page on my knee. I picked up my pen.

Dearest Jake,

I am not brave. I was going to tell you when you came last. I couldn't get the words out. They were there, in my head. My tongue was stuck. Perhaps it was that awful room, the noise. I am afraid that I may not have the courage when we are together so I am writing this to you. Then you must decide. I love you, Jake.

I stopped writing, put down the pen. Decide. Perhaps I would have to find my own way through the rest of my life, alone. Only Jake could share it.

Our son's last day in the park. He loved the trees. Instead of running along the path he was on his birthday bicycle. It was big, the bicycle but that was not it. And he was so excited about the snow.

I called the bike the green monster, but Adam was a strong little boy and determined. He quickly made it his own. Perhaps I resented it, saw it as yet more evidence of the daddy/son club. What a jealous woman. I am wandering from my confession.

You have always teased me about my short legs. That's the view of a man with super-long legs, one of the many things I love, for I do love you, Jake.

He was going too fast, excited, his legs turning like a small wheel. I was holding onto the back of the saddle, begging him to slow down, but you know how stubborn he could be. My thumb and forefinger were turning numb, slipping. He kept screaming at me, "Let go, MumMum, let go." He turned his head around, still tearing on along the path, his face a couple of feet from mine, a screwed-up, furious face. His sunglasses fallen off. The front wheel wobbled. He opened his mouth and screamed into my face.

'I hate you. I want Daddy.' Those were his last words.

I took a deep breath. The worst was to come. I sat utterly still, for a long time, pen unmoving in my hand.

I lost it. I screamed at him, 'Go then,' and I pushed the bike away from me. I fell. I saw him speed up and disappear around the bend down the path to her and her big car.

The thing I had tried to bury deeper than anything else in my life. I had held on to those two words too long.

I sent him to her, to that road. It was his birthday.

I ran after him but it was too late. Through the trees and the space opening up to the light and the road. Adam flying across the road, the squealing of brakes and the noise that tore out my heart.

I have asked myself every day, many times a day, how I could have done that, if I could have stopped him, if things could have been different and we would still have our lovely boy. I will never know. Those two words.

Can you forgive them, forgive me?

I pray that you are there, outside the prison gates, but I will understand if you are not.

Your Alice

I'd always thought of myself as brave. No longer. I had survived, had been like sand, falling, trickling, blown from somewhere to nowhere.

I sealed my words in an envelope with Jake's name on it, then sealed it in another, addressed to his secretary at his London office. She would see it reached him in time.

55

I put down Beth's letter. I had longed for her to make me laugh, tell me I would survive in here. We'd laughed together before, not enough. Everything now was before or after.

She had loved Adam.

5th May 1993

Dear Alice,

Forgive me. I could make excuses, blame the boys, or work.

I haven't visited as much as I should. That doesn't mean I haven't been thinking of you, worrying about you there.

The boys are teenagers now and you know what that means. Girls. They aren't working very hard but how would I know? I don't see much of them. Kids, you have to let them go. They are both happy and beautiful.

That's me, all mouth, going on about my boys. I could say it was too long a drive to visit you, or work, the usual excuses, but I blamed you, Alice, for the other little boy, whatever your grief. Perhaps because I have two boys. I couldn't understand it, yet I should not have abandoned you, Alice. It broke my heart to see you in court. You looked so angry, indifferent to what was happening to you, lost and lonely. And I have to say it, proud.

I can't imagine how it has been for you; hell, I expect. My few visits were not good. I have always been short on imagination.

I want to put my arms around you and drive you to the seaside when you get out. Will we do that?

I still think of darling Adam.

I promise I will make it up to you if you will let me. Please.

Love and hugs,
Beth

She had been honest, my friend. I didn't have many outside, plenty inside now, and I had loved her since we met a few weeks before Adam was born.

I send her a short note: *You were right. I know that now. The seaside it is.*

Love, Alice

'A favour,' Carol said, very quietly. There was no one else at our table just then. We had lingered and surprisingly the screws had not moved us on. I put that down to Carol, not me. Everyone liked Carol.

313

I smiled at her. She had a reputation for never asking for help. 'You, I don't believe it.' I touched her hand.

'Will you go and see my mum for me?' she said. 'Tell her I think of her all the time. It doesn't matter that she doesn't visit. She writes, every week. I don't want her to see me here but she is still my mum. She gave up a lot for me, including my dad.'

I would do that, with love. Perhaps make up a little for the mother's love I had recklessly refused.

She added, 'I've told her about you. You will like her.'

'Of course,' I said. 'She will remind me of you, my friend. I owe you.'

I might have said I owed many.

'Don't come and visit me. We have our memories. Write. That would be good.'

I would write. Prison had taught me much. Perhaps an odd thing to think but I was more whole for it. I would never have the same joy as I had known with Adam, but there are different lives to be lived, different joy and love.

I leant over her wheelchair and hugged her.

I would not forget Mary. We had touched each other and that was a beginning on the return journey for me.

'Another letter for you, Miss,' the officer said. It was three days before I was to be released.

I ran my fingers over the envelope, squeezed it, opened it.

It was a card; thick, expensive, had an elegant bunch of flowers on the outside and written underneath was *Good Luck* in cursive gold letters. The paper was thick, creamy. Inside, in strong, clear handwriting:

Dear Alice,

*I hear you are about to be released. I would like to wish
you everything you hope for. We will not meet again,
although our lives are forever interwoven.*

Best wishes,
Rosamund

I had so many Rothko postcards on my wall that some were
repeats. Over the past months, Jake and I had written to
each other frequently; gossipy letters, steering away from the
thing that mattered most.

Sometimes I caught myself talking to Adam, happy
talk. He didn't answer but he often didn't back then,
either.

I'd had more than enough time to mark the path through
my life. It started with my father, love did. It should have
been my mother, but I understood that too late. Love and
betrayals. He taught me to hunt and to run away. He taught
me carelessness. I outdid him in all.

We don't plan for what we don't know; for what obstacles,
people, loves, disappointments we will meet. They all leave
their little scars. We are malleable, changelings, different
people each day.

Anger had driven me. Jake assuaged it, and Adam for
a while drove it off entirely. Outside, I would be able to
properly see the stars. Perhaps the boy was watching us. I
liked to think so. He would know my love for him.

I had promised Adam we would grow old together. It
was not to be.

I heard him calling, 'MumMum,' running towards me.

I had to believe that Jake and I would grow old together. He would paint my toenails. I would feed him up.

I looked round my room. It was bare without Adam's drawing and the photograph and Jake's cards. I had grown accustomed to its size, to the routine and was a little fearful of my life outside. I was forty-nine. I would not go back to Wimbledon but to Jake's flat. I would miss the heron. And the common.

I wrote letters for the women up to the day before I left.

When I got out I would send most of my books here, to the library, if they would have them.

Two years in prison. Perhaps outside I would find the feisty Alice I believed I had been once. I had embraced the dark. Adam had loved life. I would too; I would not allow those two days, each with a small boy, to destroy me.

I might read about Rosamund Beresford in the newspapers, might even bump into her. We would smile at each other.

Was I ready? I did not know. I used to be quick to anger, believed in absolutes, not anymore. Truth is a slippery thing.

Adam and Jake made me. I unmade myself.

I no longer had stones in my pocket. VW would live on the bookshelf, although Mrs Dalloway was still with me. I would not return to the library, except to see my friends and borrow books.

I would float into the sky to touch Adam, hold his hand. He would giggle and the questions would start. If I was a betting woman, which I was not, I would bet on the rainbow question, hear his high-pitched laugh as I said,

'Seven colours,' and his riposte, 'Not if it's a double rainbow, silly.'

And then he might say, 'Look, MumMum, no shadow.'

'Time to go, Oldfield,' the officer said, with a smile.

I picked up my bag. I had given most of my belongings to my friends: clothes, toiletries, food, tobacco.

We walked through the narrow gate, through another, until we left the wing behind, then crossed a yard and waited at a small side gate, accompanied by the rattling of keys and the banging of gates, the song of prison life. The last corridor, the final metal door facing me.

'Good luck, Miss,' the officer said.

Prisoner number A45306

I took several deep breaths, words on a loop in my head: *Be there for me, Jake.*

And I stepped outside.

The door slammed shut behind me.

What's past is prologue.
William Shakespeare, *The Tempest*

For exclusive discounts on Matador titles,
sign up to our occasional newsletter at
troubador.co.uk/bookshop